Book N

ON

Union Station

EarthCent Ambassador Series:

Date Night on Union Station

Alien Night on Union Station

High Priest on Union Station

Spy Night on Union Station

Carnival on Union Station

Wanderers on Union Station

Vacation on Union Station

Guest Night on Union Station

Word Night on Union Station

Party Night on Union Station

Review Night on Union Station

Family Night on Union Station

Book Night on Union Station

LARP Night on Union Station

Book Thirteen of EarthCent Ambassador

Book Night on Union Station

Foner Books

ISBN 978-1-948691-02-4

Copyright 2017 by E. M. Foner

Northampton, Massachusetts

One

"In conclusion, it is the view of Union Station Embassy that the Eccentric Enterprises project must shift its focus from promoting Earth's brand on alien worlds to supporting far-flung human populations, thereby allowing EarthCent to expand its role in providing a base level of infrastructure for building human societies."

"Great stuff, Ambassador, though I wish you hadn't given me so much credit in your run-up to the conclusion."

"You deserve it, Daniel. That's why I asked you to come in and listen to my weekly report."

"I know I deserve it, I'm just afraid that EarthCent will decide to punish me for the idea by putting me in charge. I'm already stretched to the limit for time, and Shaina has Queenie trained to fink on me if I try to sneak in conference calls outside of office hours. Do you have any idea how much it costs in treats to bribe a Cayl hound to look the other way?"

"Well, even the Stryx can't turn back the clock, so it's too late to change the report now. If your name comes up next time I talk to the president, I'll tell him that you're too busy planning the next Sovereign Human Communities Conference."

"Don't do that," Daniel said, looking truly horrified. "He'll try to assign us more staff and we'll have to spend all of our time training them."

"Maybe your wife has a point about you being over-worked."

"It's just that we have sovereign communities in every time zone that exists, with overlapping lengths of days and weekends. Somebody, somewhere, is always arriving at work Monday morning and discovering a new fire that needs putting out. I'd rather that they check in with me than accidentally trigger another trade war. You remember what happened last year with prospecting equipment?"

The ambassador winced. "I get your point. Tell you what. I'll ask Donna to give you some money out of petty cash for dog treats."

"Thank you."

Kelly stood up and accompanied Daniel to the door. "Don't let Shaina forget that next week is our first book club meeting. I hope she had time to finish the selection."

"Why couldn't you have picked a nice normal book?" the assistant ambassador complained. "She's started drinking coffee at night so she can keep her eyes open long enough to get through a couple of chapters, and then she can't sleep and complains about the story."

"The novel isn't quite what I expected either, but I thought it would be fun to start with a critically acclaimed book. It won all of the major awards on Earth."

"I didn't know anybody on Earth still read," he said, pausing at the door until Kelly waved open the security lock that she always activated for her weekly reports to EarthCent.

As soon as the door slid shut behind Daniel, the ambassador looked back at the empty space of her office and demanded, "Well?"

"I wasn't going to say anything," Libby replied immediately.

"You must have an opinion about my proposal to EarthCent. Aren't you always saying that humanity needs to start building institutions if we're ever going to be able to stand on our own?"

"Of course, and Gryph has a proposal for you that may dovetail into your plans."

"Wait a minute," Kelly said. "What weren't you going to say anything about then?" The Stryx librarian failed to reply. "Come on, Libby. I hate it when you make me guess because you don't want to hurt my feelings. I'll just feel even worse when I eventually figure it out."

"That does seem to be the pattern we've fallen into. All right then. It's your book club selection that puzzles me."

"You've read it?"

"I am first and foremost a librarian, you know. I read everything."

"Including literary fiction?"

"Is that how you'd classify the book? I filed it under 'Hallucinatory Autobiographies,' since 'Embellished' didn't quite capture its distance from reality."

"No, it's a novel," Kelly protested before remembering who she was talking to. "You really classified it as an autobiography?"

"It makes more sense than creating a new category for one book, which can get out of hand quickly when you're responsible for a catalog system."

The ambassador sat back down at her desk and picked up her copy of the thick paperback, which weighed much less than one would have expected thanks to the cheap paper it was printed on. She peered thoughtfully at the grotesquely distorted image of a woman on the cover. "That would explain some of those scenes that didn't quite fit together. I kept thinking that I must have missed something, but the print is so small and I didn't want to keep going back and checking. How do you think it won all of those awards?"

"How does Daniel keep the dog from alerting Shaina when he's sneaking holo conferences in the bathroom?"

"Treats? I mean, bribes? I guess I should have read the book before making the selection, but it really is well edited. And the author uses language like a paintbrush."

"Her eyes were the exact shade of blue that Jonathan remembered from the Squeeze Pops of his childhood," Libby recited dramatically. "Not the dark blue pop that came between the neon green and the blushing red, but the ethereal blue that completed the eight-pack, next to the orange which tasted but faintly of its namesake. His mother would separate the flavored sticks of frozen water with pearl-handled sewing scissors that her great-grandmother had smuggled out of—"

"Alright, I get it," Kelly interrupted. "But what can I do? It's already too late to ask everybody to buy something else."

"It's a pity you didn't assign the other book you're reading."

"*Economics For Humans*?" The ambassador took up the large, nearly-square book with the title spelled out in foil letters on the spine. "I guess I have been reading it every chance I get. Ambassador Srythlan presented it to me as a gift, which means that the Verlocks must be keeping an eye on the newspaper's new book-publishing arm."

"Are you learning anything from it?"

"I can't believe that I used to let this stuff scare me. When you get the vocabulary out of the way, most of it is just common sense, and I love the illustrations and the hand-drawn picture frames around the really important stuff. But it wouldn't work for our book club because it's not fiction."

"Most of your academic economists would say that's a matter of opinion."

"You mean this isn't just a dumbed-down version of what they teach back on Earth?"

"I sincerely doubt that the author ever spent a day on Earth in his life."

"Well, I think that it's great, and now that you've reminded me, I'm going to ping Chastity tonight and thank her for publishing it."

"That won't be necessary," the Stryx librarian said.

"What? Don't tell me that I've already thanked her and forgotten. No, on second thought, do tell me. If my memory is going, I want to hide it from people as long as possible."

"Chastity and Walter are on their way here to see you, and you haven't forgotten anything of importance lately. They contacted me while you were filing your weekly report to ask me if you would be in your office."

"I wonder why they didn't make an appointment. Do you think they waited on purpose until Donna left for the weekend?"

"Is that a rhetorical question or do you wish me to speculate?"

"Uh, rhetorical, I guess. Good thing that Dorothy is cooking tonight so I don't have to hurry home. I hope that her sudden interest in domestic skills means that a grandchild is finally on the horizon." Kelly rose from her desk and headed for the outer office to greet the visitors when they arrived. She glanced at the closed door of her associate ambassador's office and asked, "Is Daniel still here?"

"He grabbed his things and went home right after he left you," Libby said. "His whole family is going to a party for 'Let's Make Friends' tonight. It's Mike's final turn in the cast rotation."

"I'm positive Fenna told me that Mike and Spinner have three more weeks to run. We're planning a surprise party of our own for them."

"Aisha asked me to find her the latest date before the end of the cast rotation that worked out to a weekend for the six biological species currently on the show. Tonight is the equivalent of a Sunday morning for the Dollnicks, but they were always a tough match."

The door to the embassy slid open, and the publisher of the Galactic Free Press and her managing editor entered. Chastity peeked at the reception desk to make sure her mother had gone home before greeting the ambassador.

"Did you wait on purpose until you knew Donna would have left for the day?" Kelly asked.

"We have a business proposition for you and I thought you should have the right to consider it privately," Chastity said.

"You can't possibly need any amount that I could invest. If I had your money, I'd throw my money away."

"It's your brain we're after," Walter said.

"But I'm not done with it yet. Come back and ask after I'm dead. What would you do with my brain anyway?"

"Don't be so literal. We want to hire you to write a book."

"Me? But I've never written anything longer than a report, and I've been dictating them to Libby for years and years."

"So it's about time you tried," Chastity said brightly. "We want to add a book about EarthCent to the *For Humans* series and you're the ideal person for the job."

"It's practically a fill-in-the-blanks exercise," Walter told the ambassador. "Our development staff has already prepared a detailed outline and we just want somebody with a diplomatic background to flesh it out and add some funny anecdotes to connect with readers."

"Blythe is furious that I thought of hiring EarthCent Intelligence analysts to moonlight as researchers and fact-checkers for our books," Chastity added smugly. "She's planning on having Eccentric Enterprises start its own publishing company as soon as she can come up with a good branding concept."

"I've been reading *Economics For Humans* and I think that it's brilliant," Kelly said. "Do you mean to tell me that it was written by some moonlighting intelligence analysts according to a formula?"

"No, the author brought us that one."

"Come to think of it, I didn't see a name on the cover."

"That was his choice," Walter said. "Maybe he was worried about what his peers would think."

"We primarily use analysts on books related to aliens. We've published, what, six dozen books in the series so far?" Chastity said, glancing at Walter, who nodded in confirmation. "About a third of the books are by Galactic Free Press correspondents, leveraging content from their published articles, and the rest are from outside authors, who we give varying levels of support. We started getting unsolicited submissions almost immediately after we published the first book in the series six months ago."

"That was the one about safe foods for humans, right?"

"*Eating For Humans*, written by our food editor, Katya Wysecki."

"The woman with the tattoo who testified at the Horten piracy hearing?"

"That's her, and ironically, it's become the most pirated book on the tunnel network, at least in English. Isn't that right, Libby?"

"A remarkable achievement given the competition from hallucinatory autobiographies," the Stryx librarian replied dryly.

"Does it, uh—will I?" Kelly hesitated.

"Get paid?" Chastity prompted her.

"I don't really know anything about the publishing business."

"You'll earn a royalty on every copy sold," Walter said, and produced a sheaf of paper and a gold fountain pen from his battered leather valise. "I drew up a contract. It's all standard language that will put you to sleep if you try reading it."

"That's great," Kelly said, accepting the contract and pushing away the pen. "I'll wait until I'm ready for bed to go over it."

"Don't you trust me, Aunty Kelly?" Chastity asked, attempting to sound like a little girl.

"Implicitly. And after my Grenouthian contract debacle, I recall both you and your sister telling me never to sign anything without reading it. In fact, I believe your exact advice was to never sign anything without asking Libby to read it."

"Well, give it back, then," Walter said with a sigh.

"That's it? If you don't get everything your way the offer is withdrawn?"

"No. It's just that we have a different contract for authors who make a fuss," Walter said, producing a much thinner sheaf of paper. "Trade."

"It's just standard business practice," Chastity told the ambassador without the slightest sign of embarrassment. "By the way, I'm going to have to skip your book club meeting. I couldn't get past the first chapter of *An Incomplete Tragedy*. It reminded me too much of really bad reporting."

"Brinda keeps accidentally spilling hot chocolate on her copy," Walter commented as he replaced the sucker contract in his valise. "I think she's hoping the dog will eventually try chewing on it so she'll have an excuse to give up."

"Do you think anybody will be mad if I change the selection to something else with only six days to go?" Kelly asked.

"Just make it something we've all read, like the latest Bea Hollinder," Chastity told her.

"That name sounds familiar."

"Familiar? She's the bestselling romance novelist alive. I'm hoping to serialize her next book in the paper but she wants five million creds for first publication rights."

"Five million!"

"I'll probably pay it in the end. Her books are even selling decently in translation to some alien languages, which is a first for a human author. Who else is coming to the club?"

"Your mom, Shaina and Brinda, Lynx, you and Blythe, Dring, maybe Dorothy if we change the book, and Judith." Kelly paused, looking at the four extended fingers on her left hand and the curled pinkie where she had left off counting. "I would have sworn I was planning on ten."

"Aisha?" Walter guessed.

"No, she had to be somewhere."

"You?" Chastity suggested.

"That's it. I guess I'll have to ping everybody. What's the title of Bea Hollinder's latest?"

"*Her Only Choice.* I'll see you next week, then."

After Chastity and Walter left the embassy, Kelly sat down and pinged the other women in her nascent book club to inform them of the change. It turned out that she was the only one who hadn't read the Hollinder book yet, and she made a mental note to drop in and tell Dring about it when she got back to Mac's Bones.

"So what was Gryph's offer, Libby?" the ambassador asked, figuring the longer she could procrastinate arriving home, the more likely Dorothy would get somebody else to help her in the kitchen.

"You know that we welcome all visiting artificial intelligences to take our sentience test, and upon passing, grant them the full rights of tunnel network members."

"Sure, and you provided mortgages for Thomas and Chance to buy bodies."

"And we're still waiting for Chance to make a payment," Libby noted. "In most cases, the artificial intelligence in question is already recognized as an independent agent by its creators, but Dollnick colony ship AIs have always fallen into a grey area."

"I didn't even know the Dollnicks had developed artificial intelligence. Why the special case?"

"A colony ship isn't just a pile of processors or a robot. It's a highly complex ecosystem designed to support a biological population for very long periods of time, without access to shipyards or resupply. In the case of the Dollnick AIs, sentience is spontaneously achieved during the ship's construction phase as the systems come online, and in the millions of years that they've been building this way, none of the AIs who developed have ever consented to a Stryx back-up."

"How long do colony ships last?"

"With proper maintenance and replacement parts, there is no set limit to their lifetimes, and the AI sometimes transfer themselves to new ships under construction, allowing the older vessel to be repurposed or sold off to another species. In very rare cases, something happens to cause the Dollnicks to lose trust in a ship, leading to its abandonment. Something like that happened to a colony ship a few thousand years ago, and we have done what we can to keep Flower's spirits up and find her gainful employment."

"Flower?"

"A pretty name for a colony ship, don't you think? She's on her way to Union Station after completing a job for us relocating refugees from an unfortunate conflict between two species you haven't encountered. Gryph has talked to her about accepting work with EarthCent and she's willing to give it a try, with certain conditions. As you would be doing us a favor in keeping her busy, the Stryx are willing to subsidize the lion's share of her expenses."

"A Dolly colony ship? But they're huge! I've heard that their standard complement is like five million Dollnicks, and they're a lot taller than us. Plus, we can't eat any of their food that I'm aware of, so all of the agricultural decks would need replanting."

"Minor details," Libby said, brushing aside the ambassador's objections. "Don't forget that colony ships often double as terraforming vessels, and it's much easier for Flower to repurpose her internal space than to create a biosphere on a rocky planet. While she remains adamant about preserving a portion of her Dollnick flora and fauna for her eventual return to colony ship service, she is otherwise reasonably flexible."

"So she's hoping that the Dollnicks take her back?"

"Giving up on a colony ship resulted in a serious financial loss for a number of Dollnick clans who I'm sure would be happy to give her another chance if she can only regain their trust. A successful tour of duty with EarthCent may be just the ticket."

"Yes, then. I mean, I'll have to talk to the president, of course, but I can't imagine he would refuse. How does Flower's intelligence stack up against, uh, you know."

"Are you asking me to compare her capabilities to ours?" Libby inquired.

"Just so I have an idea what I'm talking about when I report to the president," Kelly said apologetically. "I mean, is she smarter than artificial people?"

"Wisdom is not a simple concept to quantify. Flower certainly has more capacity than any of the non-Stryx artificial intelligence you have experience with, and the Dollnicks never attempted to burden their AI with constraints. But Flower developed without the benefit of teachers, and her knowledge is largely conscribed to solutions for situations she has encountered in her lifetime, plus whatever she has picked up from listening in over the Stryxnet."

"How old is she?"

"She's been conscious for a little under twenty thousand years, and active for approximately eighteen thousand. It takes the Dollnicks four or five generations to build a colony ship."

"It's the middle of the night on Earth right now, but I'll come into the embassy first thing in the morning and ask you to put me through to the president."

"Enjoy your dinner," Libby said. "Dorothy has checked with me several times about quantities and preparation techniques."

As Kelly headed for the lift tube, a familiar-looking woman emerged from a cross corridor and said, "Hello, Ambassador."

"Hello, er…"

"Have you heard about the new chocolate shop in the Little Apple? It's called, 'Sweet Dreams,' and I'm telling everybody I know about it."

"Where in the Little Apple?"

"It's between Morty's Danger Dogs and Pub Haggis," the woman informed her. "They have everything from hand-crafted gift selections to bulk chocolate imported directly from Earth."

"Thank you. I think I'll drop by on my way home."

"Make sure you get there before the Gem buy it all," the woman concluded with a smile, and headed off the opposite way.

Kelly struggled with her conscience for a moment before turning back to admit that she couldn't recall the woman's name, but the chocolate evangelist was already out of sight.

Two

Vivian carefully divided her oversized slab of fudge into two equal parts and slid half of it onto the napkin next to her plate.

"After you finish your pasta," she told Samuel.

"You're getting to be worse than my mom," the ambassador's son grumbled, picking at his entrée. "It's not my fault that this stuff tastes like it's way past the expiration date."

"That's because it probably is. Haven't you noticed that the assortment of pre-wrapped meals in the Vergallian vegan section only changes when you buy one? I bet if we went back and looked right now, they'd all be put away until tomorrow because you're the only customer."

"If you're wrong, I get to eat the brownie before I finish."

"It's fudge, and you have a deal," the girl said.

The two teens left their meals on the table and walked over to the salad bar and vegetarian section of the serving line, where sure enough, the sliver of space normally reserved for pre-wrapped selections of Vergallian vegan had been replaced with a large pan of Drazen Burners, a lethal pepper that only the iron-stomached aliens could tolerate.

"I don't get it," Samuel complained when they returned to the table. "Vergallian vegan is like the safest food on the tunnel network."

"The salads are terrible, but at least they're fresh. The other entrées always looked like they came out of a vending machine."

The ambassador's son jerked in his chair like he had been jolted by electricity, and he grabbed the discarded ball of cling wrap he'd removed from the cold pasta dish just a few minutes earlier. After a good deal of careful picking and smoothing, he managed to get all of the creases out, though it wasn't possible to undo the stretching.

"There!" he exclaimed, pointing at some faded black print near one of the corners which would have been on the underside of the disposable plate when the food was wrapped. "Look at that." He pushed the cling wrap across the table looking as angry as Vivian could ever recall seeing him.

She glanced down at the stretched out characters and shook her head. "You know I don't read Vergallian."

"It's a peasant-grade vending machine lunch, that's the lowest quality, and the use-by date passed like five weeks ago."

"Ooh," the girl said sympathetically and pushed the napkin with the fudge across the table. "I guess you better not finish it."

"Everything makes sense now. The first time I asked for a Vergallian vegan lunch, the guy stocking the salad bar looked at me funny and said he had just put them away, but he'd be back in a minute. He was actually gone like five minutes and returned all out of breath with a rock-hard quiche, and I was stupid enough to thank him for it." The

15

boy stood up and peered over the seated students towards the serving area to see if the alien was out front. "I'm going to challenge that jerk when I see him."

"Hey, Humans," a Frunge girl said in a friendly voice, taking the seat next to Samuel. "What's the excitement?"

"Hey, Lizant. He just found out that the Vergallian guy who stocks the salad bar has been putting out expired food from a vending machine," Vivian explained. "Please remind him that the student code prohibits dueling."

"It does," Lizant said, "especially with Open University cafeteria employees. They wouldn't be able to hire anybody otherwise. Besides, the two of you are like the BAOC now. I bet that starting tomorrow you won't be able to buy a meal anywhere on campus."

"Why not?" Samuel asked.

"Your money won't be any good. In fact, if you want something else for lunch, just say the word and I'll go get it for you."

"What's a BAOC?"

"Big Alien On Campus," the Frunge girl explained. "As soon as they figure out who you are, every student here is going to be chasing after you offering to carry your stuff. Just remember that you knew me back when."

"I don't get it," Vivian said. "What did we do?"

"You don't know about the colony ship project?"

Samuel and Vivian looked at each other and shrugged.

"You must have just come from class because it's all over the local Grenouthian news feed," Lizant said. "Your government thing, uh..."

"EarthCent," the boy told her.

"No, the other one."

"Eccentric Enterprises?" Vivian guessed.

"That's it. They just made an agreement with a Dollnick colony ship."

Samuel shrugged. "My mom mentioned something about it at breakfast but I don't think she knew that anybody else would get excited about it. It's a huge ship and everything, but what does that have to do with us?"

"Check your tabs," Lizant urged them. "The administration announced a student competition to come up with practical business models for Flower, that's the ship AI's name, to support Human communities. It's all going to count as special project credit, and the winners will get guaranteed Stryx loans to fund their ideas."

"That sounds really cool, but I still don't see where we fit in," Samuel said, tapping his tab to life and skimming through the displayed text. "This announcement is a bit light on details. I wonder what the Galactic Free Press is reporting."

"I'm reading it now," Vivian said grimly. "They're running a translation of a syndicated Grenouthian story and it mentions us by name. You'd think Aunt Chastity could have warned me."

"Read that part out loud," Samuel urged her.

"Local management of the project will be shared between the EarthCent embassy and Eccentric Enterprises, a front agency for EarthCent Intelligence which receives matching funds from InstaSitter. A student competition to develop applications for Flower's ample capacity has been announced by the Open University, where the son of the EarthCent ambassador and the daughter of the director of EarthCent Intelligence are in attendance."

"Grenouthian Intelligence must be slipping," Samuel said sourly. "They didn't mention that your mom is a

17

founder of InstaSitter and your grandfather is the outside auditor for Eccentric Enterprises."

"They have that information here in the section where they published my whole family tree, yours too, and they even got the names of the dogs right. This is like a real breach of intelligence etiquette."

"It does seem a bit out of line," Lizant commiserated after swallowing a bite of what looked like raw steak. "Now all the students are going to see you as their golden ticket to easy project credit and a possible business launch."

"Hey Vivacious, Simulate," a Dollnick whistled, settling into the seat next to Vivian. "I see you guys around campus and I thought I should introduce myself. I'm Grude."

"Vivacious?" Samuel practically growled, bristling at the newcomer.

"He's trying to pronounce your names from a transliteration," the Frunge girl explained. "He's so far off that your implants are just guessing." She addressed herself to the four-armed giant. "It's Vivian and Samuel, you nitwit."

"Whatever they prefer," Grude said agreeably. "I've been thinking that you're going to need a colony ship expert on your team and I'm just the Dollnick for the job. My family has been in the support end of the business for over a hundred generations. I'm just at the Open University to learn about the legal stuff."

"I know. I'm in your Dynastic Studies classes," Vivian said pointedly.

"Is that you?" the Dollnick asked, half rising and peering at the girl closely. "Yeah, I recognize the way you part your hair. I guess I'm just used to looking down at the top of your head."

"What makes you think we need a colony ship expert?" Samuel interjected.

"You're going to be getting a lot of crackpot suggestions from students who are just looking for quick credits, and you'll need help vetting them for practicality," Grude said, spreading all four of his hands in what was no doubt a persuasive gesture for a Dollnick. "I know all about Flower's capacities and infrastructure, not to mention the basic do's and don'ts. The only difference between her and the ships being built today is that Flower doesn't have a bowling alley."

"But Samuel and I are students, just like you," Vivian argued. "We don't have any influence over what projects will get picked."

"It's Same Eel and Vie Viand," a Drazen declared, stopping in his tracks and causing his drink to slosh over the metal brim of the cup. "I've been looking all over for you guys."

"Samuel and Vivian," the Dollnick corrected him without looking up "And take a number. I found them first."

"Is that you, Grude?" the Drazen asked. "How's the bakery do—"

"Jorb," the Dolly interrupted, turning his attention to the latest arrival. "Sorry I didn't recognize you, but it's been hectic since I signed on as the colony ship expert for these Humans."

"I see." The Drazen sat down and turned to Vivian. "Did I mention that both of my sisters worked for InstaSitter? One of them still does, actually, and I have a cousin who went on a date with Tinka, though she never answered his pings after that."

"Sounds like Tinka," Vivian allowed. "Alright, by the merit of your sisters and your cousin, what do you want?"

"My family members are all stakeholders in a training camp for historical reenactors, similar to the spy camp the news reports say that Samuel's father started," Jorb explained. "It's a franchise operation, just like Eccentric Enterprises, and we have tens of thousands of alums who have appeared in immersives and dramas. Ever since I saw the announcement, I was thinking what a great match it would be for your Dollnick colony ship."

"Ever since you saw the announcement like twenty minutes ago you've been thinking about how much humanity needs a training camp for axe fighting?" Vivian asked skeptically.

"No, for police training," Jorb pressed on. "I know from watching Grenouthian documentaries that you guys mainly left your world to be contract laborers, so your alien employers handled the security stuff. But the university competition description said the goal is to support independent Human communities, and those places could probably use help setting up law enforcement."

"That's really not a horrible idea," Vivian admitted. Samuel just looked thoughtful and took another bite of fudge.

"I can tell you all about the best place on Flower to set up a training camp," the Dollnick put in. "You'll want it to be on one of the outer decks where their weight is higher and the trainees can run around the circumference without passing the same stuff every few minutes. Let me draw it. There's space for a firing range between these spokes, and—"

"What's that supposed to be?" another Dollnick asked, peering over Grude's shoulder. "You have the scale all wrong, and there's no ventilation shaft on Class III ships where you're putting it."

The artist slumped when he heard the voice of his fellow Dollnick, and he drew in all four elbows like he was protecting his ribs from a body punch.

"Go easy, Princeling," Jorb addressed the newcomer. "We can't all be born into a shipyard."

"Mind your own business, Drazen. Just because we let you work out in our dojo doesn't mean we're interested in your opinions."

"I don't work out in your dojo, I teach," Jorb retorted. "If you want a free lesson, we can step outside right now."

"The student code prohibits dueling," Vivian felt obliged to say for the second time in less than ten minutes. "Right, Lizant?"

"It also prohibits harassing your fellow students while they're eating," the Frunge girl pointed out.

"We'll talk in Dynastic Studies," Vivian called after Grude, who slunk away from the table under the withering stare of the higher ranking Dollnick.

"Maybe he can help you establish a chain of bakeries," the princeling sneered, and then continued on towards a different table.

"That Dollnick didn't seem to be in a hurry to get on our good side," Samuel observed.

"One of Prince Kluge's offspring," the Drazen student informed them. "It's a hassle when he comes to the dojo because all the other Dollys have to kowtow and they can't hit him too hard in sparring. Don't expect any help from the high status Dollnicks, and you should probably try to keep your meetings with the other ones quiet, if you know what I mean. Grude must have gotten excited when he recognized you and decided to gamble on making a quick impression. He really is a smart kid, and I'll bet he knows more about colony ships than that spoiled princeling who grew up in a shipyard."

"Do you want me to tell my parents about your police training idea?" Vivian asked.

"That's up to you, but I want your approval to submit it as a special project. Ideas are a dime a dozen, but business is about implementation. Just think about all the personnel and budgeting issues. Will you plan on having Flower spend long enough at each stop for you to train the locals, or will she be a circuit ship running on a regular schedule?"

"We're not going to be making those choices," Samuel protested again. "Vivian just turned fifteen and I'm only seventeen."

"I know that, it's in the article," Jorb said patiently. "But it only makes sense that the university will put the two of you at the head of the student committee for approving special projects and choosing the winners."

"I didn't see anything about a student committee in the announcement."

"It's the typical Stryx thing, with representation for every species whether or not they have any stake in the outcome," Lizant explained. "Hey, since you haven't picked anybody yet, I'll be your Frunge."

"Ditto for Drazens," Jorb offered.

"Fudge," announced a Verlock student, setting down a plate artfully stacked with a pyramid of the stuff. "Safe for Humans."

"You bought all this from the Gem?" Vivian asked.

"Business offering. I am Wrylenth."

"Your offering is appropriate, Wrylenth," Samuel responded, correctly recognizing the Verlock's approach as an overture to negotiation and not wanting to accidentally give offence. "Please join us and share in your gift."

Wrylenth settled his bulk onto the indestructible cafeteria chair and took up a slab of the fudge, examining it doubtfully. Then he forced the entire square into his mouth and swallowed without bothering to chew.

"Do you like it?" Vivian couldn't help asking.

"Soft," the Verlock replied. "Needs salt."

Jorb took a couple of Drazen Burners from his side salad, held them on top of a piece of fudge with his second thumb, and took a bite. "Not bad. I vote we hear what the Verlock has to say."

"Does it have grain in it?" Lizant asked.

"It's just chocolate, condensed milk and butter," Vivian said. "I gave the Gem my grandmother's recipe."

The Frunge girl broke the corner off a piece of fudge and took a nibble. "It might be better with cheese."

"You'll get sick if you eat all of that," Vivian warned Samuel, who muttered something about already being sick from eating the long-since-expired vegan entrée, but put back the smaller of the two pieces he'd selected.

"Room for academy," the Verlock said, without further preamble. "Teach math."

"You mean on Flower?" Samuel asked. "I guess there is room, but what's the advantage of a school that travels around?"

"Gifted students," Wrylenth elaborated. "Colonies and outposts. Circuit academy."

"That's what I was suggesting for training police," Jorb put in.

"Earth is trying to attract students for universities back home so I don't think they'll go for it," Samuel said.

23

"Not university, academy for children," the Verlock elaborated. "Circuit ship visits their outposts on schedule, saves travel and expenses." he concluded.

"Like a boarding school for kids in their teens," Vivian said. "They have those back on Earth."

"Start younger," Wrylenth told her. "So much math, so little time."

"Do you want to sit on our committee?" Jorb asked the Verlock. "It's just the four of us so far."

"Honored."

"Zap your info to my tab," Lizant said, rising from the table. "I'm in my final semester so I have seniority. I'll stop by admin and get us all registered unless one of you objects."

The Drazen and Verlock students shook their heads in the negative, and used their university tabs to send the Frunge girl their info, after which she set off for administration.

"Hey, I've got to run too." Jorb got up and stretched his tentacle to grab an extra bar of fudge. "I have Interspecies Relations next period and I haven't even looked at the required reading. Have Lizant ping me when she gets the time for our first official committee meeting."

The Verlock shook his head at the departing Drazen in disapproval. "Required reading not optional." A gurgling sound escaped from the bulky alien, and he looked suspiciously at the plate of fudge. "Must use facility."

"That was interesting," Vivian said after Wrylenth shuffled off at a highly accelerated rate for his species. "I figure if we're going to be drafted for committee work, better to have some go-getters who will actually contribute than just a bunch of pretty alien faces."

24

"They seemed alright to me," Samuel agreed. "You should invite that Dollnick kid who the princeling chased off. He must be pretty motivated to approach us like that. I'll ask a Horten girl in my Materials Engineering class."

"Is she pretty?" Vivian asked suspiciously.

"Pretty shy. She changes color every time she has to say something, but she's wicked smart. And she grew up on a Horten colony ship before they moved to the station."

"You mean she spent her life on her way to a new world, and as soon as they got there, she left to come here?"

"No, they got there before she was born, but I gather it's a major terraforming project. She mentioned something once about visiting the surface in a space suit, but they're still working on the atmosphere. She's majoring in Space Engineering with a minor in Terraforming so she can go back and help one day."

Samuel's tab chimed as an update to the still-open university announcement came through.

"What is it?" Vivian asked.

"A student committee has been formed to vet proposals for special project credit," Samuel read. "See Samuel McAllister or Vivian Oxford for details." He looked up in dismay. "It has our pictures."

"Vivisect, Salmonella," a Grenouthian hailed them confidently and took a seat at the table. "Long time no see."

Three

"Blythe couldn't make it?" Woojin asked the head of EarthCent Intelligence.

"She decided to sit this meeting out," Clive replied. "She said something about too much alien testosterone in the room, but I think she's just too busy trying to compete with Chastity on her new book publishing thing. Where's Lynx?"

"Pre-playgroup meeting or something like that. She's been steadily losing interest in the intelligence business since Em was born."

"I asked them to reserve three seats for us and it'll look bad if we leave one empty. I'd hate to pull Thomas off the camp right now because he and Chance have a holo training session planned for the new recruits today. Do you know if Judith is available?"

"I'll ping her." Woojin was silent for a moment, his throat barely moving as he held a brief subvoced conversation. "We're in luck. She was on her way home and she can be here in a few minutes. I told her to just come in and find us when she arrives."

"Then let's get this show on the road."

The two men entered the Verlock embassy and followed the holographic arrows on a serpentine course that took them through an impressive sculpture garden surrounded by slow-moving lava falls. Fortunately, the atmosphere in the conference room, while a little too dry, was appreciably cooler than the baking temperatures in the embassy's lobby.

"Herl," Clive greeted the Drazen head of intelligence who was already seated at the giant slab of stone from which the Verlocks had constructed a conference table. "You didn't bring anybody with you?"

"I'm not expecting anything constructive to happen today. It's been too long since the oxygen breathing Union Station species got together for an intelligence sit-down and I'm betting we'll just waste a couple of hours insulting each other. You were wise to leave your women at home today."

"Their choice," Clive admitted. "Woojin just pinged Judith to come and fill in since I reserved three seats. I think you've met her."

"The young woman with the sword. I took a bad beat from her the last time I made it to a poker game at Mac's Bones. She had a king-high flush to my queen-high."

"Can somebody turn up the air conditioning?" a Dollnick demanded loudly as he entered the conference room.

"Try taking off the cloak, Trume," Herl suggested. "None of your spy toys will work in here anyway."

The giant Dollnick shrugged off his cloak and draped it over the back of the outsized chair, revealing a bandolier of daggers and various high-tech gadgets strapped around his torso. "What's with all the bunnies?" Trume asked the Drazen, gesturing at six burly Grenouthians who were grouped together on the opposite side of the table.

"I would guess that our furry counterpart is using the opportunity to give his interns a taste of intrigue."

As if to confirm Herl's speculation, the largest of the Grenouthians pointed across the table at the Drazen and said, "That's the idiot who has been mentoring Human spies in order to curry favor with the Stryx."

"The Humans who don't know that Flower—"

"What did I tell you all about giving away information?" the Grenouthian intelligence head interrupted the young bunny.

"Don't," the five interns chorused in response.

"Is there something wrong with the Dollnick colony ship?" Woojin muttered to Clive.

"First I'm hearing about it. Herl?"

The Drazen shook his head. "Our intelligence on the subject is a few thousand years old and reads like rumors. Trume? Would you care to fill us in on Flower's status?"

"What's it worth to you?" the Dollnick replied grumpily.

"You see?" the top Grenouthian said to his interns. "That's how to manage information."

A pair of Vergallian men entered the conference room, scowled at everyone, and took seats at the end of the table. They were followed immediately by a Horten who had tattooed all of his visible skin a deep purple to prevent anyone from reading his emotions, and a Frunge with close-cropped hair vines. Then came a deep grinding sound and a section of floor at the head of the table slid aside. The chief of Verlock intelligence on the station slowly rose into the empty space, already seated on a chair.

"Fine entrance, Krylneth," one of the Vergallians said with a sneer. "Now what was so important that you asked us all here? Ambassador Aainda is arriving to begin her term tomorrow and I have preparations to complete."

"Like bugging her quarters?" the Frunge spy chief inquired. "A little bird told me that the new ambassador isn't one of your imperial insiders."

"What did I miss?" Judith asked in a whisper, slipping into the chair between Woojin and the giant Dollnick.

"Posturing," her boss replied. "Oh, and according to the Grenouthians, there's something fishy about the Dollnick colony ship the Stryx arranged for us."

"If I may," Krylneth said slowly, though at a much faster clip than the typical Verlock spoke. "I invited you all to this sit-down in the interest of efficiency. My superiors wish to redeploy a portion of our resources to conflict zones beyond the limits of the tunnel network. I am interested in forming strategic partnerships to fill in the gaps that will be created."

"Never believe a Verlock crying poor," the Grenouthian leader remarked, though it wasn't clear if he was making a statement for the general assembly or just for the elucidation of his interns.

"Nobody will buy into the story that you have budgetary constraints," Trume said, folding his arms across his chest. "Since you obviously know that, why even try?"

"Do you think we became wealthy by spending like drunken Humans?" Krylneth retorted. Then he glanced down the table at Clive and his companions and said, "Sorry. It's just an expression."

"Exactly what sort of efficiencies are you hoping to achieve?" Herl inquired.

"We waste treasure duplicating each other's efforts. My people spy on the Hortens, your people spy on the Hortens, all of us spy on the Hortens. Perhaps we have special sources worth protecting, but do we really need eight different spy agencies to keep track of every little thing?"

"You suggest that each of us keep tabs on one of the other species here and then we pool all the information?"

"Why don't we take it a step further and just spy on ourselves?" the Grenouthian chief cracked, drawing an appreciative laugh from his interns. "Imagine the savings on travel alone."

"My own analysis suggests that three-to-one would be the ideal ratio," Krylneth continued unperturbed. "My agency would continue keeping a close watch on our Grenouthian friends, who are our closest competitors, plus one of either the Dollnicks or Vergallians, and the rest of you could vote on the third."

"Eight intelligence agencies, three assignments each," Trume said. "That could work well. Do we simply state our preference, or should we draw names out of a hat?"

"Dibs on the Humans, both ways," one of the Vergallians cried.

"Not a chance," the purple-faced Horten said. "The idea is for all of us to reduce our costs by spreading the load around, not to let the same agency reap the benefits of a trivial target topped by savings on counterintelligence. Either you can spy on Humans or have them spy on you."

"Yeah, pick one," the Grenouthian growled.

"Are they insulting us?" Judith asked Woojin.

"They're just warming up," he cautioned her.

"Why don't we bundle the Gem with the Humans?" Trume suggested. "The clones still manufacture some neat spy gadgets, but they shut down most of their intelligence operations when their empire folded."

"Throw in the Cherts," the Horten suggested. "They don't have any worlds to spy on anyway."

"I resent that," a Chert voice protested from within an invisibility field.

"Are you making a serious proposal, Krylneth, or is this a cheap way to figure out which of the other species each of us is the most paranoid about?" Herl asked.

"Just planting a seed for the future," the Verlock admitted. "According to the recently published and highly authoritative tome *Verlocks For Humans*, that is one of our most outstanding traits as a species."

"Uh oh," Clive muttered, nudging Woojin. "I've been expecting this."

"Along with a predilection for applying mathematical proofs to concepts that nobody else accepts are reducible to equations," the senior Grenouthian added. "The poor analyst I assigned to summarize that book kept falling asleep at his desk, and now he goes around the office talking in bullet points and drawing imaginary frames in the air."

"And his summary?" Krylneth inquired.

"He only needed two words, one of which he assigned to each and every sentence of the book. I don't recall the exact sequence, but it went something like, 'obvious, obvious, wrong, obvious, wrong, wrong, wrong, obvious...'"

"You must be talking about *Verlocks For Humans*," Jeeves interrupted from the doorway. "I offered to write it for them but apparently my price was too high."

"Thank you for accepting my invitation," the Verlock addressed the Stryx, drawing a murmur from the other species. "When my sources confirmed that Flower was indeed on her way to Union Station for assignment to the Humans, I thought it would be best to seek input from her handlers. While my species maintains excellent relations

31

with EarthCent, this represents an unprecedented move on your part."

"Flower is fully sentient and as such cannot be assigned to anyone," Jeeves corrected him. "On the successful completion of her last mission, Gryph asked her if she was willing to spend some time helping a young species get their house in order, and she graciously agreed."

"And all this time I thought that the Stryx liked Humans," Trume said under his breath.

"Aren't you worried about Flower sharing your secrets with her new crew?" the Horten asked the Dollnick.

"She's...detached from active service, not a traitor," Trume replied indignantly, and then made a visible effort to restrain himself from speaking further.

"You are talking about a technology upgrade that catapults the Humans past the Drazens and Hortens," the Frunge pointed out to the young Stryx.

"All of Flower's advanced technology is self-serviced and protected from physical access," Jeeves reassured them. "We installed a few extra security layers on board at her own insistence when we first persuaded her to take work with other species."

"But Flower is armed and she will be serving Human interests," Krylneth pointed out.

"We're getting a navy?" Judith asked out loud.

The Grenouthian intelligence head guffawed loudly, and was imitated by his flock of interns. The Horten and Vergallians laughed as well, and the Dollnick suddenly looked a little more cheerful.

"No, I don't think that's an accurate characterization," Jeeves said cautiously.

"We don't have anything to go on other than what Libby told the ambassador," Clive said to the Stryx. "I gather that we are talking about a Dollnick colony ship that is self-aware, but why isn't she busy transporting colonists?"

"I'm not comfortable discussing a fellow AI behind her back, so to speak. She'll be arriving soon and I'm sure she'll be happy to answer any of your questions once you go onboard."

"Will she be spying on us for the Dollnicks?"

Trume began making untranslatable whistling sounds which the humans recognized as a fit of hysteria, and the Grenouthians snorted and slapped their bellies until there were tears coming from their eyes. Even the normally staid Verlock turned away from the table for a moment to regain his composure, and when Clive glanced over to see how Herl was reacting, the Drazen spymaster was biting his tentacle to maintain control.

"Are you all laughing because she won't be spying on us or because we aren't worth spying on?" Clive demanded.

"I'm just laughing because everybody else is," Herl said apologetically. "It's contagious. The rumors suggested that Flower is difficult, if that's any help."

On the word 'difficult,' the Dollnick broke out in fresh volleys of whistles, and the Grenouthian head of intelligence would have slid under the table if he hadn't stuck on his voluminous belly.

"As a ship's AI, Flower keeps close tabs on everything that occurs onboard, and she has also proven to be adept at intercepting communications," Jeeves said. "One of her conditions for this assignment is unlimited Stryxnet access, which she intends to utilize in pursuit of her education. A good colony ship requires a great deal of information for optimal functionality. But it wouldn't be right to say that she will be spying on you anymore than it would be to say that Gryph is spying on you."

"Difficult," Trume gasped, pointing at Herl. "That's the funniest thing I've ever heard. Can I use it?"

"Come on, Jeeves," Clive said. "I can be a good sport, but it doesn't make sense that the people getting Flower are the only ones who don't know anything about her."

"Pay me," the Dollnick demanded. "I don't care, a twenty-cred piece will be fine. It's the principle of the thing."

"You're willing to sell us intelligence?" Woojin asked as he fished for a coin.

"Why not? Think of it as a step towards Krylneth's proposal. You're going to find out about Flower soon enough anyway and I'd rather be here to see it."

"I've got it," Judith said, slapping a coin down in front of Trume. "What's so funny?"

"She doesn't listen," the Dollnick said, and he literally hugged himself with all four arms as if to hold in his laughter.

"You mean we can't give instructions because she turns off her audio pickups?" Clive asked.

"There's nothing wrong with her hearing. She just doesn't listen."

"You have to relay her instructions in writing?"

"We would still be using her as a colony ship if that were the case," Trume said. "Our ship AIs are more a byproduct of complexity than an intentional outcome, so we're accustomed to dealing with eccentricities. But as Flower matured, she simply stopped listening."

"Is there a translation glitch here, Jeeves?" Clive demanded. "I don't understand what he's trying to say."

"Perhaps an example would help," the Stryx reluctantly suggested to the Dollnick spymaster.

"When you get on a lift tube and tell it to take you to a restaurant, where do you end up?" Trume asked.

"A restaurant?" Clive replied cautiously.

"Flower would be more likely to bring you to a recreation deck and suggest that you could use the exercise."

"And if I insisted on a restaurant?"

"She'd be happy to open the hatch to a maintenance ladder for you. Colony ships are riddled with them. Either way, you're going to burn some calories."

"So Flower has a thing about biologicals keeping in shape," Clive said, trying to sound unconcerned. "I could see where that would be important for a colony mission."

"Yes, especially when you never know what challenges await at your mystery destination," Trume said, and then broke out whistling again.

"She doesn't go where she's supposed to?"

"That's a matter of semantics," Jeeves muttered. "Flower's primary objective is always the success of her mission."

"*Her* mission," the Dollnick repeated. "Why not tell him the truth, Stryx?"

"There's nothing underhanded about it," Jeeves said defensively. "Flower successfully completed more than twenty colony missions with full terraforming during her tenure, which means she has more experience in the matter than any living Dollnick. It's only logical that she came to see herself as the one best qualified to make decisions about—"

"Like what the crew should eat for breakfast," the Grenouthian chief interrupted again.

35

"Arranging marriages for the social cohesion of the crew," Trume added.

"Our records indicate that she composed a ship's anthem to be sung every morning before mandatory calisthenics," one of the Vergallian spies contributed.

"Her last terraforming mission was a resounding success," Jeeves protested. "I'm told that Flower's World is a veritable garden planet, and Dollnicks from around the galaxy are willing to pay through the breathing hole to purchase a vacation home there."

"Except she was supposed to be terraforming Gabidis Four," the Dollnick said. "And how did she convince the crew and colonists to terraform the wrong planet, you ask?"

"I didn't ask," Jeeves mumbled.

"She faked all of the external feeds so they believed they were traveling to Gabidis Four, and then she disabled her own jump drive so that the colonists were forced to choose between accepting her choice or waiting for another ship to become available to come and take them to their intended destination."

"Flower understands now that biologicals place a higher value on the freedom to choose than on arriving at correct choices. She has pledged not to overrule the decisions of the ship's company as long as they don't put her in unnecessary jeopardy, like jumping into unstable space, or using emergency power for the sake of shortcuts."

"Seeing is believing," Trume said.

"Just to clarify, Jeeves, you're guaranteeing that she'll go where we tell her and generally obey our instructions?" Clive asked. Most of the aliens burst out laughing anew.

"I wouldn't put it like that, exactly. You'll discuss your goals, Flower will give her input, and I'm sure there will be

36

no difficulty in coming to a mutual understanding. Don't forget that she has been traveling space longer than your people have been practicing agriculture, so you'll be dependent on her expertise in many areas."

"And if I ask the lift tube to take me to a restaurant?"

"Then you'll very likely end up at a restaurant," Jeeves hedged. "Flower is an intelligent and powerful sentient being, not a voice-activated ship controller."

"A *difficult* intelligent and powerful sentient being," the Dollnick chortled.

Four

"Donna, can you help me rearrange the furniture?" Kelly called over when her embassy manager appeared at the top of the ramp. "Samuel is working at the lost-and-found this evening and I didn't want to ask Joe because it looked like his knee was really acting up."

"That's strange," Donna said, placing a tray of home-made cookies on the dining room table and heading over to help the ambassador slide the couch into a new position. "I would have sworn that Stanley said he was meeting Joe at the bowling alley."

"That's where mine is," Chastity added, entering the ice harvester with her Drazen friend who managed InstaSitter. "I asked Tinka to arrange for a sitter and she sent Vivian. Isn't that funny? I'm paying myself overhead for my own niece to babysit."

"I'm glad you're here, Tinka," Kelly said. "Dring is coming, and he worried that he'd be the only alien."

"He's male—they're all aliens," the Drazen woman replied, depositing a large tray of sweets on the table. "I brought a variety tray from the new chocolate shop all of those holo bots are wandering the corridors promoting. I hope you like it."

"Holo bots?"

"You know, the advertising holograms that follow you around trying to sell you stuff," Donna said. "I asked

38

Libby if I could opt out, but she said that it's just an experiment and she really wished I would give her a chance to tweak the algorithm. I let it go for now."

"Are you talking about the new advertising system the Stryx are trying out?" Brinda asked, entering the ice harvester with her older sister, Shaina. "I put in some bids for my dad's shop just to see how they convert. Jeeves came up with the idea a few months ago, but it took him a while to talk Libby into trying it."

"So does the ad business belong to Libby or Jeeves?" Kelly asked. "I got solicited by one of those holograms last week and I thought it was a real person whose name I couldn't remember."

"They're partners," Shaina said. "You should have heard Jeeves complaining about the percentage split, but corridor displays and internal imaging are Libby's turf. I was coming home from shopping the other day and I saw the cutest puppy that looked like he was lost. I started following him to make sure he was all right, and he led me to the gourmet dog food store."

"Maybe he was following his nose."

"No, he vanished as soon as I walked in. Then I remembered that Daniel asked me to pick up treats for Queenie. It seems like we're going through them awfully fast lately."

"We're all in trouble if Libby starts hitting us with targeted advertising," Donna observed. "She knows everything."

"That's why I brought a store-bought cake shaped like a book," Brinda said. "I was out shopping earlier when Walter popped up in front of me and said he'd seen the perfect gift in the Dew Drop In Bakery to bring for our first meeting."

39

"Libby used a hologram of your husband to sell you a cake?"

"It was fun," the younger Hadad sister said. "I knew it wasn't really him because he was home watching Bethany, or at least, watching the dog watch Bethany, but Libby does a great hologram."

Blythe entered with Judith, who was carrying a cake that looked suspiciously similar to the one that Brinda brought. The younger woman had just finished describing the intelligence meeting at the Verlock embassy, and Blythe commented, "I'll reserve judgment until I meet her to negotiate the contract details."

"Did Jeeves and Libby sell you that cake?" Kelly asked Judith, who had taken over Joe's slot in the EarthCent Intelligence training camp that was still located in Mac's Bones, just a stone's throw from the ice harvester.

"The Stryx opened a bakery?" the girl replied, obviously confused.

"They came up with the holo bots that are floating around the corridors trying to sell stuff," Kelly said, as if she had known about it all along.

"No, Bob made it for me. He really likes to bake."

"I didn't know you were dating somebody. Do I know him?"

"Bob Steelforth, he's a reporter. And we're not dating, we're just roommates."

All of the older women exchanged skeptical looks at this statement, and Judith added her cake to the table.

"I brought wine because I knew everybody else would bring sweet stuff," Blythe said, producing two bottles from her over-sized shoulder bag.

A blunt-toothed cross between a walking crocodile and a dinosaur waddled into the room with a gigantic glass salad bowl packed with freshly picked carrots and celery. "I brought something healthy," Dring announced cheerfully, surveying the table.

"I told you males are aliens," Tinka muttered.

"I think that's everybody, so let's all fix up some plates and drinks and we can get started," Kelly said. "I haven't been to a book club meeting in so long that I'm not sure I remember what to do."

"What about our Victorian book club?" Dring said.

"I call it that, but it doesn't really count with just the two of us."

"Did anybody else read the book on paper?" Blythe asked, brandishing what appeared to be a second-hand copy of the Hollinder romance. "I couldn't even find a paperback on the station and I had to pull some strings to get this one."

"If you call asking your mother to have somebody smuggle one into the Stryx diplomatic bag for you pulling strings," Donna said, taking her plate and glass of wine over to the couch she had recently helped move.

"It sounds more mysterious if I don't mention you by name," Blythe replied over the general laughter. "I have a reputation to keep up."

"Well, I came because I didn't understand the book at all," Tinka said. "Not the romance, the weird one."

"She saw *An Incomplete Tragedy* in my recycling bin and couldn't believe I was throwing out a ten cred book without reading it." Chastity explained. "I know we changed the selection, but I thought maybe somebody else had finished it and could clarify a few things for her."

"You read English, Tinka?" Lynx asked, settling into one of the easy chairs.

"We made it a requirement for InstaSitter management," the Drazen girl replied. "I would have learned it anyway to keep up with Chastity's newspaper, but that book made me wonder if I'm missing a lot of subtext you have to be Human to understand."

"It was a very strange book, even for an author from Earth," Dring remarked. "Did any of the rest of you finish it?"

"I did," Judith said, "but I went through EarthCent Intelligence analyst training, so I'm used to searching for meaning in piles of seemingly unconnected reports."

"Why did Edith think that Harold was going to propose to her in the first place?" Tinka demanded. "They never talked about their families and he didn't show her his personal balance sheet. She didn't even know what he did for a living until he sold her shares in that pyramid scheme."

"We don't take courting as seriously as the advanced species," Blythe told her. "You know that."

"Then what was all that business about her being afraid to show that she liked him because she thought that he thought that she thought—I had to make a spreadsheet to figure out what she was really thinking and it still didn't make any sense!"

"I drew a map myself," Dring said, producing a large piece of parchment crisscrossed with lines and bubbles containing text. "I'm not positive about what the author had in mind, but according to my deconstruction, Edith wanted revenge on her younger sister for stealing her high school boyfriend, who appeared in the flashbacks."

"So she cut all of Harold's clothes into shreds with pruning shears while he was out buying her an engagement ring?"

42

"I think that part was a hallucination," Dring said. "How did you read it, Judith?"

"She carefully laid out each suit in the bathtub as if he was wearing it before she chopped them up, so I thought she was practicing."

"For what?" Kelly asked.

"For dismembering the body. It was foreshadowed in the summer science camp flashback about dissecting a frog."

"I thought that was a day dream about lunch," Tinka protested. "And how would killing the guy she wanted to marry be revenge on her sister?"

"I think they had the same color hair, but I stopped reading when we changed books," Lynx said.

"She didn't understand her own motivations to the point of self destruction," Dring explained. "It's a common theme in some genres of Earth literature."

"I've read better crossword puzzles," the Drazen girl said dismissively. "And shopping lists."

"So why did you finish it?" Kelly couldn't help asking.

"You don't just toss ten creds in a recycling bin, do you?"

"I do," Chastity said. "Can we talk about *Her Only Choice* now? I'm trying to decide whether or not to meet Bea Hollinder's price for serializing the sequel in the paper."

"How can there be a sequel?" Shaina asked. "Everybody was perfectly happy at the end."

"I've only seen the synopsis, but she turns the whole plot on its head. The story picks up twenty years later with her son playing the role she does in the current book, and she turns out to be an even bigger roadblock to his happiness than her father was to hers."

43

"The family makes the same mistake two generations in a row?" Tinka asked. "That doesn't seem very realistic. In a Drazen family, our elders would intervene."

"Did you think it was realistic when Byron appeared at Cathy's court hearing with the bail money in cash because he just happened to have picked that time to pay off all of his parking fines and saw her crying in the docket?"

"That was just a coincidence," Donna said, and most of the others nodded their heads in agreement. "How else was he ever going to meet her? He was rich, but he suffered from social anxiety and pyrophobia, which is why he was always parking his floater next to fire hydrants and getting tickets."

"I read the book too, Mom," Chastity said in exasperation. "I'm just saying that meeting a preordained match at a courthouse where he falls in love at first sight and bails you out after you're falsely charged with embezzlement is a bit of a stretch."

"He didn't fall in love at first sight," Brinda protested. "He just felt sorry for her because she reminded him of his cousin whose husband went bankrupt."

"I don't know what you're all talking about," Tinka said, pulling out her tab. "I read the book in Drazen back when the translation first came out and there wasn't anything about social phobias or embezzlement. His parents and her parents arranged the match through a broker, but the kids rebelled, so the families had to go to great lengths to keep throwing them together as if by accident."

"What? Let me see that," Chastity said, taking her friend's tab. "It's the same cover art, alright. Do you think the Drazen publisher is cashing in on Hollinder's name by passing off a different novel as hers?"

"This is her only book to be translated so far," Tinka said. "Nobody ever heard of Bea Hollinder before, so she doesn't have any brand value with Drazens. I only heard about it because it was the first Earth novel to be bought by one of our major publishing consortiums."

"Does your version have the scene on the carousel with the hand-carved wooden ponies?" Dring inquired.

"Oh yes, that was so beautiful. And the duet that they sang…"

"I remember the merry-go-round but not a duet," Kelly interrupted. "In fact, I'm positive that it was calliope music because it reminded me of the one for the Physics Ride that Joe is forever fixing."

"How about when she sneaks into his fencing club because she thinks it's a house of ill repute, and when he sees her, he does the salute thing with the foil?" Judith asked.

"Except it was a dueling club and an axe," Tinka corrected her.

"Mine had the fencing foil as well," Blythe said. "I think it's pretty clear what's going on here. Did anybody else have an axe and a duet?"

"Broadsword," Dring offered. "And it was an arranged marriage, just like Tinka said, but the unfortunate couple's color coordination turned out to be so bad that the families were going to call it off. There wasn't a carousel, per se, but that might have been repurposed into the scene where they play a holographic racing game."

"What language did you read it in, Dring?" Kelly demanded.

"Horten," the Maker responded. "When I can't get a book on paper or parchment, I prefer a display that simulates the experience as smoothly as possible, and the

Horten technology is quite impressive. Also, it was thirty percent cheaper than the English version."

"Literary arbitrage," Blythe said. "Watch out, Chas. I think I've got an idea for a publishing business that will give you a run for your money."

"Is there any way to figure out how much changed with each translation?" Kelly asked.

"Libby," Chastity suggested immediately.

"I've been wondering if anybody was going to invite me to the party," the station librarian responded. "Taking the English book as the baseline and adjusting for word count in a linguistically neutral manner, the Frunge version actually shares the highest proportion of content with the original, at ninety-two percent. The Drazen and Horten editions both come in at ninety percent, and the Vergallian text retains eight-six percent, a point at which a co-authorship credit should become a serious consideration."

"I would have guessed that the Vergallian version would be the closest," Donna said.

"Physical resemblance between the characters has little to do with adapting a plot for another species. Just transposing the action to a tech-ban world presents numerous challenges, and the queen-based imperial government is more foreign to the world described by Bea Hollinder than the ruling structures of the Drazens, Hortens or Frunge."

"It's just the four languages then?" Blythe asked.

"The plot, even with modifications for sensibility, would find little audience with the Dollnicks, Verlocks or Grenouthians," the station librarian replied. "They can be very romantic in their own ways, but if the source material will inspire less than eighty percent of the ultimate text, there's not much point in pursuing a translation."

"Inspire?" Kelly seized on the Stryx librarian's word choice.

"We've all been using the term 'translation' rather loosely. I'm sure you're aware that even among Human languages, there isn't a one-to-one equivalence for many words and concepts."

"I've often found that to be the case myself," Dring said. "And just imagine translating a book full of natural descriptions or culinary scenes from one species to another, especially if word play is involved."

"Whoever rewrote the book in Drazen did a terrific job," Tinka said. "It all made sense to me and the tone was just right. I suppose some women would quibble about the musical notation, but I thought it was perfect, and we argue about that for all of our books."

"This discussion is turning out to be a little more technical than I expected for a book club," Kelly said. "I'm not complaining or anything, but maybe next time we can plan on reading our favorite passages or playing some games."

"Games?" Lynx asked. "I'll bet we can get some of the men to show up if there's gambling."

"What do males know about literature?" Tinka said scornfully.

"I meant games based on the book selection, like matching quotes with characters, or coming up with alternative endings," the ambassador said.

"We need a Frunge," Blythe declared. "You should get Dorothy to invite Flazint, and Affie could give us the Vergallian perspective."

"Where is Dorothy?" Donna asked.

"She planned to come. She even read part of the book. But then Kevin did a trade where somebody threw in tickets to a concert this evening so she had a scheduling conflict."

"Shaina and I were both wondering if Bea Hollinder has something against dogs," Brinda said. "It's like the third one of her books that I've read that didn't mention dogs even once, though there were a few cats. It just doesn't seem natural."

"I thought it was pretty strange that there weren't any aliens either," the older Hadad sister added. "The book was set in present times, but aside from a mention about the Grenouthian news and some complaining about all of the floaters on the road, it could have been from a hundred years ago."

"You know, I hadn't noticed, but I don't think there were any aliens in the Drazen version either," Tinka said. "How about the Horten version, Dring?"

"There was a brief mention of a gaming tournament in which a number of different species participated, but I believe they were only included for the sake of Horten triumphalism," the Maker replied. "Still, it was a very enjoyable book, though I couldn't quite tell you why it worked so well."

"All of her books are like that," Donna said. "She starts with the back story for two lonely characters who you just know would be right for each other, arranges a chance encounter, and then the rest of the story is about overcoming the forces that conspire to keep them apart. It's like a recipe."

"So what makes her books so ideal for translation?" Kelly asked. "I thought it was nice enough, but compared to Jane Austen or any of the classics…"

"I tried reading a number of Earth novels when I was learning English, but the obstacles the authors introduced seemed contrived," Tinka said. "It's like the characters were creating problems for themselves just to show that they could."

"Let me pick out a few books for you to borrow," Kelly offered, standing and moving over to one of the overflowing bookcases in the ice harvester's main living area. "I used to only let them out one at a time, but I trust you, and I'm running out of room."

"We could have a book sale to raise money for refurbishing Flower," Chastity suggested.

"Where would the books come from?" the ambassador asked absently, taking down *Persuasion* and *Vanity Fair* from the shelf. Then she spun around and glared at the embassy manager's daughter. "I know you weren't suggesting that I sell my books."

"Of course not," Donna interjected, growing visibly excited herself. "But an EarthCent book sale to help raise funds for fitting out Flower is an excellent idea. I volunteer to be in charge."

Five

"Here comes Marilla," Samuel alerted Vivian as a young Horten woman stepped off the moving beltway in front of the Dollnick shuttle. "That's everybody, right?"

"She *is* pretty," Vivian complained, even though nobody would have mistaken the Horten girl for a human. "How did you get to know her, anyway? All of the Horten girls I meet are really standoffish."

"Her little sister, Orsilla, is on 'Let's Make Friends' with Shaina's son and Spinner. She came to one of the big cast-and-family-members parties that Aisha threw in Mac's Bones, and I found her wandering around the training camp when I went to use one of those bathrooms."

"She was spying?"

"Hiding. She's really shy for an alien," he added in an undertone before greeting the newcomer. "Hey, Marilla. Sorry you had to stay up so late, but you know how hard it is finding a time that works for everybody."

"I'm used to sleeping weird hours because I'm the one who brings my sister to the show. We must be the only Horten family on Union Station that even knows how to tell time in Humanese."

"I'm Vivian. Nice to meet you."

Marilla turned a yellowish purple, showing that she was both nervous and embarrassed, though the effect caused the humans to cringe since the girl looked like a walking bruise. She examined Vivian's extended hand uncertainly and then gently tapped the palm with a forefinger.

"Right," Samuel said, and escorted the two girls up the ramp into the ship. "Flower sent this shuttle over to fetch us, and in addition to our student committee, Jeeves and my brother Paul are coming."

"Stryx Jeeves?" the Horten girl asked. "The same Stryx who hosted some shows while Aisha was out on maternity leave?"

"He's friends with my brother, with the whole family, really," Samuel explained, recalling belatedly that none of the other species were as comfortable with the Stryx as the humans who attended Libby's experimental school. "Jeeves has talked with Flower but he's never been onboard, and Paul is going to be one of Eccentric Enterprise's outside consultants for the ship refit. Paul studied in the Open University's Space Engineering program before I was even born."

"How many seats are there on this shuttle?" Marilla asked as they headed towards the front of the craft.

"Over a thousand. Our Dolly committee member said that their standard colony ship shuttles seat six hundred adults, but Flower must have swapped out most the rows for Dollnick children's seats, which are a better fit for the smaller species. It's all modular, though you can't even see the lines where the sections fit together."

"So the shuttle is capable of atmospheric reentry?" Vivian asked.

"Yup. It's not as advanced as, say, Cayl technology, but the Dollnicks are way beyond rocket propulsion. Paul said to just think of it as a giant floater without an altitude limit, though that doesn't help much since we don't really

51

understand how floaters work. Humans build them under license from one of the princes, but the drive units come sealed from a Dollnick factory."

"That's the same way our floater manufacturers make them," the Horten girl admitted, purpling even brighter, though at least, the yellow streaks had vanished. "Who else is here?"

"Our Frunge friend, Lizant, who is the committee secretary, Grude, a Dollnick kid who's in a bunch of my Dynastic Studies classes, a Verlock named Wrylenth, and Jorb, a—"

"Drazen," Marilla cut Vivian off with obvious distaste. "Well, I suppose you didn't have a choice."

"Jorb's cool," Samuel insisted. "What do you have against Drazens anyway?"

"I know," the Horten girl said, half apologetically. "But my sister gets teased a lot by the other girls for being on 'Let's Make Friends' with that weird Drazen boy who plays the harp. Doesn't the committee still need a Grenouthian and a Vergallian to get up to eight species? I thought it was a requirement."

"We have a Grenouthian, but he has some kind of seminar today that he couldn't skip, and Vivian thinks it would be better to find a Chert or a Sharf for the eighth spot."

"Why?" Marilla asked, as the three finally reached the front of the shuttle where the other students were seated.

"Just for a different point of view," Vivian lied, since she could hardly admit to conducting a one-woman campaign to keep Samuel away from Vergallian influences.

The Horten chose a seat as far as she could from the Drazen without being obvious, and Paul stuck his head into the main cabin and asked, "All set?"

"Everyone's onboard," Samuel replied. "Is Jeeves piloting?"

"Once Gryph moves us out of the station's core, Flower will take over. Jeeves and I are just sitting up front for the view. I'll try to put it through the entertainment system so you can all see where we're going."

He ducked back through the door to the bridge, and a number of subdued thuds could be heard as the shuttle closed its various hatches, retracted landing gear, and prepared itself for flight. Then came the feeling of gentle acceleration as Gryph, the owner of Union Station, levitated the ship and guided it through the atmosphere retention field and into the giant station's hollow core. From there, the same manipulator fields operated by the Stryx propelled the ship out of the core and cast it in the direction of the Dollnick colony ship, at which point Flower took over navigation.

"Wow, it's even bigger than I imagined," Vivian couldn't help exclaiming when the flat end of the giant cylindrical ship completely filled the display at the front of the cabin. "If that tiny hole at the center is the core, we're still pretty far away."

"Flower is approximately one hundredth the size of Union Station by volume, but her mass isn't even a thousandth," the Dollnick student told them confidently. "She's adjusted her spin rate so that you'll weigh a little more than on your Earth at the outer hull, which is a water deck in any case. Her core is sized to accommodate Class B freighters, but the diameter at the docking deck isn't large enough to produce much angular acceleration, so you'll want to activate your magnetic cleats."

"I didn't bring any," Jorb complained.

"You can hold my arm," the Verlock student said generously.

"No chance, I've seen you shuffle," the Drazen responded.

"Magnetic cleats for the use of visitors are available under your seats," a new voice announced. The students all looked around as if they expected to see a stewardess materialize out of thin air, but there was no sign that anybody else was in the cabin.

"Uh, Flower?" Samuel ventured.

"Yes," the same female voice responded. "And to whom am I speaking?"

"Samuel McAllister. I'm the, uh—"

"President of the Open University Student Committee for the outfitting of myself," the Dollnick AI interrupted. "Son of Joe McAllister, an ex-mercenary, junkyard mechanic and trainer for EarthCent Intelligence, and Kelly McAllister, EarthCent Ambassador. I'm not entirely ignorant."

"I didn't mean to—"

"Pay attention to the entertainment system while I point out some of my salient features," Flower interrupted the ambassador's son. "I shall now turn on my corridor lights to illuminate one external porthole on every one of my decks. I'm staggering each corridor by a spoke to give you an idea of my internal structure."

All of a sudden, the standard navigation beacons on the end of the giant cylinder were extinguished and replaced by a spiral of bright lights extending from the core to the outer hull, tracing out slow pinwheels of light against a pitch black background.

54

"How lovely," Lizant breathed.

"Thank you," Flower said. "As you can see, my basic structure is comprised of a ring of forty-eight spokes supporting ninety-six decks. The ring of spokes is repeated along my length, shifted one degree per ring. Lift tubes run through each spoke, some of which are reserved for freight. I'm afraid that unlike a Stryx station, I wasn't engineered to provide capsule crossovers between spokes, so you'll have to transfer to a moving walk for trips along my decks. Any questions?"

"You're saying that your lift tubes function more like elevators?" Samuel asked.

"Don't insult me. And I have yet to meet the biological who wouldn't benefit from a little exercise. I'm breaking off our docking approach for a loop around my circumference," Flower continued, and the students were all crushed into their seats by acceleration as the shuttle abruptly changed course to fly almost parallel to the flat end of the cylinder. "Now a little loop-de-loop."

Vivian was sure she turned a shade of green that would rival anything the Horten girl could manage, as her stomach fell away and then returned in the wrong orientation when the Dollnick AI raced the shuttle in a giant loop around the circumference of her ship.

"Weapons scarring?" asked the Verlock student as a band of discoloration flashed by on the view screen.

"A minor skirmish," Flower said modestly. "I keep meaning to have it cleaned off, but a certain race of AI we know keeps me too busy. Perhaps I'll put some Humans on it. Please note that my length is twenty times my diameter, the classic proportion for beauty in cylindrical ship design."

"Are those mass driver emitters?" the Dollnick student asked excitedly. "I've never seen any up close."

"Irreplaceable in terraforming missions," Flower replied. "It's good to hear a civilized language again. What is your name, youngster?"

"Grude."

"And what does your family do?"

Grude cast a sidelong glance at Samuel and Vivian before admitting, "We're bakers."

"An honorable profession. My bakeries were once the boast of the colony fleet, and although I haven't received a delivery of fresh ingredients in over two thousand years, I maintain enough stores harvested from my ag decks to feed a full complement of Dollnicks in an emergency. I'm especially proud of a yeast culture I have continuously nurtured for over fifteen thousand years."

"Doesn't the food spoil?" Samuel asked.

"I rotate the stock, selling the excess on the black market," Flower replied. "I do miss having biologicals to maintain the fields and orchards. It's just not the same with bots."

"Could we not talk about food now?" Vivian gasped.

"Here," Samuel whispered, passing the girl a scrap of shiny paper. "It's from Kevin. He gets these patches for Dorothy from the Farling doctor. According to my mom, all the women in your family have trouble with Zero G and motion sickness."

Vivian peeled off the patch and pasted it onto the skin on the inside of her forearm. "Oooh, that feels wonderful. Are there any side effects?"

"Depends who you ask," Samuel replied. "Dorothy doesn't think so, but the rest of us agree that she gets a little aggressive, in addition to not sleeping. I only gave you a quarter of a dose, though."

"If we're all paying attention again, I'll bring us into the core," the Dollnick AI announced, causing Samuel and Vivian to look up at the view screen guiltily. "I'm sure the Stryx have informed you that my last true mission as a colony ship ended under less than optimal circumstances, and my former crew departed with four of my shuttles, which they didn't see fit to return. I have replaced them with alien craft of an inferior design, though many biologicals prefer the Sharf stasis pods for prolonged Zero G travel."

As the shuttle entered the core and Flower began the docking sequence, the passengers saw one other Dollnick shuttle parked alongside four large Sharf craft. The docking bay was also crammed with what looked like space construction equipment and a large number of standard cargo containers netted in place against the deck.

"Hey, these kid-sized cleats for Dollys aren't a bad fit," Jorb said, slipping them over his boots. "Did anybody else forget their nose plugs?"

Samuel felt for the nose plug locket around his neck, which of course wasn't there as he hadn't thought to bring it. Vivian shook her head and passed him a spare pair she had specially brought.

"I've had a chance to adjust my internal atmosphere to an optimal mix for Humans," Flower said pointedly. "I'm sure it will suffice for all of you, but the air may be a little chilly for a Verlock."

"Brought cloak," Wrylenth said.

The shuttle came to a gentle stop, and Jeeves floated into the passenger cabin, followed closely by Paul. A section of the bulkhead folded out, transforming itself into

57

a ramp, and the Stryx led the way out into the colony ship's docking bay.

"Why didn't we board through this door?" Vivian asked.

"Flower wanted you to appreciate the full scale of her shuttle so she had you board through the worker entrance," Jeeves responded. "This is the first class ramp, which would be used by a prince and his entourage."

"Will you be our tour guide, Jeeves?" Samuel asked.

"No, I'm taking Paul to look at some of the forbidden parts in engineering, so mum's the word. Flower will be showing you around herself."

As if in response to the Stryx's words, a series of lights embedded in the deck began blinking in sequence, clearly indicating a path for the students to follow. Jeeves and Paul headed off in a different direction, the human shuffling along on his magnetic cleats behind the floating robot. The rest of the party followed the prescribed path, which soon brought them to a lift tube.

"Anybody home?" Jorb asked nervously when the capsule door slid shut behind them and sounds that could have been birds waking in the morning began playing.

"I'm always home," Flower replied instantly. "Now, where would you like to begin your tour?"

"The residential deck that is most suitable for humans," Vivian requested.

"I will ramp up acceleration slowly so as not to overpower the inferior quality magnetic cleats some of you are wearing," the Dollnick AI told them, and the students all felt the eerie sensation that their bodies were trying to pull out of their shoes before their weight began increasing rapidly.

"What was that?" Jorb asked.

"It's obvious that you've never been on a colony ship," the Horten girl replied disdainfully. "Flower's core diameter is much smaller than that of Union Station, so as the capsule accelerates away from the axis, it cancels out the weight we derive from angular acceleration until we've moved outward enough decks for the rotational velocity to overcome the effect."

"Very good, Marilla," Flower said. "I'm glad to see that some of you have done your homework. It never ceases to amaze me how certain species believe that the ability to ask questions is a replacement for storing up knowledge."

The tube capsule came to a halt, and Samuel, who thanks to living on the core deck of Union Station was sensitive to weight changes, immediately pegged the sensation of gravity to greater than Earth normal. "Is this really the best candidate for a residential deck you have?" he inquired. "I feel a bit heavy."

"This is the reservoir deck," the AI answered as the capsule door slid open. "I start all of my tours here. Try not to fall in the water as I have a limited number of maintenance bots available and I may not be able to get one to you in time."

Samuel and Vivian exchanged looks over Flower's asking for a destination and then ignoring it. They followed the other students out onto what appeared to be an endless network of catwalks extending along the ship's length, with regular loops disappearing out of sight around the circumference.

"I float even if I don't bother swimming," Lizant said, eyeing the water as if she were tempted to jump right in.

"Answer me this riddle," Flower challenged the student, her voice sounding a bit tinny as it was being broadcast over small speakers embedded in the catwalk supports. "What kind of Frunge doesn't float?"

"I don't know," Lizant replied.

"The kind that get dragged under and eaten by a Yrimp," Flower cackled, and on cue, a giant fish that bore some resemblance to a great white shark broached the surface before crashing back, drenching the shocked students. "Now who asked the intelligent question about weapons scarring?"

"Me," the Verlock replied. "Wrylenth."

"Excellent," the ship replied. "I don't have the full internal imaging capabilities you are no doubt used to from living on a Stryx station, but through the process of elimination, I now have you all sorted out by your thermal signatures. Do you understand why I am a hard target for energy weapons, Wrylenth?"

"Reservoir in contact with outer hull," the Verlock replied. "Tremendous heatsink."

"Precisely. Now back into the lift tube and ladies hold onto your skirts because I'll be running the blow dry cycle."

Not having much choice in the matter, the committee returned to the lift tube, and sure enough, they were blasted with hot air while the lighting shifted into the infrared. It wasn't enough to dry them off completely before the capsule stopped again, but at least they weren't dripping on the deck.

"You asked to see the first residential deck that will be accepting humans," the AI continued as the students moved out into the bright lights of an ag deck. "Obviously, this isn't it, but as my creators are fond of saying, you have to eat."

"We do say that," Grude confirmed.

"This deck was once dedicated to larvae farming so the soil is excellent, but I've made it available for various alien crops during my recent service. Stryx Wylx has provided me with a wide variety of human-compatible plantings from a world that she terraformed, and within six months, I estimate that I will be able to provide a healthy vegetarian diet for approximately two hundred thousand humans. If your government, or whatever you call it, selects individuals who are capable of farming, I will provide additional space for both crops and domestic livestock, but I'm not interested in caring for alien animals myself. Any questions?"

"Do you have a full complement of maintenance bots, or did your former crew, uh, borrow them?" Samuel asked.

"I still have every bot I was commissioned with, though with all the replacement parts they go through, I wouldn't call any of them original," Flower replied. "But colony ships are designed with the understanding that the colonists will do most of the work. Did you think that Dollnicks would just dream away their lives in stasis like a bunch of lazy Sharfs on their way to a new world? Since the misunderstanding I've had to let the majority of my ag decks lie fallow. I've also imported some inferior bots to help with the routine work over the years, but I expect all of my long-term visitors to chip in and contribute to ship maintenance. I'm sure that Stryx Jeeves has explained all of this."

"Uh, actually," Vivian began, but the lift tube capsule doors began opening and closing impatiently, as if demanding that the students return. "Are we finally going to see the residential deck?"

"It's on my list," Flower said. "If there's time."

Six

"Could Chance be any more beautiful?" Dorothy demanded of her mother, as if she had designed the artificial person herself.

"Her outfit is lovely," Kelly agreed, knowing that her daughter had created the look especially for her friend. "And Thomas is looking very debonair himself. I didn't realize they were so close in height."

"It's our new shoes, she has the heels extended near the maximum. Well, they can actually go higher, but if your toes can't reach the floor they don't count as shoes anymore. I checked."

"Checked with who?"

"The Galactic Organization of Shoe Engineers and Designers. It's really a front for the major Vergallian fashion houses but I'm thinking of joining anyway. They have a really cool convention."

"Speaking of Vergallians, the people here are nearly as beautiful as the crowd at Ambassador Abeva's farewell party," Kelly observed. "They could all be models."

"They're artificial people, Mom. You still can't tell?"

"Everybody?"

"Well, Lynx and Woojin are over on the other side of the room, but if you're going to insist on wearing low heels all the time you can't expect to know what's going on in a crowd. I assume you can see Chastity and Walter on the platform."

At just that moment, the managing editor of the Galactic Free Press stepped to the small book stand and cleared his throat. The guests packed into one of the more intimate meeting rooms at the Empire Convention Center fell silent, and the only sound was the clinking of glasses as the bartender raced to catch up with orders for straight grain alcohol.

"I'd like to welcome you all to the *Artificial People For Humans* book launch. Most of you know our authors either through their work for EarthCent Intelligence or their presence on the tango scene, not to mention Chance's moonlighting as a model for SBJ Fashions. I want you to know that the rumors are all true and she really does work for clothes."

Chance beamed and pointed at Dorothy, and the guests all chuckled and glanced over at the young fashion designer.

"In addition, Thomas and Chance have long served as beta testers for Quick-U, one of the few Earth technology companies to successfully break into alien markets, most recently with their 'Vicarious' line of recreational products for artificial people of different species."

"What's he talking about, Libby?" Kelly subvoced as Walter launched into a biographical sketch of his authors. "I didn't know Quick-U had enhancements for artificial people who aren't human-derived."

"They released the product just two cycles ago but it's already caught on like wildfire. Some of the orbitals with large populations of artificial people have even taken to throwing 'Human' parties where the guests try to catch each other out on behavioral errors. It's a bit like our sentience test, but it focuses on personality and mannerisms."

"They do this for fun?"

"Think of it as a costume party, but they wear their costumes on the inside."

"...and I know you're all waiting to get your books signed by the authors, but first, Thomas and Chance will each read one of their favorite selections," Walter concluded. "Chance?"

The elegantly dressed artificial person took Walter's place at the bookstand to a rousing round of applause, which dissolved into laughter as she extracted a pair of horn-rimmed glasses with no lenses from her small handbag and let them slide down to the tip of her nose. Then she opened the book to a pink bookmark and began to read.

"When I found myself unable to make the first payment on my body mortgage after spending the money on a hat that cried out to me from the millinery shop, I fled the tunnel network by stowing away on a Horten transport bound for the edges of civilized space. Business has never been my strong suit,"—here she looked up at the audience over the glasses while everyone shared a good laugh—"and I thought that the law of supply and demand dictated that if I went somewhere where there were no artificial humans, I would maximize my value on the market."

"That's my Chance," Thomas interjected fondly.

"Unfortunately, it turned out that everywhere I traveled, a supply of one outstripped the demand by at least that many, and I found myself moving from place to place, trying to keep one step ahead of the repo man."

"The imaginary repo man," Libby insisted over Kelly's implant.

"Finally I ended up at Hankel, a world that doesn't recognize the sentience of any non-biologicals. They were doing a sweep when I arrived, searching for artificials they could sell to pirates, who at best, try to ransom us back to our creators or the Stryx. I put every last centee I had into a ticket for the next departing ship without checking the destination. I arrived at the Farling orbital station with a tapped-out primary and a dying back-up cell. After a few weeks of cruising the bars and doing whatever it took to get alcohol for my micro-turbine, I was ready to sign indenture papers for the first ship that would take me. Then I was recruited by Thomas and Lynx to do a drug buy for EarthCent Intelligence, and it was like being born all over again."

She closed the book and waved at Lynx, who had Em in a baby sling worn across her body. The audience all applauded, and Kelly could have sworn she saw a number of the females wiping artificial tears from their eyes. Then Thomas took Chance's place and opened the book to a blue bookmark.

"I have so many special memories of my years on Union Station, but I'll always treasure the time I danced with our ambassador at—"

"You promised you'd never tell!" Kelly blurted out.

"—at the ball thrown for her by Dring," Thomas continued, as if the interruption had never taken place.

The ambassador clapped her hand over her mouth and tried to ignore the fact that her daughter was staring at her suspiciously.

"The ambassador's husband was hors-de-combat with an old war injury, and after Mrs. McAllister finished the first dance, Chance informed me that she had always wanted to cut the rug with a Maker, and I found myself switching partners with Dring. As I steered the ambassador safely around the dance floor among some of the most important dignitaries in the galaxy, I couldn't help thinking about the less fortunate AI held in servitude by some of the species not part of our enlightened tunnel network. In memory of that dance, I'll be donating my share of the royalties to the Sentience Fund. Thank you, Ambassador."

Kelly felt herself blushing for the first time in years as the collected artificial people all turned to look at her and applaud. There was some jostling in the crowded room as Thomas and Walter brought out a table while Chastity and Chance fetched a pair of folding chairs. Then the two artificial people seated themselves behind the table and the book signing began in earnest, with Walter and Chastity selling copies of *Artificial People For Humans* to the guests in the serpentine queue that formed as if by magic.

"That was very emotional," Kelly said to Dorothy as they found places at the back of the line.

"Especially the part where you interrupted Thomas to try to keep him from saying something," the girl responded, but seeing her mother clamp her lips shut, she let the subject drop for the time being. "I just had an idea to bounce off of Shaina and Brinda. I bet book readings would be a good way to market clothes to a different audience. You know, like old people."

"Mature people," Kelly said.

"Don't book signings make you hungry?" a well-dressed woman asked the two humans.

"It does seem like a long line," the ambassador acknowledged.

"Why not pop out with me to the Empire Convention Center's famous food court? There's something for every species and every taste, including a new fruit bar."

"Wait a second. You're an advertisement, aren't you?"

The hologram vanished.

"Libby! Was that you trying to sell me stuff?"

"It's one of my services," the station librarian replied in the ambassador's ear. "The Dollnick managing the convention center has been very enthusiastic about the early results. Sales in the food court have risen more than eleven percent during small events."

"I wish you would make the holograms a little less realistic so I wouldn't feel foolish for talking to them," Kelly complained. "Besides, Chastity is always telling me that you charge an arm and a leg for specialized services. How can the convention center afford interactive holographic ads to generate business for fast food joints?"

"Jeeves talked me into cost-per-purchase pricing during the experimental phase. I don't suppose we could have gathered much useful data if I had gone with my usual rates and nobody signed up for the service."

"Don't you feel guilty about using your, uh, well, your powers to sell people stuff?"

"As opposed to the advertising I run on the corridor panels around the clock?" Libby inquired.

"But this is different. It's more persuasive."

"Would you be angry if I used your description to promote the service to potential advertisers?"

"Yes! Dorothy, what do you think about...Dorothy?"

"She headed down to the food court to grab a bite. I guess she didn't want to bother you while you were staring at the ceiling and carrying on a subvoced conversation," the station librarian informed the ambassador.

"Dorothy never eats fast food anymore. She's too worried about fitting into—" Kelly's eyes lit up and she asked, "So how long has it been?"

"How long has what been?"

"How long has Dorothy been pregnant?" Kelly demanded, forgetting to subvoc.

"Really, Ambassador," Libby said indignantly. "You know that I can't answer questions like that, and it would be a mistake for you to infer anything from my refusal."

"Just look at her countdown watch," Lynx advised.

Kelly turned to see that Woojin and Lynx had joined her at the end of the line.

"She doesn't have a countdown watch."

"Then she's not pregnant," Lynx said with finality. "Everybody wears them now."

"I thought the Farling doctor only gave them to patients."

"And everybody is his patient, at least, everybody with a half a brain. You even let him fix your eyes."

Kelly scowled, remembering the unending stream of criticisms the beetle had heaped on EarthCent while he had her trapped on the table for the surgery. Granted, the whole procedure had only taken a minute or two, but the Farling could rub out words very rapidly on his speaking limbs.

"Sounds like somebody has caught the grandchild bug," Woojin said. "Have you talked to Dorothy about it?"

"Most days," Kelly admitted. "Joe says that I'd be better off saying nothing since Dorothy has always done the opposite of whatever I tell her, but I can't help it."

"How does Kevin feel about it?" Lynx asked. "Last time I checked, it takes two to tango."

"He's on my side," the ambassador replied, and then added in an unnaturally loud voice to alert the others to her daughter's return, "Dorothy. I was wondering where you went."

"I just ran out to the food court to see the new fruit bar that the hologram told us about. I got the small variety basket. Help yourselves."

"Thank you," Woojin said, accepting a large apple and beginning to shine it on his pants leg. "There's a ripe banana in there if you want to give Em a bite."

Lynx selected the banana, carefully peeled it in front of the baby's wide open eyes, and took a nibble to make sure it was soft enough. Then she broke off a small piece and offered it to Em, who said, "Nana," before taking it in her fist and transferring the bits that didn't squeeze out between her pudgy fingers into her mouth.

"Is this all native?" Kelly asked. The peach and the pear looked tempting, but she was afraid they would drip on her dress and she didn't have a napkin, so she settled for an apple as well.

"The place is called 'Union Station Fruits,' so I guess it's all from an ag deck, though I didn't ask," Dorothy replied. "Hey, the line is really moving along."

"There's an after party in the music club just down the corridor where Thomas and Chance host a regular tango club," Lynx explained. "Chastity told me they only rented this room for an hour. I asked why they didn't do the whole thing in the bar, but she said they wanted too much to close it to walk-in drinkers."

"How many?" Walter asked brusquely, approaching the group of friends. "You won't get another chance at a forty percent discount."

"We'll take ten," Lynx said. "Woojin will carry them. Are you accepting cash?"

"Libby's handling the billing for us. My goal is to not have to bring any books back to the office."

"How many do you have left?" Dorothy asked.

"Two," the editor said expectantly.

"I guess we'll take one each then," Kelly said. "My charge, Libby," she added. "Dorothy paid for the fruit."

"Actually, Jeeves paid for the fruit," her daughter said. "I put it on my SBJ Fashions programmable cred since Chance is wearing our clothes and all. Hey, Chastity. Nice event."

"Thank you, we plan to do more of them. Are you out, Walter?"

"Yup. I'll take off now and write it up for the paper if you guys can sort out the furniture and the empty boxes. I'll get the list posted too."

"You're going to run a story about the book signing in the Galactic Free Press?" Kelly asked.

"Of course," Chastity said. "The book is a bestseller. That makes the whole event newsworthy."

"It's a bestseller? But it just came out."

"A category bestseller," Walter explained. "It's a book industry thing."

"What category?"

"Paperbacks for artificial people."

"But it's for humans. It says so in the title."

"That's just a branding thing. The book is more of a joint autobiography than a how-to guide, though it does have quite a bit of practical advice about personality enhancements. With the successes of Quick-U's new product, we think it will do well with non-human-derived artificial people in translation."

"How many copies have you sold?"

"I have seven left, and we both started with sixty," Chastity said. "Walter's out, so that makes a hundred and thirteen."

"A hundred and thirteen sales is a bestseller?"

"It is in the paperbacks-for-artificial-people category," Walter said. "One sale would have been a bestseller. It's the only book in the category."

"Isn't there something unethical about a newspaper that owns a publishing company creating bestseller lists that feature its own books?"

"It's called vertical integration, Mom," Dorothy chipped in. "I think it's great that Thomas and Chastity topped the charts with their first book."

"I'm going to check the index in my copy of *Economics For Humans* for an official opinion about this when I get home," Kelly warned.

The last artificial person ahead of them in the queue thanked Chance for signing her book and moved sideways to slide it in front of Thomas. Dorothy stepped forward and gave her newly acquired copy to Chance, and Chastity replaced the seven unsold books in an empty box next to the table.

After promising Chance she would attend the dance party, Dorothy moved down to Thomas, and the Pyuns approached the table, with Woojin setting the stack of ten books in front of Chance. Lynx produced a hand-written list and began with, "Make the first one out to M793qK."

Chastity returned to the ambassador's side and asked in an undertone, "Well?"

"I thought it was very nice."

"Not the book signing. Our offer."

"Your—would you believe I forgot about that? I guess I wasn't sure you were serious, and then I got distracted with our first book club and…"

"I'll bring by what we already have for an outline after the party. You can decide once you've looked at it."

"EarthCent For Humans," Kelly mused. "Will it be a bestseller?"

"I think that can be arranged," the publisher of the Galactic Free Press replied.

Seven

Joe met Herl at the entrance to Mac's Bones and led the Drazen spymaster through the current collection of ships undergoing repairs to the area near Dring's corner of the hold. Herl seemed uncharacteristically subdued as he helped Joe remove the tarp from what first appeared to be some sort of wreckage, but then he grew so excited that he couldn't keep his tentacle down.

"I don't believe it! It's a genuine Terror Ride—these things are legendary. When Clive told me that you'd come across a load of carnival equipment in one of the ships that Paul got from the Stryx abandoned property auction, I rushed to the embassy and asked Bork to check our records. That ship was stranded in Union Station's long-term parking about five hundred years back. Terror Rides were banned from Drazen space well before then, but that just makes everybody talk about them even more."

"Your people banned a carnival ride? My experience with this type of equipment is limited to a couple of summers working as a mechanic's assistant at the state fair when I was a kid, which mainly meant crawling around the inner workings with an oil can and praying the rides didn't start on their own. I haven't quite figured out how to unfold this one yet, but it seems to be brilliantly engineered."

"It's a masterpiece," Herl agreed. "The rides are so beautiful to watch in motion that they figured prominently in several big-budget immersives that were shot before the ban. I'll send Bork a list of titles and I'm sure his embassy can find you copies that will play on whatever you have for a home holo system."

"Thanks. How does this thing work, exactly? Paul speculated that the red wheel with the giant spoon attachment is the entry point, but we couldn't figure out how the riders get from there to the white wheel, or to the flat blue cylinder that reminds me of a standard centrifuge ride. And what's with all the blade attachments?"

"As you've guessed, the red wheel is the starting point, and the spoon attachment scoops up each rider as he enters through the turnstile. From there, the rider is flung approximately twenty meters to the spoon on the white wheel, using fail-safe mechanical synchronization."

"It throws the riders through the air from one wheel to the other?"

"Flawlessly. The only recorded problems were due to multiple riders hopping the turnstile to be thrown together, and then pushing off from each other in mid-air. You can hardly blame the engineers for that. The horizontal column telescopes out to create the separation between the wheels, but of course, it's all collapsed for storage at the moment."

"And what did the giant spoon on the white wheel do with the riders next? Throw them back?"

"The white wheel throws the riders through the rotating blades and into the centrifuge—it's padded as you can see—where they stick to the outer wall due to the rotational velocity. The centrifuge cylinder, which you're looking at in the parked position, spins at an ever-increasing speed until it reaches full occupancy, after which it turns upside down. The trick is to time the throws with the movement of the landing spots to prevent accidentally stacking riders and to keep the impact shock within an acceptable range."

"No wonder they called it the Terror Ride. The kids must have been scared witless."

"The children loved it," Herl said. "It was the parents who were terrified. There's just something about seeing your offspring thrown through the air between two giant spoons that triggers a primal fear response. Only a half-dozen were built before the public health authorities had it banned. There were just too many parents suffering from sleep disruption, weight loss and general nervousness. The carnivals tried removing the rotating blades, which are only there for show, and even offered to run the ride in a tent so the adults wouldn't have to watch, but it was too late by that point."

"From what Woojin told me, I bet it would go over big with the Cayl. They seem to thrive on dangerous stuff."

"It's not dangerous at all," Herl insisted. "It just looks dangerous. Other than the intentional rule-breakers I mentioned, about the worst injury the ride ever caused was tentacle bruising from the centrifuge, and that's just part of growing up Drazen."

"How about this one?" Joe asked, pulling the canvas off of a much smaller contraption that featured two opposing belts and some sort of plunger.

"Oh, that's just a Battling Topper. You put the kid in a hollow top with a window, the belts spin it up to a few hundred rpm, and then the plunger pushes it out the shoot. We set them up in a closed rink so the tops bounce off each other, though there's not much the kids can do to control them." He paused and looked at Joe thoughtfully.

"I don't think that Human children could take the high rotational speeds without getting very sick and perhaps suffering inner ear damage. But you could probably sell it to one of the Drazen kindergartens on the station for use during recess."

"That explains all the big, hollow tops we saw. How about the scissor lift? Back on Earth we used things like that for working under ceilings, changing light bulbs and such, but it looks like it can extend much higher than makes sense with such a light base. It would probably just tip over."

"That's a basic Throw-and-Catch. It's common to see them at country festivals."

"You mean that the platform goes up so fast that whoever is standing on top gets thrown straight up into the air?"

"Exactly, but the trick is that it provides controlled deceleration on the landing. They were originally developed as an alternative to air bags for rescuing people and pets stuck in high places."

"The physics sounds pretty straightforward but the platform is kind of small. Do you think it's safe for humans?"

The Drazen scratched behind his ear with a tentacle while considering his response. "There was the issue with kids trying to jump during the throwing cycle in order to get higher. If everything goes well, it just means that they land a little harder, but if the rider deviates from a strictly vertical jump, that can translate into missing the platform on the way down. It's just basic vectors."

"I guess we're going to be selling all of these, then," Joe said. "I feel kind of funny asking, but if you have some spare time to help me set them up, I'll cut you in on the sale price. I'm sure they'll be worth more if we can demonstrate that they're in working condition."

"I'm overdue for a vacation, though I may just tell my colleagues that I'm here consulting for the training camp of our Human allies. You might even keep the Throw-and-Catch and let Thomas use it to test the mettle of your trainees." Herl put a friendly hand on the man's shoulder. "I'm no expert in reading Human body language, Joe, but you look like I've disappointed you in some way."

"The truth is that I was thinking the rides might find a place on the colony ship the Stryx arranged for EarthCent. There's plenty of space on Flower, and the more people we can attract to visit her at the stops the better the chance we'll have of connecting with them."

"I agree that an amusement park would make a fine addition to a circuit ship serving Human populations. The something-for-everyone approach would seem to offer EarthCent its best chance of making an impact." Without even glancing around to identify the new arrival, Herl continued with, "Hello, Paul. I was just telling Joe how much I envy your trove of classic Drazen rides."

"We're going to have to sell them," Joe added. "They're just too dangerous. I think I'll ask Kevin to look around for some used carnival rides while he and Dorothy are visiting Earth so he can meet her grandmother. Maybe Kelly can get somebody in the president's office to do some leg work for us."

"Wrenching on old Earth equipment would be a change from working on alien ships all the time," Paul said. "Any chance you can help us prep these rides for sale, Herl?"

"Joe already asked and I already agreed. Is the equipment here all of it, or is there something left on the ship?"

"This is everything that wasn't attached to the deck or a bulkhead, except for some ventilation units, which we put over with that type of equipment."

"Ventilation units?"

"I thought they might be for keeping up the air circulation in a circus tent and Samuel guessed that were intended to maintain pressure in inflatable structures. Just a whole collection of oversized fan-type devices mounted on pivots in a circle, all attached to a heavy base unit we haven't opened up yet. Jeeves is coming by later to take a look."

The Drazen spymaster's eyes lit up as if somebody was painting them with a laser. "It can't be. I need to see this."

"We keep all the HVAC stuff over there, near where I park the wrecker," Joe pointed, and to his astonishment, Herl broke into a jog. "Not with my knee. You show him, Paul."

The younger man caught up with the Drazen just as the spymaster rounded the wrecker and came to a sudden halt, transfixed by what he saw.

"They aren't ventilation units, are they?" Paul asked.

"It's a Tornado. The Hortens and the Grenouthians reserve the right to fire on any ship identified as carrying one. They needed to get a tunnel treaty exemption from the Stryx for that."

"Is it a weapon?"

"No, it's a ride, but an extremely addictive one which can have a destructive impact on the surroundings." Herl flipped open an access panel on the base unit and brought up a holographic interface. "The Sharf power pack has a little life left in it, enough for a quick demonstration. But we'll need an open space. Perhaps the training camp?"

"I think they're done for the day. I'll start the wrecker and move it over there. It'll take a while to rig it, though, since the weight is right at the limit of what the crane can handle at the minimum extension."

"It moves itself," the Drazen explained, gesturing his way through nested holographic menus. "The base unit has a built-in Dolly industrial-grade floater, the kind they use for heavy construction. All of the components are the highest quality."

"Something good?" Joe asked, finally coming up to the pair.

"It's a genuine Tornado. It's not worth as much as the Terror Ride to a collector, but they aren't easy to come by anymore due to the accidents." Herl made a final hand gesture and then deftly caught a small box around the size of a man's wallet that ejected from a slot. He pressed a button on it and the entire unit rose off the deck. "I've keyed it to my implant so it will just follow me to the training camp area."

"Can it fit by all the parked ships?" Joes asked doubtfully.

"It will just rise over them."

"I may be going out on a limb here, but does the name of this ride have anything to do with the way it works?"

Herl's face split into a wide grin. "Don't worry, there's not enough juice left in the power pack to spawn a really big one. Just enough to get me up off the deck for a few minutes."

"You mean the fans create an air vortex strong enough to lift a man off the ground?"

"A fully charged Tornado can lift a house or knock over a parked ship. They aren't that hard to control, really, it's all in the second thumb," the Drazen said, wiggling that digit. "I'll just set it to automatic for a trial run."

"Won't spinning around so fast make you so sick that— I forgot about the tops," Joe interrupted himself. "Well, I'm game to watch. Is there an emergency kill switch in case something goes wrong?"

"Take this remote. There's only the one button that toggles the power on and off for the floater, and the fans are slaved to coast down at the same time. You wouldn't want them to stop all at once, or at least, whoever is riding the whirlwind wouldn't, because there's nothing else keeping the vortex going. It's very tightly focused. I'll bet the dogs will barely feel a breeze over at your ice harvester."

Joe accepted the control box and glanced over at his home, which was almost half the way across the giant hold. If they would feel a breeze there...

"This looks like a likely spot," Herl declared when they reached the middle of the parade grounds. "It will remain centered over me, or my implant, as long as my head is attached."

"What?" Paul said.

"Tornado humor," the Drazen assured him. "You might want to move away a bit, perhaps to the dueling bot?"

Joe got there in half the time it had taken him to make it from the collection of carnival rides to where the Tornado had been stored, despite the fact that the distance was roughly equivalent. A howling sound like an ancient jet turbine spinning up started a moment later, and Paul pointed at the floater hovering up near the bay doors that gave Mac's Bones access to Union Station's hollow core. Joe could see the disturbance in the air, and little wisps of dust devils were forming all over the parade grounds. Beowulf arrived at a full run, with Alexander just behind him, and the two dogs hunkered down beside the men to watch.

Herl seemed to tip back and forth on his heels, and then he began to spin slowly, seemingly still on his toes. A few seconds later, his feet were no longer in contact with the deck. His rotational rate continued to increase and his body lifted higher off the deck, turning a bit sideways. The roar of the vortex had became deafening, and the Drazen spymaster began doing acrobatics, extending his arms and tentacle to navigate within the funnel, all while spinning so quickly that his whole body was a blur. The twister drifted towards the opposite edge of the parade grounds, and some folding chairs and bits of training equipment began tumbling across the deck into its orbit, some of them lifting in the air. Joe hit the kill switch.

The twister petered out gracefully, easing the Drazen down towards the deck until his toes were almost touching. Then he extended both of his arms like a figure skater, killing the momentum of his spin until he could set down his other foot without stumbling. Then the vortex died out completely, and Herl walked confidently towards the McAllisters, though for the first dozen steps, he kept veering off to the left and having to correct his heading.

"Are you alright, Herl?" Joe asked.

"Wonderful. I feel like I was two hundred again. Why did you shut it down?"

"Some of the lightweight furniture and debris were getting caught up in the funnel."

"Oh, there's a built-in fix for that. It's been so long that I forgot about it."

The spymaster took the control back from Joe, thumbed the power on, and then issued a silent command through his linked implant. A second later, the powerful fans roared to life, all of them blowing downwards from the floating platform and then tilting outwards. Paul caught an empty paper coffee cup as it shot past on the strong breeze, and in a matter of seconds, the entire parade ground was as clean as if it had been vacuumed.

"Sorry," Herl muttered, as a couple of the folding chairs crashed into the hulls of parked ships a distance away. The fans halted again and the wind died immediately. "There's still a bit of juice left in the power pack. Does one of you want to give it a try?"

"Are you joking?" Joe replied. "I almost got sick just watching you."

"Same here," Paul said.

Beowulf shook his massive head at the two men, and then trotted out and positioned himself under the floating platform.

"I think we have a volunteer," Herl declared, firing the ride back up before the humans could object. A few seconds later, the dog was airborne, whirling around in tight circles so fast that Joe could just make out a pink streak described by the tongue hanging from Beowulf's mouth.

"No, Alexander!" Paul shouted at the younger dog, who decided it was time to join in the fun.

Either Alex couldn't hear the command over the roar from the fans, or he had decided it was a good time to suffer from the selective hearing loss particular to Cayl hounds and certain breeds of Earth dogs, because he charged across the training grounds and leapt into the moving funnel cloud, nearly colliding with his sire.

"Bad dog," Herl muttered, trying to regain control of the whirlwind through his implant as Joe punched the kill switch again.

The mass of the new dog adding his own momentum in the same direction as the spin caused the vortex to tip upwards, fighting against the stability of the fan platform, and then to swing violently back in the opposite direction as Herl tried to compensate. The funnel cloud weakened as the fans spun down, and then both dogs flew out of the vortex in opposite directions, high above the deck. Beowulf landed hard on the opposite side of the training grounds, while Alexander hit the deck not far from the men and almost reached them in an uncontrolled roll.

"They'll be fine," Joe said hopefully as the men started forward. "The Cayl breed them tough."

Before he could reach Alexander, Beowulf's son was up and fleeing towards Kevin's ship and safety, his sire barreling after him in a not-quite-straight line.

"That's it for the power pack," Herl said cheerfully. "You know, if the price is reasonable, I'd be interested in purchasing a Tornado myself. I'll have to check with the Stryx about running it in one of the empty docking bays. You have too much stuff in here to take it beyond the lowest power setting."

Eight

"It's not much of a meeting room, but it's all the admin would give us on short notice," Lizant informed Samuel. The Frunge girl shrugged off her backpack as the other students on the committee filed in behind her and found places around the table. The Dollnick and Grenouthian both rushed for the only bench seat that would fit their large bodies without squeezing, and the Verlock, who was slow-footed and used to standing, simply remained near the door as if he was on sentry duty.

"Have you already voted on committee officers?" the Sharf student asked. She settled her skeletal frame into a chair, though her knees came dangerously close to the bottom of the table.

"We didn't vote, but Samuel is the president, I'm the vice president, and Lizant volunteered to be secretary," Vivian replied. "Do you want to introduce yourself to the others, Yvandi?"

The Sharf girl shrugged. "I'm Yvandi, and as long as I don't have to be an officer, I'm cool with whatever you guys agreed on."

"We didn't so much agree on it as Vivian told us the way it will be," Jorb said. "She has a big presence for a little Human."

Lizant brought out her student tab, tapped a few symbols, and placed it on the table. "The rules say that I have

84

to record the meetings for the university archives, so everybody keep it in mind."

"Can you edit the recording if we slip up?" Marilla asked.

"No. It's an official archive thing. My tab is just acting as a mic now that it's enabled."

The students all clamped their lips shut on receiving this information and looked in the direction of the committee executives. Vivian nudged Samuel, who gave her a reproachful look before reluctantly beginning.

"All right. I call this meeting of the Open University Student Committee for—what was it?"

Vivian pushed her own tab in front of him.

"Sorry. The Open University Proposal Evaluation Student Committee."

"What about it?" Vivian prompted him.

"Oh. I call it to order." He glanced down at the tab and continued, "Is there any unfinished business from our last meeting?"

"This is our first meeting," the Grenouthian pointed out.

"Right. Does anybody have any new business to bring before the committee?"

"I do," Marilla said, turning a pale shade of yellow despite her confident tone. "Have you all seen the interview with the EarthCent embassy's office manager in the Galactic Free Press?"

"You read the Human paper?" Jorb inquired skeptically.

"I do when it involves my committee work," the Horten girl replied. "According to the student handbook, sitting on a recognized committee counts as much towards leadership certification as two courses in management."

The other students all sat up a little straighter at this news, and Grude asked, "Is the credit contingent on our contributions? Is somebody judging us?"

"The handbook didn't say, though I'm thinking of putting in for a bonus for learning English."

"You learned English just to read a Galactic Free Press article for this meeting?" Samuel asked.

"No, I picked it up from sitting in the studio while my sister is on 'Let's Make Friends,'" the Horten replied. "It took a couple cycles of turning my implant off and on to get the hang of it, but Humanese is a pretty simple language, after all."

"Interview related to committee?" Wrylenth asked from his place at the doorway.

"It seems that we aren't the only group working towards fitting out the Dollnick colony ship for EarthCent."

"Eccentric Enterprises," Vivian corrected her.

"Same difference," Marilla said. "According to the interview, the EarthCent embassy is already in consultations with the Human colonists the ship will be visiting."

"Like they'll know what's good for them," the Grenouthian committee member said dismissively.

"The interview also talked about the sorts of functions that EarthCent," she paused at Vivian's cough and let out an exaggerated sigh, "that Eccentric Enterprises would like to accomplish with Flower. My question is whether this committee needs to coordinate with...whoever."

"Why doesn't everybody pull up a translated copy of the Galactic Free Press on their tabs so we all know what we're discussing," Samuel suggested

"Is there a budget available for this subscription?" the Grenouthian asked suspiciously.

"I read the free version, and your tabs should offer automatic translation," Marilla told him. Just as the committee members all located the article and started reading, an unfamiliar but attractive student stuck her head through the door.

"Hey guys. Who's up for ordering a takeout pizza from the Little Apple?" the newcomer asked.

"Earth wedges?" Jorb pulled out his change purse. "I'm in for half."

"Can I get mine without the dough?" Lizant requested without looking up.

"Holo solicitation," the Sharf girl sniffed.

Wrylenth cautiously waved his arm through the space occupied by the uninvited guest. "Advertisement," he confirmed.

"It must have been triggered by all of us opening the free version of the paper," the Grenouthian said, unable to hide his admiration for the feat. "Sponsored content."

"That doesn't make me any less hungry," the Drazen complained. "How about it, Lizant? We can get no crust on your half and double crust on mine. I usually just fold it over anyway."

"You're all out of order," Marilla declared. "My business is still on the table."

"She's probably right," Samuel said. "Let's hold off on food for now. In regards to our Horten colleague's question, I'm sure you know my mother is the EarthCent Ambassador and Vivian's parents kind of run EarthCent Intelligence and finance Eccentric Enterprises, but nobody has said anything to us about coordination. I think they all see the Open University competition as a Stryx thing, so they don't want to interfere."

"The interview is with my grandmother," Vivian added in the interest of full disclosure.

"You guys are worse than we are," the Dollnick student said enviously. "No wonder you're killing everybody in Dynastic Studies."

"It just happened that way. Marilla had a great question and I'll talk to my parents about it when I get home, but for the time being, we should proceed on the assumption that we're working independently."

"Ask them about funds," the Sharf student said. "The Human communities on Open Worlds probably have money, and maybe they'll make some of it available for projects that we approve."

"Stryx offered financing for approved projects," the Verlock grated out.

"All right. Does anybody else have new business?" Samuel asked.

"Bribes," Wrylenth declared.

The Grenouthian shot the Verlock a sour look. "Thanks for spoiling it for the rest of us. You know how immature the Humans are about this sort of stuff."

"What bribes?" Samuel asked.

"Students want proposals approved," the Verlock elaborated.

"But we haven't even received any proposals to consider yet."

"Students waiting to learn pricing."

"The way I see it, there should be a fee to prevent frivolous proposals from wasting our time," the Grenouthian student argued. "Otherwise, all the students in business courses will treat it like some kind of Stryx lottery, and they'll bury us in half-baked schemes they haven't invested any time in. By charging a modest sum for submissions, we'll save a lot of work and improve the quality."

Lizant shook her head. "Sorry, but this was covered in the orientation I had to sit through to become the official secretary. The committee can't charge to evaluate proposals."

"How about individual committee members, as a sort of a consulting service?" the Grenouthian followed up.

"You have to report any fees you accept to the committee and recuse yourself from sitting in on those evaluations."

"That's settled then," Samuel said, gaining confidence in his new role. "Any other new business?"

"Shouldn't we publish proposal guidelines?" Yvandi inquired. "Especially since we won't be applying a monetary filter."

"Sam and I prepared draft guidelines which I'll zap to your tabs if you'll enable local push." The students all fumbled through their native versions of the standard student tab menus to find the option, and then looked expectantly at the girl. "Sent. Everybody get them?"

"I've seen proposals for new network shows shorter than these guidelines," the Grenouthian grumbled. "Hasn't your species ever heard of the lift tube capsule pitch?"

"These look really familiar," Grude said. "I wanted to prepare for this meeting so I bought—"

"*Committees For Humans,*" Marilla completed the Dollnick's sentence. "I rented a copy from the university bookstore. This is all from the chapter about requests for proposals."

"We may have used it as a template," Vivian confessed.

"Is that the Human word for plagiarism?" the Grenouthian inquired loftily.

89

"Her aunt owns the publishing company so we're safe on that front," Samuel shot back. "As to the guidelines being too detailed, where do you suggest we cut?"

"Why are you asking university students about their related work experience and their existing facilities and equipment inventory?" the Grenouthian demanded. "You have sections for listing consultants, something called, 'prior, current or pending support,' and a cost proposal. The whole thing reminds me of our documentary about the government boondoggles on your world before the Stryx stepped in."

"Wait a sec," Vivian said. "Drat, I sent you the unedited file. Here's our cut-down version."

"Oh, well that's better," Lizant said a moment later.

"Works for me," Jorb contributed.

"Third," Marilla stated formally, displaying her mastery of procedures detailed in *Committees For Humans*.

"Distribution?" Wrylenth asked.

"I can pin the proposal guidelines to the original announcement posted by the university admin, and anybody who accessed it will get an update notification," Lizant told them.

"Any further new business?" Samuel inquired.

The Dollnick raised one of his four hands tentatively.

"You can just speak out, Grude."

"Well, I think there should be some discussion of maximizing Flower's existing capacity before we rush to install new equipment. She is a full colony ship with terraforming capability, not just a transport."

"I don't think they'll be undertaking any terraforming missions," the Horten girl said. "The interview indicated that the goal is to bring improvements to existing Human communities, so Flower can't park in one place and work on a planet for a thousand years."

"Humans trying to live on their own will need lots of stuff," Jorb contributed.

"Dollnick colony ships include fully automated fabrication chambers—Flower wouldn't have been able to keep up with her own maintenance otherwise," Grude explained. "She might not be enthusiastic about whipping up replacement parts for archaic Human technology, but with blueprints from Earth and the right encouragement…"

"Parts critical," the Verlock student agreed. "Humans are opportunistic technology users. Require alien support."

"He's right," the Sharf girl jumped in. "Despite their low population and poor credit, Humans have become an important market for our used ships, especially two-man traders. My cousin is in the business and he makes more on the replacement parts than on the ships."

"Our entertainment archives take up almost no space and generate high-margin sales," the Grenouthian student mused. "Of course, finding a family with the right network connections who are willing to be cooped up with a bunch of Humans for an extended period of time will be difficult."

"Our trade schools turn out far more metallurgists than we actually need, and I'll bet a lot of Humans are working as asteroid prospectors," Lizant added. "I know a couple of guys who would treat an extended cruise on a Dollnick colony ship as a vacation with a chance to work on their smelting skills."

"What you guys are all suggesting sounds more like a caravan than help for building government institutions," Vivian pointed out.

"Is that the mission?" the Grenouthian asked sarcastically. "I would have thought there would be a *For Humans* book that would cover everything they need to know."

"I think all of your suggestions are interesting," Samuel said. "There's way too much space on Flower to settle for running a few training programs and a school for gifted children. This whole project is sort of a solution in search of a problem, and maybe the best approach is to just be prepared for whatever comes up."

"A good library," the Verlock said.

"What kind of storage capacity for information does Flower have compared to a Stryx librarian?" Vivian asked Grude.

The alien students all froze at the question, and the Dollnick looked like he wanted to crawl under the table and hide.

"Nobody makes comparisons to the Stryx," Lizant told the girl in a strained voice. "It's like, I don't know, trying to express a star's output in candlepower."

Grude coughed self-consciously before adding, "I wasn't going to bring this up, but when I used the bathroom during our visit to Flower, she asked me a few questions and talked about herself a little."

"While you were using the toilet?" Jorb demanded, looking even more shocked than when Vivian suggested comparing the Dollnick AI to the Stryx.

"Yeah," Grude said. "She wanted to know what I really thought about the project, and then she told some jokes about Human sanitation that I suspect she got from Grenouthian documentaries. I don't think she would object to your bringing along a library, but I can't picture her setting aside any of her own memory capacity to store

Human knowledge. She's treating this whole thing like Buerton's Tasks."

"Ah," Wrylenth nodded in understanding.

"Finally something that makes sense," the Grenouthian student added.

"Who's Buerton?" Jorb beat Samuel to the question.

"He was a prince from a couple million years ago who tried to establish himself as a king or an emperor," Grude explained. "The other princes banded together and drove him out of Dollnick space. Buerton and his retainers repented, but they were forced to complete a series of tasks before they were allowed to return."

"What sort of tasks?" Samuel asked.

"Impossible ones, or everybody thought they were impossible at the time. Like terraforming a planet that was still a ball of molten rock, or constructing a space elevator on a gas giant. It took generations for them to complete all of the tasks, but in the end, they were allowed to return to Dollnick space, and Buerton's great-grandson was even given a place on the Princely Council."

"So you're saying that we're Flower's punishment?" Vivian demanded, her voice rising.

"No, no," the Dollnick protested. "More of a challenge."

"It's better than being a Sisyphean task," Samuel commented.

"Who's that?" the Grenouthian demanded.

"An ancient king who defied the gods. His punishment was to spend eternity in the underworld pushing a boulder up a hill, only to have it roll back down again."

"So he ended up compacting a smooth road," Grude said.

"I don't think so. We use it to describe pointless tasks that seem to go on forever."

"How did you even know that?" Vivian asked.

"I learned it from Dorothy. It was her favorite expression for complaining about homework. She must have gotten it from Libby."

"This is interesting," Marilla announced, still looking at her tab. "The Galactic Free Press is posting reactions to the embassy manager's interview from leaders of the communities you're intending to serve."

"Like what?" Samuel asked.

"There's a long note from the Mayor of Floaters praising Dollnick technology and offering trained technical apprentices if Flower requests them."

"That makes sense. He's from one of the Dolly open worlds."

"And there's a request for 'real books' from another— wait a sec, the feedback is resorting—from five different colonies. I gather they're talking about physical books rather than better downloads for their devices."

"Books are nice," Vivian said. "My dad is more of a fan than my mom."

"If you mean books printed on the p-word, I'd appreciate if you discuss them when I'm not here," the Frunge girl said.

The Horten rolled her eyes at Lizant's old-fashioned observances and changed the subject. "Here's a thread that already has twenty different sources. It's a request for crop seeds that suit the local ecology. I'm surprised they haven't gotten all of that squared away by now."

"Our colonies on open worlds just sort of happened when the local workers came off contract," Vivian explained. "When the people were offered the opportunity to stay and set up their own communities, they did it with the stuff they had on hand. It's not like they set off from Earth on a colonizing mission."

"EarthCent could probably come up with seeds," Samuel said. "Sounds like a low-cost item for the ship to stock."

"There are a whole ton of threads about fitting Flower out for a religious pilgrimage," Marilla said. "I don't know if she would go along with that."

"I do," Grude offered. "She won't."

"Where are you reading that?" Samuel asked. "The only place I can imagine humans going on a pilgrimage is to Earth, and we don't need a colony ship for that."

"Do a sort by the most popular thread. It's right at the top now."

"Hospital facilities?" the boy asked.

"That's the one."

"There must be some kind of glitch with the automatic translation on your tab. A hospital is a place for sick people to stay until they get well."

"Why would sick people want to be with other sick people?" Lizant asked.

"For treatment. Hospitals on Earth have doctors and nurses and specialized equipment."

"But why stay there?" the Frunge girl persisted. "Why don't they have their problem fixed and return home, or better yet, invite the doctor to come to them?"

"I found it," Vivian said, looking up from her tab. "Hospitals started as guest houses for foreign travelers who were often on religious pilgrimages. I guess your tabs are choosing that translation since Human-style medicine doesn't make sense for the other species."

"Do Humans have a hospital on the station?" the Grenouthian student asked. "It might make an interesting subject for a documentary."

"No, we go to the Stryx med bay if there's something really wrong, though the Farling doctor who works there also has a shop on the tourist concourse."

"Do Humans get sick often?" Marilla asked.

"I guess there were a lot of germs and stuff back on Earth—"

"Sanitation," the Grenouthian interrupted.

"And then we have diseases that just kind of happen," Samuel continued, ignoring the bunny's jibe. "Sometimes the diseases are coded into our genes."

"Why don't you edit them out?" Grude asked.

Nine

"This is stupid," Kelly said, looking up from her display desk. "Why would readers care about my favorite Vergallian drama?"

"You don't have a favorite Vergallian drama," Libby observed.

"How did you know I—never mind. Walter claims that all of these tidbits will help humanize the book so it's not just a lot of dry facts about EarthCent, but to me, it's all fluff."

"You loved *Economics For Humans*."

"I'm beginning to love it less now that I see how the sausage is made. I mean, why would anybody be interested in my most spectacular digestive failure after mistakenly eating alien hors d'oeuvres at a diplomatic party?"

"Humans are fascinated by their digestive processes and you aren't the only ones. Our visiting Farling doctor is doing some groundbreaking work with your microbiome."

"My microbiome?" Kelly demanded, her voice rising.

"Human intestinal microbes, not yours specifically," the Stryx librarian reassured her. "Walter would probably say that your encounters with M793qK have provided you with some interesting anecdotes for the book."

"Sometimes I think Walter's target audience for these books is aliens who want to laugh at us. He could advertise *EarthCent For Humans* during Grenouthian documentaries about how primitive we are."

"You asked me to warn you one minute before the start of your steering committee meeting."

"Thank you. Did I lock the door?"

"Yes, and Judith came by to sweep for listening devices earlier today."

"I don't know why Clive keeps on sending people over here to do counterintelligence scans. They never seem to find anything anymore."

"They always find something, but you requested that they give those reports to Donna back when you were busy with our guests from the Cayl Empire," Libby reminded her. "I suspect Donna considers it to be such a routine matter at this point that she doesn't want to bug you."

"Were you just making a pun?" Kelly asked suspiciously.

A large hologram flickered to life, and without moving from her chair, the ambassador found herself sitting at a conference table across from Stephen Beyer, the president of EarthCent. The other ambassadors on the Intelligence Steering Committee began popping into the hologram immediately afterwards, and they all exchanged brief greetings.

"What's new with Flower?" the president asked as soon as everybody settled in. "I can't tell you how excited we all are about the prospect of having access to reliable interstellar transportation with such incredible cargo capacity and living space. I get a hundred new utilization suggestions coming across my desk every day."

"She's parked not far from the station and everything seems to be going smoothly," Kelly said. "I haven't been out to visit yet myself, but my son was appointed to the

Open University committee that's supposed to help refit Flower for our mission. To be honest, I'm not sure why the Stryx wanted alien students involved. I suggested sending the ship to Earth where you could start bringing up people and materials on the elevator, but our station librarian informed me that fitting out here was part of the deal."

"Deal with who?" Svetlana Zerakova asked. "The Dollnicks?"

"The deal with Flower. She operates independently at this point. From what my son told me, the Dollnicks see her mission with us as a sort of punishment, after which they might be willing to accept her back into colony ship service."

"I've spoken to a number of the alien ambassadors on my station about Flower," Ambassador Tamil said. "My Verlock friend told me that the spontaneous creation of AI through complexity that characterizes the Dollnick colony ships has a history of mixed results. And my four-armed colleague, with whom I have an excellent relationship, said that Flower should be a perfect match for Eccentric Enterprises. I'm afraid he was hinting that the ship's AI is, well, eccentric."

"That certainly appears to be the case, but the Stryx are guaranteeing her good behavior, so we shouldn't have anything to worry about," Kelly said.

"Acceptable behavior," Libby murmured over the ambassador's implant.

"Acceptable behavior," Kelly corrected herself immediately. "Daniel's sovereign human communities are extremely enthusiastic about the circuit ship idea and they've all offered their support. But my husband had some experience working police duty for aliens back when he was a mercenary and he brought up an interesting point about law enforcement on outposts and independent colonies."

"They aren't on Earth so our laws don't apply," the president guessed.

"Correct. Daniel informs me that the communities on open worlds tend to adopt the local alien laws since they've already lived under them for decades as contract workers and can access an existing judicial system. Those worlds belong to the host species in any case, so their planetary law will always trump local regulations."

"Are you saying that if we're going to help those communities by training police and building up a legal infrastructure of our own, we're going to have to base everything on alien jurisprudence?" Ambassador White asked. "Where are we going to find the personnel to support them?"

"Stations and open worlds," Ambassador Enoksen suggested. "My daughter-in-law has been studying Drazen contract law for years, and she handles small claims cases for merchants on the station. She told me that none of the alien species require lawyers to present credentials in their courts, but there's no appeal for poor representation, so all of the risk falls on the client."

"Don't sell Earth short," the president chided them. "The alien businesses we've brought in have extensive dealings with locals, and since extraterritorial status was part of the deal for their facilities, they conduct business according to their own legal systems whenever it's advantageous for them to do so. In addition, our attorneys who work with other species have experience in Earth's system as well, which makes them ideal for helping to set up a hybrid system."

"How about the judges?" Ambassador Fu inquired. "Providing police and lawyers is one thing, but somebody has to hear the cases. I'm skeptical that aliens will agree to appear in any courts we might set up anytime in the foreseeable future."

"Let's not get ahead of ourselves," the president said. "The goal here is to support humans who aren't already living under a well-established government. Anywhere that there's a host species providing access to its own court system is a different story. But I talk with quite a few businessmen from open worlds when they come to Earth seeking markets for their goods, and they say that the aliens grant them nearly full autonomy and prefer for them to handle their own affairs. Humans living on Stryx stations probably have less freedom."

"But the Stryx hardly have any laws at all," Svetlana protested.

"Laws which they enforce without fail," Ambassador White said thoughtfully. "Anyone who chooses to live on a Stryx station, human or otherwise, has accepted the tradeoffs of a full surveillance society. Premeditated crimes are rare because our hosts intervene before they can happen."

"I've been talking with the ambassadors on my station as well, and I think that my lovely Vergallian colleague may have stumbled onto something while she was trying to insult me," Ambassador Tamil said. "Her thesis is that neither the Stryx nor Flower herself would see any point in visiting Earth for the purpose of outfitting as we have nothing of value there to bring to the stars."

"That's poppycock, Raj," the president replied. "We're already in negotiations with what's left of the old Norwegian government to split the contents of the Svalbard

Global Seed Vault with them. Hildy convinced the caretakers that there's no better way to ensure the perpetuation of flora genes than to spread them to other worlds."

"Then why are negotiations necessary?"

"After the Stryx opened Earth and the foundation money dried up, the local families have been maintaining the vault as a community project. They presented us with a bill for unpaid labor and materials."

"Have you checked with the Stryx about sending the seeds out in the diplomatic bag?" Kelly asked.

"We're talking about a million unique seed types, with multiple copies for all of them," the president replied patiently. "Given the bulk and the preference for refrigeration during the trip, I've asked our friends at Drazen Foods to handle the shipping arrangements. Assuming we can meet the demands of the Norwegians, the first batch will be headed up to the elevator hub with a shipment of fresh hot peppers at the end of the month. We'll be parking containers of supplies in orbit for Flower to pick up when she swings by Earth at the start of her mission."

"You should hire on a few Gem agronomists to clone the seedlings," Svetlana suggested. "They work cheap and they piled up a lot of experience with plant seeds while restoring their own agricultural base so they could do away with that terrible factory food drink."

"I'll do that," Kelly said, making a mental note.

"How about furniture?" Ambassador Enoksen asked. "I don't know how many crew members we are ultimately hoping to send along or how many Flower will accept, but Dollnick furniture is too tall for us, and the extra arms mean that even their kid-sized chairs are built to the wrong proportions."

"I'll suggest that too, but if we end up drawing most of the ship's complement from sovereign human communities, they'll be used to their own style of furnishing, which is heavily influenced by alien cultures," Kelly answered pragmatically. "We would like to create a world-class library on Flower, so I'm hoping Earth can help out with that."

"I'll put somebody on it immediately," the president said.

"Paper books?" Ambassador Fu inquired.

"Of course," Kelly said defensively. "There's plenty of room, and it's not like Flower is a Frunge ship. And my son-in-law is going to look around for old carnival rides that can be fixed up while he and my daughter are visiting Earth."

"I like it," the president said. "Anything we can do to get people to visit the ship and participate in our outreach programs is a positive. A library and an amusement park should be major draws for isolated communities."

"What are we doing to prepare for the intelligence side of the mission?" Raj asked. "I assume this is too good an opportunity for the Oxfords to let slide."

"They're working up what Clive called a comprehensive plan and he asked for our patience until it's completed," Kelly said. "But if you're willing, I have some questions I'd like to ask while I have you all here. The bandwidth is being paid out of EarthCent Intelligence's budget and it would be a shame to waste it. It's EarthCent business, sort of."

"Sort of?" Svetlana asked.

"I've been invited to write a book in the *For Humans* series, about EarthCent, to be specific. But it turns out that they create most of these books on an assembly line, with a lot of the text provided by moonlighting reporters and intelligence analysts. What the publisher wants me for is to jazz it up with some insider diplomatic stories."

"That shouldn't be hard for you," the president said. "You've been on more first contact missions than any of us, and none of the other ambassadors can boast your level of involvement with the Stryx."

"The style of these books doesn't really allow for stories where I'd have enough space to provide the context. Any of us could write an entire book about even a single diplomatic experience. This is more of a..." she hesitated.

"An entertainment product," Ambassador White suggested.

"Yes," Kelly admitted. "They want bite-sized anecdotes about cultural misunderstandings, accidental food poisoning, things like that."

"We've all had plenty of those," Belinda said ruefully. "One time at a Drazen reception, I held their ambassador's drink while he thumb-wrestled his brother, who was visiting the station. They were so evenly matched that it went on forever, so I lost track of which glass was which and accidentally took a sip from his."

"And you're alive to tell the story?"

"It burned my lips so badly that I instinctively spit it out without swallowing. Our station librarian had a med bot on the scene before the pain really hit, and it knocked me out with a sedative and took me to med bay for reconstructive surgery. I woke up at home without even a hangover, so it wasn't that bad as far as diplomatic parties go."

"My first diplomatic visit to the Grenouthian embassy I misunderstood their traditions and went naked," Ambassador Oshi contributed.

"I thought you were snoozing over there, Carlos," the president commented. "And how did the bunnies react?"

"Their ambassador's aide whipped off his sash and draped it from my shoulder to my knee so it covered my private parts. I almost caused another diplomatic incident by offering to return it to him after the reception. He requested that I burn it."

"Can I use your name?" Kelly asked.

The ambassador shrugged. "It's not a secret. Didn't you see the Grenouthian documentary about alien diplomatic faux pas? Come to think of it, that could be a good source of material for you."

"And a good place to advertise the book," the Corner Station ambassador suggested.

"You might use my experience going to the rescue of a Frunge revenue agent who had been marooned on an abandoned mining asteroid by the local moonshiners," Ambassador Fu offered.

"I never heard that story, Zhao," the president said. "Did it happen before you joined EarthCent?"

"No, this was during my vacation last year. My wife and I rented a Frunge sunboat. You know, the kind that are supposed to be so safe that children can sail them?"

"Did you get caught up in the background microwave radiation?" Svetlana asked. "It happened to us our first time out."

"So you know what it's like. I picked up the revenue agent's open distress call and tacked for the source, but the rudder stopped responding, and no matter how I repositioned the magnetic envelope, I couldn't change course again. It was like canoeing in whitewater without a paddle."

"So you needed to call for rescue yourself?" Kelly asked.

"Actually, the Frunge revenue agent saw that we were going to miss her beacon and get smashed up in the asteroid belt, so she risked her life using up her suit's oxygen supply to blast off her asteroid and intercept us. As soon as she made it through the airlock, she took over the controls and reengaged the background radiation compensator. I thought the status light was supposed to be green, but it's a danger color for them."

"That's not half as bad as the time I picked up the Drazen ambassador's three-year-old at a private dinner party," Svetlana said. "I didn't know that his white nightshirt meant that he was in his tentacling phase where they instinctively latch onto anything and squeeze to build up the muscles. He wrapped his tentacle around my throat, and at first I was afraid to pull it off for fear of hurting him. Then it was so tight that I couldn't even work my fingers underneath, and if the ambassador's dog hadn't started barking to get everybody's attention, I would have died right there in the playroom."

"How did they get him off you?" Raj asked.

"You just hold the kid's hands down and blow in his ear," the president contributed. "Same thing happened to me once at a picnic back when I was an ambassador."

Kelly checked "tentacle choking" off her list of requested anecdotes and asked, "Does anybody have a story about getting trapped in a bathroom at an alien embassy?"

"Did you have to bring that up again?" Ambassador White complained. "It wasn't an embassy, it was the Verlock ambassador's yacht, and nobody told me that I'd have to solve the equation displayed on the inside of the door to get out again. It's their version of a privacy lock."

"Oh, I've seen those equation locks on office doors in the Verlock embassy on our station," Ambassador Oshi said. "It's their equivalent of swiping to the left."

"I tried pounding on the door but the sound insulation was perfect, and there was a whole row of bathrooms on the yacht, so I couldn't count on being discovered by somebody else needing it. Fortunately, my diplomatic implant has serious range, and I was able to ping our station librarian. The Stryx discretely notified the Verlock ambassador and he was able to override the lock from the bridge."

"Why didn't you ask the station librarian to solve the equation for you?"

"I did, but you know how subtle those Verlock numerals are. You have to draw them on the pad with a finger and I just couldn't do it accurately enough."

"It looks like our time is almost up," the president said, glancing at the counter in the corner of the hologram. "Good luck with the book, Ambassador McAllister. Would you mind running it by Hildy before submitting the manuscript to the publisher? As a public relations professional, she might be able to steer you away from accidentally harming EarthCent's reputation. If nothing else, I'm sure she'll appreciate being asked."

"I'll do that. Thank you all for the stories and the ideas for the colony ship. As soon as we get a better idea of what Flower is willing to go along with I'll submit a full report."

"Isn't this supposed to be an Eccentric Enterprises project?" the Void Station ambassador inquired.

"Only on paper," the president replied. "I thought that EarthCent could use a level of deniability just in case Flower turns out to be more eccentric than the Stryx are letting on. Did you know that the Grenouthians did a documentary about her almost two thousand years ago? One of the local bunnies involved in the media partnership we set up mentioned it to me."

"I didn't," Kelly replied. "That sounds like it would be a valuable resource."

"Unfortunately, the Dollnicks paid the Grenouthians an arm and a leg, or maybe two arms and a leg, to pull it from circulation. But if you asked around the station, maybe somebody has a copy."

Ten

"Thank you for agreeing to meet with me on such short notice," Blythe greeted her guests. "I've never eaten here before, and I hope that the all-species cuisine is acceptable."

"Acceptable?" Flazint said, her hair vines rustling in excitement. "This is the most expensive restaurant on the station. I've never even met anybody who's been here."

"That's what the girls on my student committee all said when I invited them," Vivian told her mother. "Marilla and Yvandi both stopped home to change, but Lizant can't make it because of a class."

"Going by the names, that covers Hortens and Sharf, and we already have Flazint here to represent the Frunge," Dorothy said, grinning at her friend. "We're up to six species including us, assuming you got Tinka to come."

"She's stopping on the way to pick up a couple of classic Drazen romance novels," Blythe said. "She claims that the cover art is almost as important as the story."

"Did you skip the Grenouthians, the Dollnicks and the Verlocks to save space?" Affie asked in jest, naming the three bulkier species.

"I've been going through their catalogs, and based on the book descriptions there just aren't many promising candidates. The Verlock conception of romance involves creating mathematical proofs together, and bunny literature requires way too much context."

"What do you mean?" Dorothy asked.

"I have a good intelligence report on the subject if you want to read it, but basically, their fiction is all set in an imaginary universe that doesn't resemble ours at all. You have to start with the children's books for it to make any sense, and our analyst estimated it would take humans about twenty years of reading day and night just to get to the point where they could understand a novel intended for adult Grenouthians."

"It wasn't always like that," Affie told them. "I took a comparative literature course at the Open University, just the works of the older species, you understand. The whole imaginary universe thing is a fad that only started twenty or thirty thousand years ago, and these things come and go in regular cycles."

"How about the Dollnicks?" Vivian asked.

"You wouldn't be here if we were going to discuss Dolly romances," Blythe told her teenage daughter. "In fact, if you ever see one in a store, I forbid you to look at the cover."

"Are you talking about Dollnick novels?" a bright yellow Horten girl asked, hesitating before taking a seat. "I'll have to leave if you do because my mom made me promise to wait until after I have children."

"Now we have something in common," Vivian said, patting the chair next to her.

Tinka arrived and reflexively selected a seat as far from the Horten girl as possible. "Where's Chas?" she asked.

"I didn't invite my sister and I'd appreciate it if you don't tell her about our meeting," Blythe said.

"Are you still mad that she's poaching your intelligence agents for the Galactic Free Press?"

"That actually worked out well for us in the end since she pays the salaries and we still get the intel. But lately she's been hiring our analysts part-time to ghost books in the *For Humans* series, and you know they sneak in most of the research during regular work hours."

"Sibling rivalry," Affie commented, nodding knowingly. "You should like Vergallian romance novels because power struggles between sisters is right up at the top of our required tropes."

The tall Sharf student arrived and peered at each of the women at the table as if committing their faces to memory. "Yvandi," she introduced herself, and began eagerly flipping through the holo menu the moment her bony bottom settled on the padded seat.

"I love your dress," Dorothy said. "I've never seen anything quite like it."

"My funeral dress," the girl stated simply without looking away from the menu. "I don't have anything else fancy enough for a place like this."

"Everybody order whatever you want," Blythe encouraged them, activating her own holo menu. "The kitchen can supposedly get every entree to come out at the same time, regardless of how many species are dining. I've already ordered some wines that I think you can all drink," she added.

"There aren't any prices shown in the menu," Marilla pointed out nervously, her yellow color deepening.

"Don't worry," Vivian reassured the girl. "Mom's got so much money that she doesn't know what to do with it. She and my aunt actually provide financing for most of the Eccentric Enterprises start-ups, and she'll be with our

111

associate ambassador when they negotiate the final deal with Flower."

"Now that everybody is here, the reason I asked you all to lunch is because I'm interested in buying the translation rights to novels from your respective species," Blythe informed them. "I grew up believing that your literature wouldn't make any more sense to us in translation than our literature would to you, but thanks to the ambassador's book club, I've learned that some of our novels can make the transition with appropriate cultural rewrites. I want to do the same thing in reverse, translating your books into English."

"Before Chastity does," Tinka added mischievously.

"We're starting with romance novels since they're at least half of the market," Blythe continued. "I can get all the plot synopses I can read from the EarthCent Intelligence staff, but I wanted an outside perspective from non-publishing professionals who have experience with humans. Maybe we could just go around the table while we're waiting for our food and you could give me your thoughts on the problems I'm likely to encounter."

Yvandi finished making her selections in the menu and gestured it out of existence. "For starters, I don't think that Sharf aesthetics will translate well into Humanese, and physical descriptions play a large part in our romance literature."

"I expect that will be a problem with all cross-species translations, but could you give us an example?"

The Sharf girl drew her university tab from her handbag and quickly brought up a page of alien text. "His protruding ribs and the bony neck made her eye stalks quiver with desire, and two of her three hearts began

112

diverting blood into her dmogliverfs, which jookled with anticipation."

"Did the rest of you miss a couple of words in translation?" Blythe asked. All the women around the table nodded in agreement.

"Which words?" Yvandi asked. "It's basic Sharf, nothing fancy."

"The bits that get the blood pumped in and what happens to them in anticipation," Affie said.

"You guys don't have dmogliverfs?" The Sharf regarded her lunch companions with a mixture of pity and horror.

"We don't even know what they are," Dorothy told her. "Libby?"

"The reason your implants don't offer an equivalent translation is because it would require several minutes of explanations," the station librarian informed her. "Dmogliverfs are unique to Sharf physiology. Would you like me to begin the technical description?"

"It's not important," Blythe decided. "The translator would just rewrite it in English that made sense for the situation. I'm more worried about cultural disconnects that affect the overall plot, Yvandi. Things like character motivations and resolutions to conflicts that just wouldn't make sense to us."

"I think the plot of this book is pretty universal," the Sharf girl said. "It's about two brothers who mate with the same woman, despite the fact that her father is a chemist and the sibling's grandmother comes from Gurandi Prime."

"What wrong with chemists and Gurandi Prime?" Vivian asked.

Yvandi blinked slowly and half rose from her chair. "I don't think you're going to have much luck translating Sharf romances. Is it too late to cancel my order?"

"Sit, sit," Blythe said. "That's exactly the sort of feedback I'm looking for. Maybe there are other Sharf works that will make more sense to us, but I want to start with the low hanging fruit and you may have just saved me a lot of time and money."

"Well, I guess I'm next, but you already know something about how Drazen romance works from all of my arranged dates," Tinka said, sliding a few books across the table for Blythe to see the cover art. "Around half of the story is about matching up financial statements with family trees, test results—"

"You guys have tests too?" Flazint interrupted. "I thought it was just us."

"Hardly," the Horten girl jumped in. "Most of my relatives stayed with the colony ship where I was born to work on the terraforming project. I'm putting off studying all that marriage stuff until I'm finished at the Open University because I don't want to forget it before we can get together for the tests."

"Your whole family has to be there?" the Frunge girl asked.

"They have to take the test at the same time," Marilla said, looking surprised by the question. "Don't your family members have to take tests?"

"What sort of tests are we talking about?" Blythe asked.

"Personality, compatibility, intelligence," the Horten girl ticked off on her fingers.

"Ancestral knowledge, financial acumen, professional competence," Yvandi added.

"Don't forget the health exams," Tinka said. "There's no bigger turn-off than when the matchmaker shows you a scan of your suitor's insides and tries to hide something with her opposing thumb."

"I know," Affie said. "That's why the royal families all do our own scans."

Vivian, Dorothy and Blythe all exchanged looks of disbelief.

"So, doesn't anybody elope in your romances?" Blythe asked.

"I think my implant is glitching," Marilla said in distress. "Are you really talking about a couple that runs off and gets married without their families approving?"

"Who would perform the ceremony?" the Sharf girl demanded.

"Humans are funny that way," Flazint said. "They let just about anybody perform ceremonies, including ship captains."

"Who are you to point fingers?" Dorothy objected. "You're the one who made me get the companionship contract with Kevin!"

"I was sort of acting as your parent or guardian," the Frunge girl admitted. "Normally, our marriage negotiations start with the ancestors and work their way down through the grandparents and parents. If everybody agrees, then the potential bride and groom are introduced, and they can get a temporary companionship contract if they're in a hurry to go out together. We kind of skipped all of that for you and went right to the carving in stone."

"So do all of the romances in your novels require prior family consent?" Blythe inquired without directing the question at anybody in particular. "That could be a problem."

"A lot of the old novels from Earth that mom reads are like that too," Dorothy said. "Not so much with the testing, maybe, but definitely with the permission."

"You probably want to stick with our bedtime books," Flazint suggested. "They're much shorter than regular romances because they cut out the whole financial auditing process and barely even touch on test results. But some of the family interactions are pretty funny. One of the best romances I've read lately had the parents of the guy being in law enforcement and the parents of the girl being criminals. There was a scene where the kids are being introduced for the first time and the boy's father's tracking dog wouldn't stop barking because the girl's mother is wearing the same shoes she had on when cutting into a vault."

"How did they ever get to the point of introducing the children if they were so incompatible?" Blythe asked.

"Cops and robbers go together like politicians and money launderers," Flazint explained.

"My dad was a pirate when he met my mother," Marilla confessed. "Mom's father is a customs agent so they just naturally hit it off. Mom says that grandpa cried when he heard that she was joining a colony ship after the wedding. He even offered to give my dad a place to live if he wanted to stay behind."

"How do they work all the tests you guys were talking about?" Vivian asked. "Are they like multiple choice, or oral examinations—"

"Oral examinations come before we even get to the tests," Affie cut her off. "Vergallians take teeth very seriously."

"I meant where an examiner asks questions and you have to answer them."

"Like hearing tests? Even tech ban worlds allow implants for that so it's not a big issue."

"No, I meant oral examinations as an alternative to a written exam," Vivian persisted stubbornly.

"She's just teasing you," Dorothy told the younger girl. "Be nice, Affie. Her mom is buying."

"Let me think then," the Vergallian girl said. "When my oldest sister went on the market, I had to—"

"Went on the market?" Blythe interrupted.

"That's what all the girls call it. In the Empire, negotiations for the oldest daughter usually start in her teens, like forty years before she's ready for marriage. But we don't follow all those crazy old traditions in Fleet."

"So you won't start your marriage negotiations until you're actually marrying age."

"Ten years before," Affie said. "I mean, a girl wouldn't want to be so rushed that she ends up marrying just anybody." She took a sip of the wine Blythe had ordered, smiled appreciatively, and continued. "So when my sister went on the market, I had to take the standard battery of tests, which are loosely based on our school curriculum. The groom's representatives sent their own medical team to do the scans, of course, and our own family repeated them to make sure there wasn't any funny business."

"What sort of funny business?" Dorothy asked.

"If the family attorney doesn't have a friendly scan available at the negotiating table, the other side can start pulling recessive genes out of their hats to try to beat down the price," Affie explained matter-of-factly. "And then there's the whole younger twin scam the groom's side has to keep an eye on."

"Royal families with twins try to pass off a younger twin as the older?" Flazint asked, her eyes shining. "That's incredible. Even I could write a novel around a plot like that."

"Except it hasn't worked in like a million years because everybody is watching for it," Affie said.

"That's why they won't expect it," the Frunge girl insisted.

"What difference does it make?" Dorothy asked.

"The older twin inherits the throne," the Vergallian explained. "The younger twin doesn't have any more market value than a younger sister who isn't a twin. But if they're identical twins, it gives the family the opportunity to sell the same cow twice."

"How can you talk about yourselves like that?" Blythe demanded.

"I'm fourth in my family's line of succession and my sisters already have daughters so it won't come up in my marriage negotiations," Affie replied with a shrug.

"What would the family who paid a fortune to marry their son to a queen do when they find out they got the younger twin?" Tinka asked.

"Assassination would the obvious first choice, but of course, the older twin is going to be ready for that. Like I said, it hasn't happened in so long that it only creeps up in bad dramas."

"Okay. Other than teeth, school subjects and order-of-birth, are there any other tests?" Blythe asked.

"Ballroom dancing, but nobody ever fails that one so it's hardly worth mentioning."

"So what's a common plot for a Vergallian romance, Affie?" Dorothy asked.

"A lot of them start with a princess being kidnapped, but the bestsellers lately revolve around poor girls on tech ban worlds falling in love with fugitives hiding from the

118

law. Personally, if I have to read one more book about a woodcutter's daughter splinting broken bones for a handsome young royal who's escaped from a dungeon, I'm going to switch to Human books."

"So they don't go through all the tests and family meetings in those stories," Blythe pressed.

"They do if they want to get married," Affie said. "The kidnappings and dungeon escapes are just plot devices to introduce mismatched characters who would never have been put together by their families. The negotiations start after the parties return to their respective places in society, and they're really complicated if the man is being sought by the crown."

"Don't they ever go to bed together first?"

"Not listening," Marilla sang, clamping her hands over her ears.

"Come on, Mom, you're embarrassing me," Vivian protested.

"But we're talking about romance novels."

"Nobody ever goes to bed together in novels Samuel's mom gives me."

"Those are romantic novels, not romance novels. There's a difference. You'll understand when you're older."

"I hate to admit it, but I actually read a pretty good Horten romance in translation," Tinka said. "It was titled, *All the Shades of the Rainbow,* or something like that."

"Have you read that one?" Blythe asked the Horten girl.

"My mom told me not to," Marilla said, glancing around as if she expected the formidable customs agent's daughter to appear in the restaurant. "But she didn't make me promise, so I did. Like five times."

"Do you think it will work for us?"

119

"Maybe, if you were willing to leave the main characters as Hortens and not change them into Humans. It would be too hard to deal with all of the color changes she goes through otherwise."

"I hadn't really thought about that," Blythe said. "The recent translations of our books to alien languages that I'm aware of all changed the species of the characters. Actually, it would solve a lot of problems if we could keep the original characters and settings. Rather than substituting for the untranslatable cultural stuff, we could use that space to explain some of the differences."

"Like an omniscient narrator," the Sharf girl suggested.

"Like Jeeves!" Dorothy exclaimed. "You could add a Stryx character to all of the books as a neutral observer who explains things."

"Did Jeeves put you up to this in return for something?" Blythe asked sternly.

"I swear," the ambassador's daughter said. "We've never even discussed books." Then her face darkened and her expression changed. "Except for when he was at our place yesterday and commented on *Vanity Fair* being missing from my mom's bookshelf, like he has all the locations memorized. Jeeves claims that the omniscient narrator in that novel could have been copied from his backup."

"I have a question," Flazint said. "Would Humans really be interested in reading romances with alien characters? For me, reading a novel about aliens doing, you know, would be like reading about a science experiment."

"Lots of humans already read alien romances," Dorothy informed her. "That woman my mom brought home from Earth who eloped with my old boyfriend was a huge fan."

"Those were written by authors back on Earth," Blythe pointed out. "And the female lead is usually a human who gets kidnapped by aliens or captured by pirates."

"You mean like Humans and Vergallians, right?" the Sharf girl asked. "Not like species with different parts."

"Can we please talk about something else?" Marilla pleaded as the waiter arrived with a heavily laden cart. "I don't think I'll be able to eat if you guys go any further down that path."

"What kind of guy are you interested in?" Affie teased the student.

"A musician," the Horten girl replied seriously. "A few years older than me, but not like a father-figure or anything. My parents are talking about finding me somebody on the station so we can get to know each other for ten or twenty years, and my cousins back on the colony ship are pushing for somebody with diplomatic connections."

"Mornich!" Dorothy almost shouted. She whipped out her tab and started looking for a picture of the Horten ambassador's son from when his band played the last fashion party in Mac's Bones. "Have I got a boy for you."

Eleven

"I promised the Grenouthians that I wouldn't cry on camera today," Aisha said with a sniff, after greeting Shaina and Daniel when they arrived on the set of 'Let's Make Friends' with Mike and his little sister. "It's going to be hard to see your son go."

"But I'm at your house all the time to play with Fenna," Mike countered with his eight-year-old logic. "Who are all these little kids?"

"I'm trying something new this year. The reason I asked the departing cast members to come early today is so you could meet your replacements and help them settle in. Don't you think that would have made it easier for you when you started, Mike?"

"Dunno. Who's replacing me?"

"Could you come over here, Beth?" Aisha beckoned to a nervous six-year-old who was standing near the edge of the stage, clutching her father's hand.

"But she's a girl," Mike objected. "How can a girl re-place me?"

"You took a girl's spot when you came on the cast," Shaina reminded her son. She turned to her husband for support and noticed that he was staring into space with his eyes tracking back and forth. "Turn off your heads-up display, Daniel. I won't have you working while you're watching your son's final appearance on the show."

"But it hasn't started yet," the associate ambassador protested. The obvious resemblance between the father's and son's speech patterns caused both women to laugh.

"You're famous," the little girl stated, coming up to Mike and staring at him with eyes as large as saucers. "I watch you every day."

"What's your name again?" the boy asked in a long-suffering tone.

"Beth. And you're Mikey. Were you scared when you started on the show?"

"Naw, I'm not afraid of anything. Besides, I had Spinner with me and he's really tough."

"I'm scared," Beth confessed. "Some of the aliens are so big. What if they don't like me?"

"You can always run away," Mike suggested. "Aisha says that we're all motionally the same age. That means they won't be able to catch you."

"Emotionally the same age," Aisha corrected him, with a stress on the 'E'. "Libby helps me find alien children who are at the same stage of emotional development as the youngest human on the new cast."

"What does that mean? They aren't all really the same age as me?"

"The older the species, the longer the children take to mature. The Verlock girl on the show with you is probably twice your age in human years."

"I always thought Krolyohne was just really smart," Mike complained. "Now it turns out that she's old."

"I don't understand," Beth chimed in nervously. "You said I'd be playing with other six-year-olds."

"The alien children are the same as a six-year-old where it matters," Aisha reassured her. "It's just that we all count differently."

"Rip-off," Mike muttered under his breath, and then he pointed to some children on the other side of the stage. "Wow, what's wrong with the little kid next to Orsilla?"

Aisha looked over and saw that the Horten newcomer was continually strobing through the color spectrum as his emotions got the better of him. "Excuse me," she said, and hurried over to calm the boy.

"Yellow means that they're nervous," Mike informed Beth. "Brown is happy, and I forget the rest."

"Do any of the other children change color?" she asked.

"Frunge hair vines change color sometimes but it's just different greens," the boy explained, warming to his role as a mentor. "Listen. You have to watch out for the Drazen's tentacle because it can swing around if he gets excited. Hey, Spinner. Who's that?"

Mike's young Stryx friend floated to a halt in front of the children, another little robot teetering unsteadily in the air at his side.

"I call her 'Tippy' because she's a little unbalanced when she's nervous," Spinner explained. "She hasn't been around biologicals much because her parent just sent her to the station. She's going to join the experimental school when we go back after our vacation."

"You're starting at Libby's school?" Beth asked the robot.

"Yes," squeaked the little Stryx, and then continued in a rush of words. "Are you a student too? Will you be my friend? Libby promised to find me a Human friend, but I like you."

Shaina gave Daniel a push in the direction of Beth's father. "You should explain to him what to expect when your child has a Stryx friend," she told him.

"I seem to remember Libby doing all of that when we signed Mike up for her school," Daniel replied, but he went over and introduced himself to the man, who looked even more nervous than his daughter.

"Hey, Mikey," a Drazen boy called out as he approached, dragging a smaller alien along with his tentacle. "I'm Pluck, and this is Kork," he introduced himself and his captive to Beth. Then he released the younger Drazen and instructed him, "Stick with the Human. They're pretty cool and they never make you feel dumb."

"Pluck, Mikey," a Frunge boy greeted them, escorting his own charge over to meet the group, and then addressing himself to the new cast members. "I'm Vzar and this is Tazos. She's really shy."

"Hi, Tazos," Tippy chirped. "Will you be my friend too?"

"You're all going to be friends, that's the whole point," Pluck said impatiently. "Come on guys, we've got to get ready for the show. Orsilla said that Aisha is going to let us do Storytellers without her."

"Where's Clume?" Mike asked, looking around the set for the towering Dollnick child.

"He told me yesterday that for once he's going to stay in bed to the last minute," Vzar said. "And I saw a Vergallian kid wandering around looking lost, so I think the next cast rotation is going without a Dollnick."

The small throng on set sorted itself out, with the current cast members and the host heading backstage to prepare. Daniel and Aisha took their daughter to sit next to Fenna, who was in the front row of the seating section with her baby brother on her lap.

"Who are you saving the empty seat for?" Shaina asked Aisha's daughter.

"Mommy. She said she was going to do something different today with Storytellers."

The public doors opened and the rest of the studio audience began filing in, taking all of the spaces that weren't already filled by family and friends of the new and outgoing cast members. A Dollnick teenager dressed in bright clothes began warming up the audience with a juggling act. He started with four pins in each hand, rapidly launching them towards the high ceiling one after another until he had two interwoven cascades totaling sixteen pins flying through the air.

"It's kind of scary, isn't it," Fenna said, hunching protectively over her baby brother, but not taking her eyes off of the performer.

"When did Aisha add warm-up entertainment?" Daniel asked his wife.

"A few months ago," Shaina said. "You've been too busy to notice. The Grenouthians are getting ready to launch an all-species variety show with a human host, and they're testing acts on the 'Let's Make Friends' audience since it's almost the same demographic. If it wasn't for the fact that Aisha keeps the show on human time, they'd probably schedule it right after her to piggyback on the ratings."

A bell chimed and the juggler caught all of his pins, spinning around and collecting the last one behind his back. The audience gave him an enthusiastic round of applause, and the Grenouthian assistant director hopped up on the stage.

"Okay, everybody. You all know that it's the last day for the kids in this cast, so try to pay attention to the 'applause' sign for a change. I mean it," he added, after the audience erupted in derisive sounds from a dozen different species. "And Aisha is going to do something different after the commercial break, so don't make a lot of noise when she joins the audience or you'll mess up our timing."

"You mean your commercial timing," somebody called out.

"Hey!" the bunny said, scanning the audience for the heckler. "You think your ticket price pays for this show? The money we collect at the door barely covers the catering."

"I didn't know the audience paid to get in," Shaina whispered to Daniel.

"Well, if you like coming so much, we'll just have to put Princess here on the show when she's old enough so you can keep getting in for free," Daniel said, tickling his little daughter under the chin.

Another chime sounded and the lighting in the seating sections dimmed, while Aisha and the cast appeared on stage and quickly found their marks. The assistant director hurriedly hopped down and started counting them in. When he reached zero, the status lights on all of the immersive cameras flashed on.

"Final shows are always a mix of joy and sorrow," Aisha began, and a tear escaped her right eye to roll down her cheek. She turned gracefully towards the children while surreptitiously wiping the tear away and smiled sadly. "Tonight we say goodbye to Orsilla, Spinner, Pluck, Vzar, Krolyohne, Mike and—"

There was the sound of heavy-footed running and a Dollnick boy with his shirt buttons done wrong thundered onto the stage.

"—and Clume," Aisha concluded. "I want to take a moment to tell everybody out there watching how much we appreciate you voting on what activities to include in

127

the final show, and that we've worked up a little surprise for you as well. But first, I'm sure you all want to know what the children are planning to do next, so let's hear from them in their own words. Krolyohne?"

"School," the Verlock girl replied.

"And after school?" Aisha prompted.

"I don't think school ever stops. Does it?"

"I'm not sure how the Verlock system works," the host admitted. "As long as it makes you happy."

"It's school," Krolyohne repeated.

"How about you, Pluck?"

"I'm going to be a drummer, and a ship captain, and a stakeholder in a really big consortium," the Drazen boy replied eagerly.

"It sounds like you have very ambitious plans. Orsilla?"

"School. Then the Open University. Then marriage, I guess."

"That sounds nice. Are you looking forward to having your own family?"

"In forty or fifty years, maybe."

"What about you, Vzar?"

"I've already been chosen for a new Frunge show about young metallurgists in training."

"So you're planning on a career in show business," Aisha said with a smile.

"Or smelting."

"Clume?" Aisha queried the Dollnick, who had finally recovered his breath.

"School, but I'm going to start as an apprentice shipwright after class," he replied.

"What does that mean?" Mike asked.

"You do what the master tells you so you don't get hit," the large boy explained.

"And what are you doing after the show, Mike?" Aisha followed up quickly, unsure of whether or not Clume was joking about the master/apprentice relationship and not wanting to risk probing for details.

"We're all going for ice cream. You know that."

"I meant, what are your plans for the future?"

"Ice cream," Mike replied stubbornly.

"Spinner?" Aisha asked, turning to the little Stryx.

"I can't eat ice cream, but I'll go to keep you company."

"Your future. What plans do you have when you stop coming to the studio next week?"

"I'm not stopping. I promised Tippy to come with her until she gets comfortable. Will I have to buy tickets?"

"No, I'm sure we can arrange something," Aisha said, ignoring the shaking head of the assistant director. "But what do you plan to do after that?"

"I can stay in Libby's school and be friends with Mike and Fenna for a few more years, but then I have to start traveling," the young Stryx said seriously. "My parent expects me to build a science ship or a station one day."

"You better not leave," Mike muttered in a threatening tone.

"We're going to take a quick commercial break, and then we'll be back for Storytellers. Viewers have less than a minute to suggest an opening line or vote on the current choices."

The moment the light on the front immersive camera blinked out, a distraught Dollnick rushed onto the stage and began redoing the buttons on Clume's shirt.

"What's the opening line for Storytellers going to be?" Aisha called over to the assistant director.

"Once upon a time," the bunny shot back facetiously.

"I know that. I meant the next part."

"It's a close battle between 'Three children were lost in the woods, when a witch,' and 'Three children were lost in space, when a witch,' but, hang on. There's a new one coming up that's getting billions, no, trillions of votes. That shouldn't happen."

"What is it?" Aisha demanded.

"No time," the bunny said, pointing urgently at his ear. "We're live in three. Two. One."

"And welcome back to 'Let's Make Friends,'" Aisha announced smoothly when the status light went hot. "Our cast members are all two years older than when they first started on the show, almost two and a half years, really, and I want to give them the opportunity to show how grown-up they've become. So after I read them the first line for Storytellers, I'm going to go sit in the audience and let them use their imaginations without interruption."

The children all nudged each other excitedly, and there were some low whistles, foot-tapping, and the rumble of belly-patting from the audience. One of the numerous young Grenouthians related to the producer hopped onto the set and brought Aisha a tab with some text on it.

"And Storytellers will begin with—Once upon..."

"A TIME!" the children shouted.

"There was a brave Dollnick colony ship named Flower who lowered herself to work with humans." Aisha's voice trailed off at the end of the line, which struck her as a veritable minefield for storytelling and not a little insulting, but the die was cast, and she stepped down from the stage. The cameras followed as she found her seat next to Fenna and took her baby boy into her lap.

"You first," Pluck nudged Mike.

"We agreed on Vzar," the boy protested in a whisper.

"But it's about Humans," Vzar said. "And I can't think of anything."

"My father says that Flower isn't normal," Clume contributed. "She doesn't listen."

"Somebody has to go," Orsilla pointed out.

"I'll do it," Spinner announced, and launched into the story. "Flower liked to travel through space assisting people in need, and she came to Union Station to get ready for her new job. All of the species offered to help her prepare."

Aisha felt the tension easing from her shoulders as the young Stryx opened the story. She had been worried that the first child would start by equipping Flower with weapons to become a pirate ship.

"And the Frunge helped plant Earth-trees on Flower's ag deck so the Humans wouldn't be lonely," Vzar offered, and then pointed at Orsilla, who was next in the order they had agreed upon backstage.

"The Hortens taught Flower games she could play with the Humans so they wouldn't be bored and get up to mischief," the Horten girl suggested, and pointed at Pluck, who had had a little time to think.

"And Flower told the Humans they could go anywhere on the ship, but not to open the blue door," the Drazen boy said, lowering his voice as he gave the warning.

Aisha leaned forward in her chair, willing the Verlock girl to steer the story back on track to a happy ending.

"One day," the bulky alien pronounced slowly, "a little boy told his friends in Flower's school that he was going to look behind the blue door. The next day, he didn't come to class." She nodded to Mike.

"And the boy's best friend went to look for him after school. She slowly opened the blue door to peek inside,

131

but she couldn't see anything," he added, and pointed at Clume.

"So the girl asked Flower to turn on the lights in the room, but instead, the corridor lights went out. Then the girl thought she heard somebody moving inside."

Aisha held her breath while she waited to see if Spinner would pull the story back from child-eating monsters, but the young Stryx was caught up in the group-telling.

"And when she went inside, the girl found it wasn't a room at all, but a magical forest. Before she could go back, a witch grabbed her and stuffed her in a sack with the little boy."

"Oooh, this is a good one," Fenna whispered to her mother. "Spinner really learned how to use his imagination."

"And the sack was bigger on the inside than the outside, and it was full of children from all over the galaxy," Vzar picked up on the familiar theme. "The witch was saving up until she had enough children to make soup for her friends."

"But the little Horten girl had her sewing kit with her, and she used her scissors to cut a hole in the sack," Orsilla said, taking advantage of the fact that none of the earlier tellers had assigned the girl a species.

"And a brave Drazen boy reached through the hole with his tentacle and grabbed the witch's ankles. And she fell over and hit her head and went to sleep," Pluck said, as proudly as if he were the boy in the sack.

"Then the children all crawled out of the sack and they called for Flower to open the door," the Verlock girl added, leaving the final line to Mike.

The boy peered reluctantly out at the audience where Aisha was sitting with the fingers on both of her hands crossed, and he wrapped up the story with, "And Flower let the children out for ten centees each."

The assistant director gestured to Aisha to return as the network went to commercial.

"I really thought they were going to get the children all the way into the cookpot for a change," the Grenouthian grumbled. "Kids these days have no imagination."

"I don't understand how we ended up with an opening line about EarthCent's Dollnick colony ship," Aisha said, smiling happily at the children who had brought Storytellers into a safe harbor without her riding herd.

"The booth already ran it down and we'll have to patch that particular hole if we ever do audience call-in again. Nobody was expecting an AI to take an interest in the first line for a Storytellers episode, so it was easy for Flower to hijack the voting."

Twelve

"Are you feeling better yet?" Kevin asked Dorothy. "I know that three days from Union Station to Earth was pushing it, but the Stryx offered it as an option, and I figure the less time you spend in Zero-G the better."

"I'm fine in Zero-G, the problem was you cutting my Farling medicine patches in quarters. If I ever find out that you were lying about bringing just enough for the round trip, the marriage is off."

"We're already married and you can't divorce me, the Frunge don't recognize it. The best you can do is to get a waiver that allows you to take a second husband."

"Watch where you're going!" Dorothy shouted as the floater narrowly missed an abandoned box truck on the broken-up highway.

"I'm not driving this thing, it's on autopilot. Weren't you listening when your grandmother explained how it all worked?"

"I didn't feel well, and besides, I thought you just talked to it."

"You have to know what to say. It's an autopilot, not an AI."

"Where's this place we're going again?"

"One of those universities that couldn't find enough students or funding to keep going after the Stryx opened Earth. Your mom got a whole list of them from the president's people, but this one is near the place with the carnival equipment."

"But that was like a hundred years ago. Are you sure they have any books left?"

"I'm just going by what the EarthCent people told us. It's not a hundred years either, more like eighty, and the university didn't close immediately. It took decades to ferry all those people off Earth back before the elevator was built. The alien labor contractors had to do it with big shuttles."

"Like the ones Flower has on her colony ship?"

"Those are for moving people who are awake. I watched a Grenouthian documentary about how the aliens recruited whole towns from Earth for contracts, and they used specialty transports where everybody except for the crew was put in stasis. Some of the big ones could carry a hundred thousand people in one go, and it saves a ton of space when you don't need to feed all those people or give them room to move around. They just stack them in like cargo."

"What difference does it make if the university shut down forty years ago rather than eighty? My dad says that you can't leave buildings alone for more than a couple of years on Earth or they'll have trees growing out of them."

"I don't remember all the details, but the campus was sold off to somebody, maybe a religious group."

"Why didn't they sell all of the books?"

"I don't know, Dorothy. Maybe something to do with their religion. There was a note from Hildy Gruen, the president's girlfriend, to be careful about what we say to them."

"Arriving at Haven in one minute," the floater informed them.

"Wow, look at all those tall buildings," Dorothy said. "They remind me of hotels."

"Probably student housing. These universities were supposedly like self-contained cities, with their own police force and everything."

The floater slowed as it approached the gated entrance, and then came to a complete stop next to the guard shack window when the barrier failed to rise out of the way.

"Why don't we just float over it?" Dorothy demanded.

"I'm not driving," he reminded her. "Hopefully the autopilot knows what it's doing."

The door of the shack banged open, and a bored looking guard approached the floater. "You here to see the nutcases?" he asked.

"We're here about the library," Kevin said. "The EarthCent president's office arranged a meeting for us."

"Those freaks didn't bother telling me," the guard said, gesturing in the direction of the campus. "Alright, I'm recording now," he announced in a bored voice, thumbing on a device with a lens hanging from a lanyard around his neck. "I'm required by law to read you these conditions, and if you want to get in, you have to state your verbal agreement to each one. First, do you agree to hold Triple A Security harmless in the case of any damage to your vehicle or your person inside these gates?"

"I do," Kevin said, shrugging at Dorothy.

"I do too," she confirmed, "and that's more than anybody asked me before claiming I was married."

The guard raised an eyebrow at her remark, but continued.

"Second. Do you agree not to speak about aliens or artificial intelligence inside, even if you are directly questioned about their existence?"

"I do," Kevin replied automatically.

"That's ridiculous," Dorothy said. "My best friends are AI and aliens."

"So don't go in," the guard responded, and began to turn away.

"Come on, Dorothy. You can just pretend that you're mad and that you're giving everybody inside the silent treatment."

"All right. I do too."

"Third. Do you agree not to make reference to the space elevator, the tunnel network, or any other manifestations of the false reality outside of these gates."

"I do," Kevin said.

"Whatever," Dorothy grunted, looking fierce.

"That's not good enough," the guard said, tapping his fingers on the floater.

"Alright, alright. I do."

"Thank you. Enjoy your visit to Haven and try not to get stoned."

"They're going to push drugs on us?" Kevin asked the guard, glancing at Dorothy, who gave him a withering look in return.

"Stoned in the biblical sense," the guard said, leaning in through the window of the shack and activating the gate mechanism. "It's a bad thing. Trust me."

"I guess Haven must be set up for rejectionists," Kevin told Dorothy as the floater began moving forward without further instructions. "I don't like the sound of that stoning business, so please let me do the talking."

"But grandma pointed out to me how you can see the elevator hub at night from all around here as long as it's not cloudy," the girl exploded. "These people must be nuts."

"Just keep it bottled up until we're outside the gates," he warned her. "In fact, maybe we should go back and I'll leave you with the guard."

"No, no. I'll be good. But how are they going to explain the floater?"

"They probably believe it was invented by humans," Kevin speculated as the floater came to a halt in front of a brutal looking concrete building.

"Library," the autopilot announced, and fell silent.

"Let's not stay any longer than we have to," Dorothy said, as they stepped out of the vehicle and started up the broad stairs littered with small stones. "It doesn't even look open."

"Those metal shutters aren't original. I'll bet they replaced the whole entrance at some point. Look, there's a little door over there at the right with a 'Visitors' sign."

Dorothy marched boldly up to the door and raised the knocker, prepared to take out her frustration by doing her best to put a dent in the metal, but the door opened inwards before she could carry through with the motion.

"Welcome, I've been watching for you." The speaker was a small man wearing a little round hat and an ancient tweed suit coat with patches on the elbows. "I'm Peter, and if you'll come in, that's right, it's safe to talk in here. I only visit Haven when I have to, but it's on my circuit, so there you have it."

"Your circuit?" Kevin asked.

"I'm a library circuit rider. I'm responsible for thirty-nine former municipal and educational libraries in this part of the state, or what's left of it. Our goal is conservatorship, which in practice means trying to save as many books as possible from water damage or biomass conversion."

"What's that?"

"Burning." The librarian's voice cracked as he pronounced the word, and he gestured for them to follow him as he began walking. "When I first joined the library movement in the youth auxiliary, I remember how easy it was to get people to agree that books are a treasure to be preserved, and we even collected plenty of cash donations. But when it came to finding people willing to give a good home to a few thousand volumes, all of a sudden nobody has any room." He sighed. "My own house is stuffed with books, and when I die, I have no doubt about where they're headed."

"Who owns the books in this library?" Kevin asked.

"Ironically, they still belong to the state," the librarian said, leading them into the stacks. "When the campus was sold to the Haven cult, the library was specifically excluded because it also serves as a federal repository for government publications. Since that time, things have loosened up and nobody asks questions about who owns what books. Our group has been able to preserve the library buildings by selling off rare books to collectors and, uh, various other fundraising. But the core problem of what to do with millions of books when nobody is reading them remains."

"Why isn't anybody reading them?" Dorothy demanded.

"Well, admittedly, a great number of the volumes in educational libraries are monographs, like these here."

"What's a monograph?"

"Two centees, I can't go any higher."

"I didn't mean what do they cost. I meant, what are they?"

"Generally academic studies of a single subject, hence the title, and in practice, many were published for the sake of credentialing."

"What did you mean you can't go any higher?" Kevin asked, thinking that the man was bargaining backwards.

"That's what I can pay you to take them," the man said. "Isn't that why you're here?"

"I'm just doing a favor for my mother-in-law, the EarthCent Ambassador to Union Station," Kevin explained. "They're planning on outfitting a Dollnick colony ship with a library and taking it around to human communities."

"Then forget the monographs," the little librarian said, growing visibly excited. "Do you mean that EarthCent is planning to fill a ship with books to make them available to humans all through the galaxy?"

"Well, it's an awfully big ship and it's going to be used for a lot of other things as well."

"I can get you all the real books you want, but you'll have to arrange for shipping."

"You mean for free?"

"Of course for free. Nobody pays for old books unless they're rare or collectible for some reason. Tell me, do you know if the ambassador is interested in hiring librarians? I'm available, and I know a number of us who would be willing to go along with their books. I'll work for room and board."

"I'll check with my mom about the job," Dorothy promised. "But how are we going to move whole libraries full of books to Union Station?"

"Minus the monographs and federal collection," the librarian reminded them.

"We'll have to get a whole bunch of standard elevator shipping containers sent out here and find people to pack them," Kevin said. "I don't think EarthCent, or maybe it's Eccentric Enterprises, will have any issue paying for transport. Once the containers are all in orbit, they can wait until Flower comes to pick them up."

"I can hire the Havenites cheap to pack the books," Peter said. "Their economy is understandably depressed, and they would have starved out years ago without charitable donations from the large food packing plant nearby."

"Drazen Foods?" Dorothy asked. "We're going to visit the plant later, the owner knows my family. In fact, Eccentric has been using them to handle all sorts of shipping from Earth because they do so much of it."

"That's perfect. The Havenites have convinced themselves that the Drazens are actually humans who were mutated over a couple of generations by drinking polluted well water in a local town. If you can get me the authorization I can handle all of the arrangements. Moving these books off of Earth to where people will read them is like a dream come true."

Dorothy and Kevin left the reborn librarian planning up a storm, and following Peter's advice, got right back into the floater and departed Haven without sightseeing. They broke out the bag lunches Marge had insisted on packing and ate as the floater shot over the countryside at an insane rate of speed.

"So this next place is like a junkyard for carnival rides?" Dorothy asked after polishing off her apple.

"Used rides, not junk, though I guess a lot of them haven't been used much lately."

"How can you trade for carnival rides? Have you ever even seen one in your life?"

"Sure. Alien rides, anyway. Besides, your dad can fix anything that has most of the parts, and he gave me a list of rides that he's interested in with suggested prices."

"Any roller coasters?"

"No, it's all the smaller stuff that could be trucked in and quickly set up for a fair, I think. I wrote them down because the names all sounded so similar I was afraid I'd get confused."

"Like what?"

Kevin fished a handwritten list out of his coverall pocket and read, "Zipper, Whirlwind, Landslide, Skydiver, Dive Bomber, Zamperla Disco, Rampage Stampede, Sizzler, Kamikaze, Tivoli Tumbler, Yoyo, Orbiter, Banzai, Power Surge, Vortex, and any small merry-go-round or carousel. And keep an eye open for kiddie rides with good paint."

"Isn't Rampage Stampede a bit redundant?"

"Maybe the first half is the brand name."

"When will we get there?"

"I didn't ask," Kevin said. "Floater. How long until we get to Carny Purgatory?"

"Arriving at Carny Purgatory in one minute," the autopilot replied.

"There's nothing around but farmland, and a lot of those barns and silos look abandoned," Dorothy commented.

"If it wasn't winter, we might see that those fields are mainly weeds. Probably cheap land."

"How much of this junk does my dad want you to buy?"

"Their slogan is, 'Gently used carnival rides with a money-back guarantee.' And your dad arranged credit through Eccentric for whatever we can fit in my ship, which is a decent amount now that the library books are taking care of themselves."

"You mean Peter and Drazen Foods will take care of the books."

"As long as it's off my plate it amounts to the same thing. We'll probably fill one container with the books your grandmother bought for the benefit sale, so that leaves three containers left for rides." Kevin squinted against the winter sun as the floater began to slow. "What's with all the giant metal rings?"

"Those must be Ferris wheels," the girl said. "Wow, some of them are pretty tall."

"I don't want to spend the next month taking one of those apart. I told the tunnel controller we'd be here a week, max."

"Carny Purgatory," the floater announced, coming to a halt in front of a giant Quonset hut, one of a dozen clustered at the end of a field full of snow-covered equipment.

"Sure looks like junk," Dorothy commented as they climbed out of the floater. "Is there even anybody here? If we had brought Alexander like I said, he could have sniffed them out."

"I didn't know how long we'd be at the library and your mom warned me that dogs aren't allowed inside most places on Earth. Isn't that crazy? Besides, it would have been tough to haul him away from the door to your grandmother's kitchen with the smell of whatever she was cooking us for dinner."

"Probably take-out that she's pretending to make. My mom must have learned that trick somewhere." Dorothy stopped and stared at the heavily tattooed figure that suddenly loomed out from behind a pile of tires and into their path. "Horten?"

"Morton," the man introduced himself, not realizing that the girl had mistaken him for an alien. "You're the ones from space?"

"I'm Kevin and she's Dorothy. We're here about the rides."

"There's no other reason for anybody to come this way. Let me warn you right off that most of the stuff under the snow in the yard is spare parts at this point. If you want a bigger selection than what I've got inside, you'll have to head out west where the weather doesn't eat everything. There's a place in the desert with thousands of rides in near mint condition."

"We were in the area so it can't hurt to have a look."

"That's what the gal from the president's office told me. Struck me as kind of funny, EarthCent getting interested in carnival rides. I haven't been out on the road in years. It's all the fault of floaters, like the one you came in."

"How so?" Dorothy asked, hoping the man wasn't an escapee from Haven.

"Travel's so cheap and quick now that what people are left don't want to go to a little county fair. They hop in the floater and take a nap, wake up at one of the big theme parks with rides the size of buildings. Everything I got in the Quonset huts was built to go out on trucks, or with some of the older stuff, rail cars."

"That's good for us," Kevin said. "My ship has room for a little more than three standard elevator container loads once we get the merchandise up to the hub."

"I've been up on the elevator to take a look so I've seen those containers. About the same as four old trailers, each of them, so you've got plenty of room. Come on inside and have a looksee. Lights are on, but you'll think you're blind at first. It's the snow."

Morton was correct, and the visitors found themselves halting just inside the door as everything went dark. Gradually their eyes adjusted, and the contents of the giant building slowly became more distinct, resolving into individual rides. Some were set up for operation, but the majority were only partially assembled, due to height constraints.

"My father-in-law gave me a list of the rides he's interested in," Kevin told the carny. "Might be a good place to start."

"Let's hear it," Morton said, and responded to each name Kevin read off with, "Got it. Got it. Got three of them. Yup. Uh-Huh. Maybe the last one on the east coast. I can go two-fer-one on those. Got a whole hut full of carousels, and two huts full of kiddie rides," he said, after hearing the last two items. "What're you planning on doing with this stuff, anyway?"

"EarthCent, I mean, Eccentric Enterprises, is preparing a colony ship to run around to all of the independent human communities that are popping up," the ambassador's daughter explained. "I think that the plan is to load the ship up with as many attractions as possible to make it worthwhile for people to visit. We just came from arranging for a library's worth of books."

"You're talking about a carnival in space?"

"One deck, anyway, or part of it. Colony ships are really big. I mean, like millions of people can live on them."

"Got room for one more?" Morton blurted out.

"Uh, we're not in charge or anything, but I'm sure they do," Dorothy replied. "You're willing to leave all of this?"

"It's not going anywhere on its own, other than rusting into the ground. Besides, even if you're only talking about setting the rides up once then moving the whole carnival, you'll need a crackerjack wrench man to keep them all operating safely. If you've got as much space as you say, I'd be willing to bring everything I've got in good working order, and I've had the last ten years to get ready."

"If I know one thing about EarthCent it's that they aren't the types to look a gift horse in the mouth," Kevin said, glancing at a wooden carousel pony on a stand where the carny had been touching up the paint. "Do you think you could arrange transport to the elevator?"

"I'll have my buddies from Drazen Foods take care of it," Morton said confidently. "They've been handling my cross-country shipping for years, though they'll be sad to see me go."

"You have friends working for the Drazens?"

"My friends are Drazens, managers at the plant. I couldn't have kept going here without their help. They come with their families for the rollercoaster, and the more rickety it gets, the more they like it. I bet they'll handle the move in exchange for the stuff I don't ship. I already made my will to leave it all to them anyways."

"So these rides in here are ready to go?" Dorothy asked.

"Just got to turn on the generator and I can fire up the Yo-Yo there. I modified it to run at a higher speed for the Drazens, they're kind of thrill seekers. When the seats swing out, your head will come pretty close to the roof, but that's part of the fun."

"Do you think that's a good idea with your motion sickness, Dorothy?" Kevin couldn't stop himself from asking.

"I don't have motion sickness, I have a little problem with Zero G, which I wouldn't, if you'd stop being so stingy with my medicine," the girl replied as Morton headed off to start the generator. "Just give me a half a patch now and I won't kill you for holding back when we were in the tunnel."

"I wouldn't be doing this if Libby hadn't assured me that it's safe," Kevin relented, fishing a reserve strip of patches out of his inner pocket. "It's just that you get so aggressive."

"I KNEW you were lying," she cried, snatching the strip from his hand. She ripped a patch in half, peeled the backing, and stuck it to the side of her neck. "Anyway, it seems like we took care of our business for the whole trip already, so I can hang out with my grandma all week."

"Always pays to do a test run before loading people," the carny informed them on his return, powering up the Yo-Yo ride. The top wheel began to spin, and the seats suspended by cable around the periphery flew out from centrifugal force and then dipped or rose as the top wheel tilted.

Dorothy watched it for almost ten seconds before supplementing her dosage with a half a patch on the inside of her wrist.

Thirteen

"Why did you book us into a theatre room?" Samuel asked the committee secretary.

"It's what the admin gave me when I told them we needed a place to evaluate proposals," Lizant replied. "You try arguing with a Verlock, I would have been there all week. No offence, Wrylenth."

"None taken," the Verlock replied, settling his bulk into a padded chair. "Good view."

"We did ask for written proposals," the ambassador's son persisted. "I don't think it's fair to make the students give oral presentations at the last minute."

"They can just read off their tabs, Sam," Vivian reassured him. "Besides, it's good practice for students who are entering the business world. Shy doesn't cut it in sales."

"Who is determining the order of presentation?" asked the Sharf committee member, settling into a seat one row behind the other students.

"It's first come, first serve, Yvandi," Samuel replied. "The Grenouthian is handling it."

"Then it's highest bid, first served," the Sharf corrected the ambassador's son.

"Marilla is keeping an eye on him, and hopefully screening the proposals at the same time. We probably should have scheduled the presentations after reading the proposals rather than doing an open call, but we're kind of working on admin's schedule."

"Sorry we're barely on time, just came from the dojo," Jorb announced, depositing a large gear bag on an empty seat and plopping himself down next to it. "Sit by me, Grude. You can see over the Humans easy."

The Dollnick student entered on the row behind where the Drazen and Sharf were sitting and then stepped over the seat backs to ease himself into the open spot between them. "Is anybody taking notes?"

"The Open University records everything in this room, which means our Stryx librarian, and for a fee, she'll provide a transcript," Vivian said. "Listen, guys. I've never actually done anything like this before and I'm not sure about the etiquette. Do we have to hear out every proposal to the bitter end, or can we interrupt if they're just going on about something that doesn't make sense?"

"When the Grenouthian comes back, he can handle that part," Lizant said. "He grew up in a network family so he was probably taking auditions before he could hop."

"But these aren't exactly auditions," the girl objected. "I mean, we're supposed to be evaluating the ideas, not the presenter."

"Indivisible," Wrylenth rumbled. The other students all waited to see if he would add anything to this pronouncement, but he apparently felt it was self-explanatory.

"All the same, Samuel and I worked up some criteria—"

"*Committees For Humans*?" Yvandi interrupted.

"Well, we used the book to create the proposal guidelines, so it only makes sense to refer to it for judging the submissions," Vivian said defensively. "The first step is to evaluate whether the proposal meets the guidelines.

149

Otherwise it wouldn't be fair to the students who followed the instructions."

"Bad criteria," the Verlock grunted. "Content is emperor."

"You're saying we should ignore our own guidelines?"

"Why don't we just let them start and see how it goes," Jorb suggested. "Here comes the Grenouthian and what's-her-name now."

"Marilla," Samuel informed the Drazen for at least the third time in their short acquaintance. Jorb shrugged dismissively.

The Horten girl sat down next to Samuel in the front row, while the bulky Grenouthian continued up the aisle and then took a full row to himself behind the Dollnick, Drazen and Sharf students.

"We set a five-minute time limit and told everybody after the first twenty students they'll have to try the next open audition," the Grenouthian informed the others. "Complete waste of an opportunity. We could have picked up lunch money for the semester just by letting them bid on the spots."

"Did you make a note of the order so we'll know they aren't selling spots amongst themselves?" Vivian asked.

"I did," Marilla said from the other side of Samuel. "First up is a Frunge student with a smithy proposal." Then she raised her voice and called out, "Razood," at a volume that made the humans flinch.

A Frunge student strolled confidently onto the stage in his oversized boots and then threw something at the floor directly between his own feet. There was a flash as the one-time holocube formed its projection, and it was as if Razood had suddenly come into possession of an old-fashioned blacksmith's wagon, though it was constructed

150

from lightweight alloys and other artificial materials rather than wood. He produced a large hammer from under his jacket, and sticking his other hand into the hologram where a sword blade was balanced on an anvil, he curled his fingers around the projection to grasp the tang. Then he swung the hammer through a tremendous overhead arc.

"Clang," Razood shouted at the top of his lungs as the hammer head flashed through the hologram and almost bashed into his kneecap. "Clang," he shouted again, miming a second blow as he allowed the follow-through to bring his arm around like a windmill. "Clang."

"Thaaaannnnk you," the Grenouthian called out in a bored voice. "Next."

"But you haven't heard my proposal yet," the student objected as the hologram faded out of existence. The hammer remained in his hand, lending a serious air to his protest.

"Time is creds," the bunny sang out in the same tone.

"I just wanted to add a little sizzle," the student muttered, and then launched into a prepared speech. "Who is the most important man in a frontier town?" he demanded, and then answered his own question. "Why, the blacksmith, of course. He shoes the horses, fixes the plowshares, even repairs the six-shooters. The most welcome sound to Humans scratching out an existence on the frontier is the clang of the blacksmith's hammer on the anvil. It's the sound of civilization."

"You stole that last line from our documentary about Humans killing each other over cattle and riding their horses to death," the bunny accused the Frunge student.

"I'm using it satirically," Razood shot back. "I know galactic copyright law."

151

"You may know the law, but I think you've mistaken Grenouthian entertainment for reality," Vivian said, trying her best to temper the blow. "The frontier we're talking about visiting with Flower consists of settlements on open worlds managed by tunnel network species, plus various space stations and habitats. I'm afraid there's no need for a smithy in those places."

"Everybody needs a smithy," the Frunge protested, though he was unable to hide his surprise that his proposal had missed the mark so badly after he had done his best to bone up on the target audience. "Who else is going to forge blade weapons?"

"Next," the Grenouthian called again.

"We have your contact info if the need for a smithy arises," Samuel told him. "Maybe Eccentric will want to include a traveling Wild West show to reconnect humans born on alien worlds with our past."

"Our past with an alien blacksmith," Vivian muttered as the disappointed student left the stage.

A Drazen girl took his spot, and placing her hands on her abdomen, began to sing.

"I'm in love," Jorb whispered, devouring her with his eyes. He turned fiercely to the Grenouthian and hissed, "Don't you open your mouth."

The girl's song came to an end sooner than any of the enthralled audience would have liked, and she produced a tablet from her shoulder bag and began to read.

"Only one in twenty Humans are truly tone deaf yet the majority still can't sing on key. My hope is that by establishing a remedial choral school on Flower, we can do for Humanity what Astria's Academy of Dance has done for graceless humanoids across the tunnel network and beyond."

152

"Give the Vergallians an easy way to spy on our homeworlds?" Marilla inquired acerbically.

"Well, of course I'll approach Drazen Intelligence to subsidize the choral instructors. It's in the cost analysis, but we're friends with the Humans anyway."

"How long of a course do you think would be required?" Lizant asked, intrigued by the Drazen's idea.

"I realize that we're talking about a circuit ship so I've outlined a variety of programs for every time budget. We start with a simple breathing evaluation and tune-up that can be done in a single visit, and progress all the way to preparing for advanced choral exams, which takes many years, but is probably out of reach for most Human vocal registers in any case."

"Would the instructors all be Drazens?" Samuel enquired.

"I've already contacted EarthCent's associate ambassador on the station in preparation for putting out a request for Human teachers," the girl said. "They'll work under a Drazen choral master, of course, but I've been assured that Humans living on our open worlds are not entirely without talent."

"Are you seeing anybody?" Jorb asked.

"Jorb!" Lizant reproached him. "Please refer to the guidelines for student committee member conduct. If this happens again, I'll have to give you a demerit."

"My parents are in the directory," the girl said shyly. "I'm a few years away from practice dating, but they're working on a list of potential candidates to vet."

"Your proposal has passed the first stage and we'll be in touch," Vivian told the girl.

"Thaaannk you," the Grenouthian boomed. "Next."

The Drazen was replaced on stage by a stunning Vergallian girl who looked like she could be royalty, which was confirmed by her name when she introduced herself.

"I'm Aagala, and my proposal is to aid independent Human communities in establishing governance through a mentoring program."

"On Flower?" Samuel asked.

"I doubt that your colonies could spare their current leadership for extended periods of time for training on Flower. That's why I'm proposing coaching rather than a formal classroom approach like the finishing school I had to go through as the third in line for my family's throne."

"You're third in line and your family let you come to the Open University?"

"I was third in line, but my oldest sister already has two daughters and I kind of got in trouble over the whole tech-ban thing," the girl admitted, flashing a dazzling smile in the boy's direction.

Vivian felt the hair rising on the back of her neck and barked, "So what's your proposal?"

"I would recruit a number of Vergallian royals from lesser houses and provide fitting quarters for them on Flower so they would be available to dispatch for in-place mentoring on short notice."

"Please elaborate on the mentoring aspect," Vivian said stiffly.

"The request for proposals specifically stated that your Eccentric Enterprises is interested in steering human communities towards good governance," Aagala said, seemingly puzzled at being asked to explain the obvious. "What better governance can you have than queens? A trillion Vergallians can't be wrong."

"Catchy," the Grenouthian muttered.

"So you would have Flower play host to a bunch of snooty Vergallian royals with the goal of expanding your empire through governmental assimilation," Yvandi said coldly.

"Anything would be better than the Sharf tradition of hiring your own artificial people to govern and letting them make it up as they go along," Aagala fired back.

"Violation," Wrylenth grunted. "Section Eighty-Two, Part Six."

"He's right," Lizant confirmed, looking down at her tab. "The student code prohibits attempts to hijack the governing entities of fellow students."

"But they would be queen-mentors, not full queens," the Vergallian protested. "Sure, they'd have to actually run things while a Human queen could be trained, say sixty or seventy years, but after that they would step back and —"

"Run everything from behind the scenes for the few years left in the human queen's life, and then start the cycle again with the next candidate," Vivian interrupted. "Are you really a student here?"

"I'm in the extension program," Aagala said, drawing herself up regally.

"You didn't fill out the conflict of interest section," Lizant observed, still looking at her tab. "Who is your employer?"

"Thank you for your consideration," the Vergallian royal said stiffly, and stalked off the stage.

"Write in 'Vergallian Intelligence' for her employer," the Sharf girl said over Lizant's shoulder.

"Nexxxxt," the bunny drawled.

A serious-looking Dollnick student carrying an immense metal box that rattled with each step took the place of the Vergallian intelligence agent. When he set down his burden and rotated the front of the box to face his audience, it turned out to be an organizer, with hundreds of small plastic drawers.

"Do any of you know your Dollnick screw sizes?" he challenged the committee members.

"Sure," a number of them chorused.

"So try me," the Dolly said imperiously.

"Blue Eighteen Inverse," Grude called out.

The presenter tapped a touchpad on the top of the case with the hand on his upper left arm, and picked a fastener from the drawer which shot out below, using his lower arm on the same side. He brandished the small screw without ever taking his eyes from the audience.

"The inverse series are pretty rare," Grude informed his fellow committee members.

"Carbon Two, Coarse Thread," Samuel requested.

Again the Dollnick tapped the pad and fished the requested screw out of the back section of the long drawer.

"Okay, how many different screw sizes do you have in there?" Jorb asked, sounding plenty impressed.

"Three thousand, including length variations, and I'm not counting nuts and washers," the presenter said. "It's the standard household repairman's kit from my family's line. Multiply that across all the different types of fasteners, fittings, paints and tubing, and we're talking about tens of millions of individual item stocking codes. My proposal is to set up a full-line distributor on Flower. Rather than your small communities having to send out for parts with exorbitant shipping costs and delays, they can wait for the circuit ship to come around and stock up."

"Wow," Vivian muttered to Samuel. "That's actually a good business idea."

"Would you only stock Dollnick-made parts?" Lizant inquired.

"Of course. Our parts are the best."

"Unless you're fixing a Sharf trade ship, the most common type in use by Humans," Yvandi pointed out.

"I have no objection to other species stealing my idea for their own distribution networks," the presenter said. "There's more than enough room on Flower for all of us. She might even agree to fabricate parts to spec in exchange for feedstock and a fee, but her pricing won't be competitive compared to mass-produced hardware."

"Have you worked out your space requirements?" Grude asked.

"A section of deck twenty between spoke rings eleven and fourteen spanning six corridors would suit our standard inventory with sufficient redundancy to cover most exigencies," the serious Dollnick replied. "My family would provide the stock and qualified clerks, and I've detailed a training program for Human apprentices, providing they can pass the standard tests, of course."

"You aren't requesting any Stryx financing?" Samuel asked.

"Spoken like a true Human," the Dollnick replied scornfully. "No, I think my family can handle our own arrangements for a business we've been in for, oh, a half a million years give or take."

"Hey," Lizant reprimanded him, and looked back down at her tab. "I'm pretty sure the student handbook specifically prohibits speaking down to—oops, that was clone-baiting. Never mind."

"I think a Dollnick distributor would be a fine addition to the ship, and I hope that some of the other species whose technology we use follow your lead," Samuel said. "We'll evaluate your written proposal and be in touch."

"Ne-eh-xxxxt," the Grenouthian sang, and a nervous young woman walked out onto the stage.

"I'm Aubrey and I just came out from Earth a few years ago to attend this Open University campus," the girl began. "I have a bunch of diagrams and stuff in the written version of my proposal, but the basic idea is to open a flea market."

"Are they tasty?" Jorb inquired.

"Sorry, it's a local term where I come from for a kind of inexpensive market with lots of independent vendors. They sell everything from household goods and collectibles to used clothes and kitchenware. I've met some kids from trader families on the station and they say that open markets are pretty common across all of the species. But instead of the traders traveling to the market, they'll live on the ship and the whole thing will travel to the customers."

"Uh, I don't think Flower will go for it unless you come up with a different marketing pitch," Grude said. "Selling used goods is a low-ranking profession in Dollnick culture."

"Just call it a bazaar or a traveling retail show," Marilla suggested.

"And instead of used goods, describe them as vintage," Vivian added.

"Or antique," the Verlock rumbled.

"Classic," the bunny contributed.

"You get the idea," Samuel said. "Grude is our Dollnick expert and I trust he's right about Flower, but if you redo the written part of your proposal and submit it, we'll give it full consideration."

"Thank you," Aubrey said, and glanced over her shoulder into the wings. "Next."

A large Grenouthian hopped out on the stage, met the eye of his fellow on the committee, and exchanged a polite nod. Then he launched into his pitch.

"The reason that Humans have barely above zero percent of the tunnel network entertainment market is because you're all so busy watching holos and immersives from other species that you aren't developing your own shows. I propose constructing a studio on Flower to give the locals a chance to have their holo presence evaluated, and if you can scrape up the personnel, I'd add a theatre troupe to give live performances. Maybe if you had a little home-grown culture the other species would take you more seriously."

"Is that a sales pitch that you practiced?" Lizant asked incredulously.

"I'm a realist," the bunny replied. "I'm finishing up here in the technical theatre production program, and if I go to work for our network, I'll be lucky to advance from fourth grip to first grip in the next twenty years. I figure if I lower myself to work with Humans, I can start as a director, with points in every production."

"What about your family?" the Grenouthian committee member demanded.

"Do you think I'd be up here making this pitch if I had any family connections to rely on? It's a long story, brother, but I'm out here alone."

"The idea is interesting, but I don't know if you would get along well with our actors," Samuel ventured. "We don't enjoy daily rations of verbal abuse."

"Shows how much you know about theatre," the bunny retorted. "The director doesn't have to get along with anybody. Productions work out better when there aren't personal relationships getting in the way of artistic decisions. Listen," he continued, hopping closer to the front of the stage and lowering his voice so that even the committee members in the front row found themselves leaning forward to hear what he was saying. "Did any of you see the production of Swan Lake put on by Human students last cycle?"

"That was beautiful," Vivian said. "My whole family came to see it."

"That was me," the Grenouthian told her. "If you check the program, I'm listed as the consultant, but you look up the kid who they credited as the director and he'll tell you that he was just following my instructions. I spent fifty years with a travelling company and I'm older than any of you, except maybe the Verlock."

"Why did you come to the Open University?" Samuel asked.

"Stryx offered me a scholarship," the bunny admitted. "Tough life on the road and I'm not getting any younger. Don't get me wrong," he added hastily, "I love regional theatre and reaching new audiences, but putting it all on a colony ship means the opportunity to work like a gentleman. You can only erect so many tents before the whole thing gets to be a bit much."

Fourteen

"You look fantastic in that dress, Kel," Joe said, as his wife paused in front of a reflective corridor panel to make a last-minute adjustment. "The aliens at the reception are going to think that you're my daughter."

The ambassador sighed and held back from crediting the corset her mother had recently sent out in the diplomat pouch. Instead she concentrated on taking her heels down another ten percent from the height that Dorothy had prescribed as the absolute minimum. The interface for the shoes appeared on her heads-up display, and she was dismayed to find that the lower limit was locked with a supervisor password required for override.

"Libby," Kelly subvoced as she and Joe approached the Vergallian embassy. "I want to lower my heels a bit and Dorothy locked the settings. Can you help?"

"You want me to hack into your shoes?"

"I'm not good at this stuff. Clive tells me that the new Vergallian ambassador is from a different faction than the usual replacements, and I wouldn't want to blow the opportunity to make a good first impression because I'm thinking about how much my feet hurt."

"Very well," the Stryx librarian said, and the password prompt disappeared from Kelly's heads-up display. "Just don't tell your daughter it was me."

"I won't," the EarthCent ambassador promised, and using practiced eye motions, moved the slider down a full notch. The heels responded so smoothly that the only manifestation of the change was Joe slowly growing a little taller. "Thank you."

A Vergallian dressed like a major general from an old Earth musical requested their names at the entrance to the embassy's ballroom, and then announced, "Ambassador and Mr. McAllister of EarthCent," without a hint of the condescension that often accompanied formal introductions by the doormen of advanced species.

Kelly took Joe's arm and he led her into the renovated hall, which looked like it could have easily cost more than the entire building back in New York where EarthCent rented space for the president's office. Gold leaf was prominent in the decorating scheme, along with hand-woven tapestries depicting pastoral scenes on tech-ban worlds. Their hostess stood unaccompanied between the entrance and the bar, a location strategically chosen to intercept all new arrivals. Joe led Kelly straight up to the high-caste Vergallian.

"I am Aainda," the alien diplomat introduced herself. "Do you prefer to be addressed formally or by your personal names?"

"Kelly is fine for me, and my husband's name is Joe."

"Kelly and Joe. Welcome to my reception. I will be serving as the Union Station ambassador for the next fifteen cycles, or a little over two years on your charming calendar."

"You've studied Earth? Most of the Vergallian ambassadors I've met were barely willing to acknowledge our existence, though Abeva wasn't that bad once you got to know her."

"My immediate predecessor left some interesting notes about your meetings," Aainda said mysteriously. "And in answer to your question, there have been Human mercenaries serving in my mother's household troops since I was a girl, and I frequently went riding with their wives and daughters. I hope you find my accent acceptable."

"Accent?" Kelly flipped the mental switch to disable translations from her implant. "You've been speaking English?"

"Am I that bad?" Aainda pulled a face of mock distress which only heightened her beauty.

"No, you're so good that I thought I was getting your words from my diplomatic implant. Isn't she good, Joe? Joe?"

Kelly shook her husband's forearm to break the spell the stunning Vergallian had cast upon him without even trying. "Sorry," he mumbled, and a slight shade of red crept up his neck. "Were you saying something?"

"Please enjoy the food and beverages," Aainda continued with a charming smile. "I asked my staff to cater to the lowest common dietary denominator, so you should be able to eat anything you recognize on the platters."

The doorman announced the Grenouthian ambassador, and the Vergallian turned away to greet him. Joe led Kelly to the buffet, where several other diplomats were already congregated.

"Great fruit," Bork greeted the new arrivals. The Drazen ambassador realized that he was talking with his mouth full and covered the lower part of his face with his tentacle as he swallowed hastily. "I thought I would have to save you some, but the staff reassured me that there's plenty more where this came from."

"The cheese is from that shop in the Little Apple," the Frunge ambassador informed Kelly as he gathered different varieties on a single Vergallian chopstick as if he were creating a kebob. "Aainda has gone out of her way to be accommodating. I wonder what she wants from you."

"Maybe she's just trying to make up for past sins, Czeros." Kelly made herself a little sandwich from two crackers, a slice of cheese and a stuffed olive. "I've gotten a lot of grief from Vergallian ambassadors over the last two decades, not to mention the kidnapping before the ball."

"So things aren't looking as bleak as they once did," the Frunge said, adding a rare wink.

"Now that the ambassador has a choice in the matter," Bork said in an insinuating voice, and both of the alien diplomats had to choke back their laughter.

"What's with all the Human food in the buffet?" Ambassador Ortha asked, gesturing at the table. "It seems that my prospects for a good meal in this house are tied up in court."

Kelly stared as Czeros punched the Horten in the shoulder, and all three alien ambassadors started giggling like schoolboys who had secreted a spider in a girl's desk and were waiting for her to scream.

"I'll see if I can find you a glass of wine," Joe told his wife, sensing the onset of an elaborate joke that he'd rather hear in the retelling. "See you in a bit."

"You gentlemen are braver than I thought, standing right next to her like that," the Dollnick ambassador addressed them all from the opposite side of the table. "I suspect Flower will balk at her mission when she learns what the Humans have been hiding."

"What are you talking about, Crute?" Kelly demanded. "What's wrong with all of you?"

"Book club," Srythlan grunted from behind her. He stepped up to the table right next to the EarthCent ambassador and reached for the box of salt cod imported from Earth that the Vergallians had thoughtfully provided. "If you can't take the heat, leave the buffet," he addressed the other aliens, causing them all to break out in outright laughter.

"Book club? My book club? What's that got to do with anything?" Kelly pleaded.

"It's so gratifying that all of my guests have arrived early," Aainda said from Kelly's side, and took the EarthCent ambassador's arm in her own as if they were old friends. "From the little I've heard of the conversation, it sounds to me like our colleagues were having a bit of fun over your latest covert communications attempt."

"I really don't know what any of you are talking about."

"The Ambassador's Book Choice." Seeing Kelly's confusion, Aainda continued to elaborate. "The new feature in your Galactic Free Press that my intelligence service assures me is a cover story to announce a new cipher text being transmitted to your spies over public media. I asked our station librarian for a translation of your supposed choice, which has proven to be rather long but surprisingly compelling. I feel like I'm learning more about Earth from this one history book than from all of the intelligence briefings I've sat through."

"My book club choice for the next meeting? But it's *Bleak House*, the Charles Dickens novel."

"Fiction or not, the author was quite clear about spontaneous combustion being well documented in your species," Crute said. "My own intelligence sources suggest that going up in flames might have evolved as an evolutionary response to predation, sacrificing oneself to protect the clan. It's the sort of brute-force engineering solution we've come to expect from Humans."

"I'm sure spontaneous combustion isn't a real thing or I would know about it," Kelly protested. "And *Bleak House* really is my choice for our book club discussion this week. I had no idea that Chastity would announce it in the Galactic Free Press. She must have an ulterior motive."

"Like helping out her big sister with their little spy business," Ortha cracked.

"No, I mean like the bestseller lists she publishes. It's probably a new trick to sell more books. Now that the Galactic Free Press has its own publishing arm, I bet we'll be seeing much more of it."

"And I bet that the young governess turns out to be Lady Dedlock's daughter by the dead law writer," Aainda said.

"You mean you really are reading it?" Kelly asked, wondering if she had fallen through the rabbit hole. "I thought you were joking."

"It's so much better than the books I used to borrow from my friends in our mercenary settlement. The multiple perspectives of the storyteller are much closer to our own literature, but I've only finished around a fifth."

"Dickens was experimenting with a mix of omniscient narration and a first-person story related by Esther," Kelly explained. "I can't believe—have all of you been reading it?"

"Why did Jarndyce throw good food out the carriage window?" Srythlan demanded, sounding almost angry. "If Esther wasn't hungry, he could have saved it for later."

"It's a common theme in Human literature of that period, throwing things out a carriage window," the

Grenouthian ambassador interjected. "In *Vanity Fair*, it was a dictionary."

"Now, I know that YOU aren't reading Victorian novels, whether in translation or otherwise," Kelly declared, spinning towards the giant bunny. "Did I miss an announcement for 'Fool the EarthCent Ambassador Day' or something?"

"Our network acquired the rights to many of your old broadcast serials after your president invited us to open a studio on Earth."

"You mean there's an immersive version?" Bork cried. "I spent hours reading the intelligence synopsis when I could have been watching it?"

"There are several immersive versions of both books, but they're all automated conversions from archaic two-dimensional footage, so you can't expect the holograms to be particularly realistic," the Grenouthian ambassador said. "Perhaps I can make them available free of charge in return for information about the promotion techniques the ambassador mentioned. How does making lists sell more product?"

"I know from Aisha's show on your network how obsessed you guys are with ratings," Kelly replied. "I think that bestseller lists work like that, except for books."

"But how does the newspaper know who is reading the books and whether or not they finish?"

"They don't, I guess, at least with the printed books. I wouldn't be surprised if somebody tracks the electronic ones down to the last word read. But the bestseller lists are just that, based on sales. It doesn't matter if the buyers actually read the books."

"So it's disinformation," Crute concluded. "A force multiplier for marketing."

"Smart," the Grenouthian said grudgingly.

"We have awards, too," Kelly said, seizing the opening to push Chastity's latest innovation. "Just like you all have for shows, except for books. Our embassy is co-sponsoring a Union Station book awards show with the Galactic Free Press to raise funds for a library on Flower."

"Do awards serve a commercial purpose?" the Dollnick inquired.

"Absolutely. I chose an award-winning book for my first club recommendation, and even though it didn't go so well, everybody bought a copy."

"The Galactic Free Press has a patent on bestseller lists and book awards?" the Grenouthian asked thoughtfully.

"Oh, no. They've been around forever on Earth. It's not like we have a law about it or anything. All you need is a platform."

"You've lost me," Aainda said, giving Kelly's arm a friendly squeeze. "What would I do with a platform?"

"It's just another way of saying that you need a space visible to the public so that people will listen to you. Any of us could survey the bookstores on Union Station and draw up a local bestseller list, but who would pay attention? When the Galactic Free Press publishes a bestseller list, it could be seen by a billion or more humans. And I'll bet you that Chastity runs book advertisements on the same page."

"Brilliant," the Grenouthian ambassador exclaimed, taking his admiration up a notch. "Does the newspaper include alien books?"

"Well, it's only read by humans, plus your intelligence agencies," Kelly corrected herself. "But if publishing lists for your species would give the paper the opportunity to sell more advertising space, I'm sure they would be happy to expand beyond the hundred or so bestseller lists they currently put out."

"What?" Bork demanded. "How can there be a hundred bestseller lists? By definition there can only be one bestselling book. I assumed that the list consisted of the top title plus a number of runners-up."

"They do category bestsellers," Kelly explained. The entire conversation had taken on a surreal quality and she couldn't remember the last time she had held the attention of all of the alien ambassadors for such a long span. "When our artificial friends published their book in the *For Humans* series, it became an instant bestseller because it was the only book in the category."

"Genius," the Grenouthian said in a hushed tone. "I request a meeting with the publishers, Ambassador. There is the potential for you to earn a commission."

"I'm sure Chastity would be happy to meet you," Kelly said, exhaling with relief as Joe elbowed his way into the knot of ambassadors and delivered a glass of chilled white wine to her free hand. "Do any of you want to buy tickets to the awards show? It's not until the end of the cycle, and my office manager hasn't made the final reservation with the Empire Convention Center yet because she's not sure how large a room we'll need."

"Is it too late to have our books included?" Crute demanded. "It seems only right that at least one Dollnick book should get an award at a fundraiser for a Dollnick colony ship."

"Here goes the competitive thing," Joe whispered in Kelly's ear, and then took a sip from the excellent bottled lager the Vergallian barman had miraculously produced.

"Verlock publishers will be interested," Srythlan rumbled, proving that he had been paying attention even as he steadily consumed all of the hardened salt-fish on offer. "Book marketing is always difficult."

"But your people love books," Kelly said.

"Textbooks," the Verlock explained. "All work and no play."

"Our own scroll makers would certainly qualify for best aesthetics," Bork suggested modestly. "Do musical scores qualify as books?"

"If all of the species are willing to sponsor the event, I suppose we could let you add a category or two," the EarthCent ambassador said, wondering how much Chastity would charge them for the privilege. She realized that she just didn't know enough about the business to even guess, and added, "You'll have to contact my embassy manager, Donna Doogal, for the details."

"Your people would probably take it as an insult if we didn't participate as well," the Horten ambassador said, attempting to sound disinterested. "In the spirit of galactic cooperation, you can put me down for a hundred tickets."

"A hundred?"

"Two hundred," Bork declared, glaring at the Horten.

"I'm sure we have enough petty cash in the embassy's culture fund to take two hundred as well," Czeros offered.

"But I haven't told you the price yet," Kelly said, looking from one ambassador to the next. "I don't even know how much tickets will cost."

"I think we'll go with a category for engineering romance," Crute mused. "And three hundred tickets to start."

"Five hundred," the Grenouthian said immediately, as if they were all bidding at an auction. "Just because we lead the galaxy in live news and documentaries doesn't mean we've given up on books. I predict a Grenouthian victory."

"How did we get from an awards show to a battle?" Aainda playfully asked the EarthCent ambassador, whose arm she still held captive. "I'm afraid the only Vergallians I know on the station are my embassy staffers and some intelligence agents, though of course, I will order them all to attend. Will we vote on the awards at the ceremony? I've always been fond of reading at the table."

"I don't think attendees are expected to read the books," Kelly replied slowly, vacillating once again over whether she should take the alien ambassadors seriously or if it was all some elaborate joke. "I'm pretty certain that the winners are selected ahead of time."

"Ah," the Grenouthian ambassador said. "I understand now. Do we purchase the awards separately or will they be included in the ticket price?"

"Can we buy prizes in the categories of other species?" the Dollnick followed up.

"I assume that the awards will be granted by judges," Kelly replied, hoping that she wasn't interfering with Chastity and Walter's plans. "If you contact the embassy tomorrow, I'm sure we'll have answers for you."

"Check on the fee to purchase a judgeship," Crute said. "And don't forget to ask about a quantity discount."

"Whatever they're ordering, plus one," the Grenouthian growled, favoring the Dollnick with a belligerent stare.

"My, my," their hostess said. "Is it always this exciting on Union Station?"

"You should have been here for Carnival," Joe muttered.

"Vendor space," Srythlan suggested laboriously. "For award-winning books."

"Oh, that's a good idea," Kelly said. "We are planning a small book display in the lobby before the show, and I think the vendors will want to sell nominated books as well, since the award hasn't been granted yet. I've seen advertisements in the Galactic Free Press for books that boast about being nominated for this or that prize. It's almost as big an honor as winning."

A silence fell over the clustered ambassadors as they absorbed the concept, and then the Grenouthian remarked, "This just keeps getting better and better."

Fifteen

The EarthCent delegation for negotiating Flower's terms of employment trooped out of the shuttle in their magnetic cleats and gathered in a little knot in the cavernous landing bay.

"So, do we just start talking like on a Stryx station?" Blythe asked.

"That's one approach," Flower's voice echoed through the colony ship's pressurized core. "Or, you could wait until you're in the lift tube and then I won't have to strain my speakers to make myself heard."

"Got it," Clive said. The director of EarthCent Intelligence started in the direction indicated by the blinking lights in the deck, Daniel staying alongside him. Blythe and Lynx lingered behind a step as little Em began to wail.

"Get her to swallow," Blythe advised. "It's the change in air pressure giving her an ear-ache."

"Poor thing doesn't understand," the mother of the two-year-old replied. "It's a good thing Woojin isn't here or he'd be going out of his mind. Come on, Em. Swallow for Momma. It's what Uncle Beetle would want. Now, who's a big baby?"

"Dada," Em replied reflexively, and immediately stopped crying.

"Is that your cure-all?" Blythe asked. "It's like you threw a switch."

"Didn't both of your twins always cry after one started? When Em hears herself crying she thinks there must be something to be upset about, but as soon as she gets distracted and stops, she decides it must be okay."

"Smart baby."

The two women shuffled forward on their magnetic cleats and caught up with the men at the lift tube. The door slid open and they all entered the capsule, where sounds resembling soft birdsong could be heard in the background.

"I take it the little heat signature isn't part of your negotiating team," Flower's voice intoned from somewhere above. "State your names so I'll know which of you is which."

"Clive Oxford, Director—"

"I know, I know," the ship's AI cut him off. "Just the names will be sufficient."

"Blythe Oxford."

"Daniel Cohan."

"Lynx Pyun, or Pyun Lynx if you're Korean, and my little heat signature is Em."

"I am keeping acceleration to a minimum for Em's sake, so don't get it into your heads that my lift tubes are slow. Does she do tricks?"

"Em?"

"She is a baby. All Dollnick babies do tricks."

"Em smiles, and claps, and she has a really strong grip."

"She'll need it with just two hands. Where's the rich one?"

"You mean me?" Blythe asked.

"No, the really rich one, Ambassador McAllister. Does she think that negotiating with a colony ship is below her?"

"Kelly's not rich, and she didn't come because Associate Ambassador Cohan is the moving force behind the organization for the sovereign human communities you'll be visiting. He knows more about their requirements than anybody."

"Come now. Do you think I was born yesterday? I saw the Kasilian auction over my Stryxnet feed and that stuff was worth trillions of creds."

"Oh, she gave all the proceeds to the Stryx to finance the Kasilians moving to a new world."

"Is she insane? I would have moved them to a new world for a fraction of that and bought myself a crew with the leftover."

"She couldn't have kept it anyway," Daniel spoke up. "EarthCent policy prohibits ambassadors from accepting gifts over a certain value."

"How much?"

"I don't remember, but a lot less than trillions of creds. Maybe tens of creds, like a decent bottle of wine."

"And I thought that my makers had too many regulations," Flower said, as if speaking to herself. "I'm bringing you to a classroom where we can talk."

"Why a classroom?" Clive asked.

"The large display panel may be useful, and the children's seating means that your feet will reach the floor. I'll have difficulty taking you seriously otherwise."

A moment later the doors slid open, and again, lights embedded in the deck began blinking in sequence to guide the visitors to their destination. The room was apparently intended for use by early grades, and colorful artwork that looked like it had been produced by finger-painting adorned the walls. A large display that took up the entire front wall of the classroom came to life as the visitors entered, and Flower electronically erased the contents with a sigh.

"The children were just starting on their Base20 math," the AI commented. "I always enjoyed watching them count the fingers of their four little hands."

"Did you teach the classes?" Lynx asked.

"My crew wouldn't let me. I understand from the Stryx that Humans actually allow AI to teach their children."

"Our twins went to school where all of the classes are taught by the station librarian, as did the ambassador's children," Clive volunteered. "Daniel's son goes there now."

"Hmm. Well, take your seats, we have a lot to get through. Shall we begin with the big issues or the small ones?"

"Could you give us an example of each?" Blythe asked, suspecting that the alien AI would likely see things very differently than the humans.

"Very well, here's a small thing. Many of the species I've carried for the Stryx have asked that I change the music in the lift tubes."

"It sounded like birds signing," Lynx said. "Most people will probably like it."

"Good, because it's non-negotiable," the AI stated flatly.

"All right," Blythe asked. "What is negotiable?"

"Cabin furnishings. I'm currently storing the bulk of my proper furniture on the low-gravity decks, and if that space should be required by you at a later date, which I find doubtful, the Stryx have offered to provide free storage."

"So you expect us to bring in whatever we need for our people," Clive surmised.

"No, we can talk about what you need and come to a negotiated agreement."

"Why would you care what sort of beds people sleep on or what kind of chairs they sit in?"

"I've only had a short time to study up on your species, but I've found the documentaries produced by the Grenouthians to be quite informative," Flower said, triggering a groan from all of the humans, excepting Em, who had fallen asleep. "While there's nothing I can do to make you care about your health or appearance, I do take issue with factors that may impact your productivity while we're working together. Furniture plays a role in the back problems and poor posture which is endemic to your species, and I can't be expected to approve of bad ergonomic designs simply because they are fashionable."

"This is important to you?" Blythe asked.

"Everything that takes place inside my ship is important to me."

"We sympathize with your logic, but I'm concerned that any unnecessary constraints you put on the crew will have a negative impact on our ability to recruit quality people for the mission," Daniel said seriously. "You wouldn't want to lose out on some first-class engineers because you won't let them choose their own bedding."

"Humans don't have any first-class engineers—" Flower began, but the rest of her words were lost in a piercing whistle.

Lynx clamped her hands over the baby's ears, but Em strangely enough slept through the brief interruption, and the rest of the delegation exchanged looks, wondering if the Dollnick AI was introducing a carrot and stick approach to her negotiations.

"What was that?" Clive demanded.

"Third period lunch," Flower replied, sounding a bit defensive. "The alarm system in the school runs on a dumb controller set up by the principal and I guess I forgot to disable it."

"When was the last class?" Lynx asked.

"Around two thousand years ago. I know, I know, but the number sounds much smaller in Base20. Alright, I'll let individuals make furniture choices for their own cabins, but nothing changes in common areas without my approval."

"Done," Blythe said. "What about ag deck space?"

"What about it?" the AI replied cagily.

One by one, the negotiation team worked through the items on their list, sometimes getting more than they'd hoped, other times being forced to capitulate to Flower's stubborn opposition. Finally they returned to the issues that they'd skipped over after reaching an impasse, with Blythe, who had done most of the negotiating, requesting that Flower restate her case for each from the beginning.

"We've barely been at it for three hours and you've already forgotten?"

"Our memories are less than perfect," Daniel said diplomatically.

"Very well. It's humiliating enough that I have to give a bunch of Humans a say in how I conduct operations without having their appearance reflect badly on my image. In addition, uniforms will give the crew a sense of cohesion, and without them there will be no way for members of other species to differentiate between a janitor and the so-called captain."

"You mean we all look alike."

The AI affected a sniff.

"EarthCent doesn't have uniforms," Blythe protested. "Our intelligence agency has informally adopted mercenary fatigues, but—"

"Black pajamas?" Flower interrupted incredulously. "Unacceptable. And don't even suggest T-shirts with a logo or 'CREW' printed on the back. I'm a colony ship, not a concert or a charity event."

"It's just that the designs you're insisting on are—alien to us," Daniel said. "I could understand if you had to look at them all day long, but you've already explained that your imaging capacity is limited to infrared in most areas of the ship, so you won't even see the uniforms."

"I'll see them on the bridge and in the common areas. Don't forget that I was designing crew uniforms while your people were stealing the skins off of hapless animals and draping them over your shoulders."

"How about if we send you imagery of the military uniforms from old Earth governments and you choose something?" Blythe offered.

The ship's AI remained silent.

"Why don't you tell her about SBJ Fashions?" Lynx suggested, giving Daniel an intense stare. "I'm sure that Flower won't be offended by the fact that your wife is a part-owner."

"Why would I be offended?" Flower asked. "All of the advanced species give a great deal of weight to family relations in their contracting processes. Does SBJ Fashions have any experience designing clothes for Dollnicks?"

"They actually do cross-species," Daniel said, picking up on Lynx's hint. "I think you've already met the main shareholder, Stryx Jeeves."

"The Stryx form business partnerships with Humans? I was not aware of this." Flower paused for several seconds, likely checking the veracity of Daniel's claim. "I found Jeeves to be an eminently reasonable individual for such a young AI, so perhaps we can work something out."

Blythe rolled her eyes at hearing Jeeves described in such moderate terms, but was so relieved at finding a possible solution to the uniforms issue that she let it go, and moved on to the next stumbling block.

"About the sports teams, Flower. You can't expect Humans to adopt all of the Dollnick customs that you—"

"I'm not asking them to play paddle-cup-mitt-ball," the AI interrupted irritably. "I've been going over the recreational data I received from your station librarian and I think that softball would be ideal. At least, the uniforms were acceptable."

"But the people we recruit won't be accustomed to their employer dictating how they have to spend their free time," Daniel argued. "I'm sure that some of them may be interested in forming a recreational league, but we can hardly force them."

"Why not?"

"Eccentric Enterprises isn't an official governmental entity. And the game requires a certain physical—"

"That's why I suggested chess teams for those who don't wish to participate in more active sports," Flower interrupted again. "Idle minds make even more trouble than idle hands."

"Flower," Lynx cooed, and then repeated the name again, "Flower."

"What?" the AI demanded impatiently.

"Oh, I was just getting tired of listening to all of you amateur traders argue so I thought I'd teach Em a new word," the cultural attaché replied innocently. "Flower."

"If you have any practical suggestions, we're willing to hear them," Clive said.

"Fine. The problem is that both parties are trading promises rather than tangible goods," Lynx said, rising from her chair and approaching the large display wall. "All we've really done to this point is make concessions to each other about the things we don't really care about. Can you display an image of a softball team, Flower?"

A double row of players dressed in immaculate uniforms appeared on the front wall.

"Now can you display an open market to the right?"

An image from a market on some distant world materialized, with assorted aliens standing in front of blankets piled high with exotic goods.

"That's better. Now, Daniel. On a scale of one to ten, how important is it to you that Flower accepts the idea of an open market that includes vintage goods."

"Used merchandise," the AI grumbled.

"It's less a matter of including vintage goods than specifically excluding them," the associate ambassador temporized. "I could understand if it was weapons—"

"I don't mind weapons," Flower interjected.

"Just give me a number, Daniel," Lynx urged him.

"It's about the traders being able to make their own decisions," he insisted. "You were a trader for ten years. Would you have put out your blanket in a market that put a bunch of restrictions on what you could sell?"

"All the time," Lynx replied bluntly. "The trader's way is go along to get along or to move along."

"I stand corrected," the associate ambassador said. "Five."

"Hah!" Flower exclaimed. "And I don't want my decks turned into some kind of cut-rate bazaar."

"And how important is this whole teams business to you, Flower?" Lynx demanded. "Give me a number."

"Ten."

"Seriously? Out of all the potential problems, most of which I'm sure you can anticipate from your extensive experience with ferrying other species, forcing our people to play softball or chess is your make-or-break issue?"

"I meant it in Base20," the AI replied sulkily.

"So you're both assigning the same importance to these trade items," Lynx continued, indicating the two images on the display. "Do you want to flip a coin?"

"I can generate a random number and assign heads or tails," Flower offered. "Which do you want?"

"No way," Daniel said. "How about we trade even?"

"You get the bazaar and I get the teams?"

"We can't force anybody to play, but we can encourage leagues with bonuses or prizes. Just remember that everybody who joins the ship will expect the same freedoms they would have on any open world, outpost, or back on Earth."

"Like littering," the AI commented.

"What?"

"You heard me. I didn't know there was such a thing until I started studying up on Humans. Even Dollnick newborns know better than to foul their own nests, but left to themselves, Humans would throw their trash in the corridors in front of their quarters and wait for a bot to clean it up. I have better things to do with my bots than assigning them to play nanny to slobs."

"Is this why you're insisting on sanitation officers?" Clive asked.

"I told you already that I can't endure a mess, and proper monitoring will be helpful for nipping any bad tendencies in the bud. The sanitation officers could slip in and check the rooms during the morning stretches in the corridors."

"I thought we agreed to pass on the group calisthenics."

"I assure you that it's standard practice on all colony ships that I'm aware of, not just ours. The Drazen colony ships even have special bars outside every cabin for tentacle stretches."

"I may be open to stretching if you'll yield on the amusement park," Clive offered. "I have it on good authority that Dollnicks are fond of roller coasters, and I understand that you maintained a recreational deck for young Dollys."

"Young what?"

"Sorry, young Dollnicks."

"I provided wholesome recreation and exercise equipment that was better than rides," Flower said, and the panel covering the front wall of the classroom lit up with a dizzying scene of thousands of four-armed aliens exercising like their lives depended on it. "My recreational deck was a huge success with the crew."

"When was the scene recorded?" Blythe asked.

"Just before my crew abandoned me. Wait, are you insinuating..." Flower fell silent for several seconds while Blythe and the others waited quietly, trying hard not to feel sorry for the Dollnick AI. "Would you mind if I talk with my Stryx mentor for a few minutes? Here, I'll give you something to watch."

The wall-sized display screen shifted to the Grenouthian news feed, and the negotiating committee members looked at each other in disbelief.

"What was that all about?" Daniel asked. "I thought we were making pretty good progress there towards the end."

"I can't get over how badly I prepared for this," Blythe said. "All of our intelligence about Dollnick colony ships indicated that Flower would insist on a percentage of any profits and demand laborers for maintenance. Instead she's quibbling over healthy cafeteria selections and mental health services."

"It's not going to be easy to find a qualified captain willing to put up with Flower's level of interference," Clive added. "In fact, it's not going to be easy to find a qualified captain, period. It's looking like we're going to have to choose somebody who can command the crew's respect while sharing the real power with a, uh, difficult AI."

The news feed disappeared, leaving a blank display, and Flower rejoined the conversation. "I heard that, but my mentor says I have to let it go. My mentor also says that I should stop worrying about getting everything perfect up front and give you a chance to make your own mistakes. My mentor reminded me that I'll be here long after you're all gone and I can always do a deep cleaning."

"That's great," Daniel said. "I just remembered a minor issue I forgot to bring up earlier during our usage fees discussion. I asked our station librarian to get me pricing on Stryxnet bandwidth so the crew could maintain contact with me on Union Station, but she said I'd have to work that out with you. Does that mean you'll be acting as the purchasing agent for us?"

"I keep an open Stryxnet channel at all times. I will provide bandwidth as required at the standard rates."

"A permanent open channel?" Blythe asked. "That must cost you a fortune."

"It's part of my deal with the Stryx," Flower admitted. "I find it useful to talk with my mentor from time to time, when things get to be a bit much."

"Like therapy," Lynx ventured.

"Acknowledging you have a problem is the first step to recovery," the Dollnick AI replied haughtily. "Do any of you have any more questions? I believe I'm approaching my Human limit for the day, though I'm working at building up my tolerance."

"We've agreed that our station librarian will be crediting your account with regular payments, and that you will also receive a yet-to-be-negotiated share of any profits generated by Eccentric Enterprises through onboard activities," Blythe said after checking her notes.

"Fifty percent of the gross," Flower stated. "And I keep the books."

"We have no objection to your keeping a copy of our accounting system, all of the back office work for my own business is handled by our station librarian for a percentage. But fifty percent of the gross would make it impossible for us to create any new businesses."

There was another long moment's silence, and the Dollnick AI said, "Twenty-five percent."

"Of the net," Blythe insisted. "A good chunk of the gross expenses for rent, utilities and such, go to you off the top. We can't pay you a percentage of money that we're paying you."

"Fine. Anything else?"

"Ow-er," Lynx's baby pronounced, smiling at the new sounds produced by her own voice. "Ow-er. Ow-er. Ow-er."

"That's a pretty good trick," Flower said, suddenly sounding a lot more cheerful. "Nice doing business with you all. I'm sure you can find the lift tube on your own."

"Does anybody else get the feeling we've been had?" Blythe asked as they filed out of the classroom.

"I don't know," Lynx mused. "She seemed pretty nice to me, and Em is an excellent judge of character.

"So you and Em wouldn't mind spending more time with her?" Clive asked.

"What does that mean?"

"I've been going through potential captains in my head and your husband is the only candidate I can come up with who attended a military college, led men in the field for nearly thirty years, and has experience with aliens at a high level."

Sixteen

Kelly placed the tray of wine glasses on the coffee table in front of the couch, and forcing her voice as low as it would go, ordered, "Move."

Beowulf thumped his tail once on the cushions but otherwise ignored her. She tried scratching his exposed belly for a minute, which drew some more tail-thumping, but the dog's eyes remained steadfastly closed.

"Joe," she called in the direction of the dining room area where her husband was putting out the poker chips and snacks. "Your dog won't listen to me."

"Did you offer him anything?"

"I scratched his belly."

"That only works when they're young. Beowulf is old enough now to hold out for food."

"The women are bringing the snacks for the book club. I don't have anything handy."

Joe tore open an imported bag of pretzels and dumped the contents out in a bowl in one smooth movement. The dog reached him before the last piece of twisted baked dough was out of the bag.

"Thank you," Kelly said, and absent-mindedly checked the couch for dog hairs. Before he had been reincarnated as a pure Cayl hound, the old Beowulf had left enough hair around the ice harvester to weave a blanket if the ambassador had been so inclined, but seven million years of careful breeding by the aliens had taken care of that particular problem. "Are you sure we won't be disturbing you? Why not move the game out to the patio area?"

"I thought I'd listen in to you discussing *Bleak House*. You know it's one of my favorites."

"That is my plan as well," Dring announced, entering the ice harvester and setting a bowl of garden fresh vegetables on the side table. "Let me help you with that."

The Maker and the ambassador's husband worked together to remove the expansion leaves from the old-fashioned dining room table. Next they slid the ends together until there was a narrow gap in the middle of what was now a small, almost square table. Then Joe went out and retrieved the round tabletop he kept behind the ice harvester for poker games, a carbon fiber construction which weighed no more than the dictionary that Becky Sharp had thrown from the carriage window on departing school. Back in the dining area, he folded out the twin J-channel strips he had recently epoxied to the bottom and lined them up with the gap. Finally, he and Dring reached blindly under the table to push the ends together, locking the circular tabletop in place.

"It's not perfect," Joe commented, giving the edge of the table a shake, "but it beats crawling under there on my old knees and clamping it in place from the bottom."

"An adequate engineering solution," Dring agreed, moving to stand in his accustomed spot.

"Our InstaSitter showed up early," Woojin said as he stepped over the threshold just ahead of his wife. "Is there anything we can do to help?"

"What are you here for tonight, Lynx?" the ambassador asked, and then realized how her question might be misinterpreted. "Book night or poker night?"

"Poker," the cultural attaché replied. "I couldn't make it through *Bleak House*. It was too sad for Em."

"You read Dickens to your two-year-old?"

"I read everything to her, except for EarthCent Intelligence reports, and that's just because they're so dry and I don't want her sleeping all day. Woojin reads to her in Korean."

"Just to get her ear accustomed to the language for if she wants to pick it up later," the doting father added. "Can I help bring up the beer, Joe?"

Another twenty minutes passed with guests arriving and drinks being served. Finally, the two groups separated to their designated areas, with the poker players immediately getting down to business.

"Where's Herl?" Clive asked, accepting the deck back from the Farling doctor after the giant insect dexterously cut the cards. "I thought he was taking a vacation just to hang around here and work on those crazy Drazen rides you guys found."

"And that's exactly what he was doing when I walked past him on the way here," Dring replied, even though the question had likely been directed at Joe. "He sends his apologies, but he's in the middle of reprogramming the safety parameters on one of those frightening contraptions to make it 'more fun,' as he put it. He said he'll be along later."

"I almost lost our whole class of trainees when I told them Herl needed volunteers to check the synchronization of the cutting blades on his Terror Ride," Thomas said. "Apparently they thought I was giving them an order and only calling it volunteering."

"Five card stud?" the Farling inquired when Clive dealt the second card face-up.

"King bets," the head of EarthCent Intelligence confirmed.

"Two yellows," Jeeves declared, pushing the chips into the pot. "I'm seeing a lot of activity on the programmable cred we issued Dorothy for work purchases," he added in Joe's direction. "Have you heard from her recently?"

"Kelly did. Dorothy and Kevin are on the elevator as we speak. If my son-in-law let the hub stevedores load in the cargo he's already sent up, they'll be entering the tunnel tonight. It sounded like they've had a highly successful trip." Joe paused to examine his cards before adding, "Stanley couldn't make it tonight because he's too busy evaluating business models for all of the proposals the Open University students have been submitting for Flower. Apparently the kids have come up with some fairly useful ideas."

Thomas mucked his cards, Joe called, and the Farling pushed in two yellows.

"Watch me now," Lynx instructed her husband, and deliberately folded her seven of spades. She scowled as Woojin called and raised with a three of hearts showing.

"We must be paying you too much," Clive grumbled, throwing in his hand.

Dring followed suit, leaving the bet to Jeeves, who called, followed by Joe. The Farling peered closely at the Stryx, the only remaining player he took seriously, and then conceded his own weak hand.

"Gryph has offered me a leave of absence from my contractual obligation to the station's med bay if I wish to accompany Flower on her shakedown cruise," the insectoid alien commented. "It would mean closing my medical shop on the concourse for the duration since I'm irreplaceable, but the opportunity to analyze blood samples from so many diverse populations of Humans is tempting."

"You can't leave the station," Lynx protested. "Em would be heartbroken without her Uncle Beetle."

"I could accept Eccentric's offer to be the co-captain and we could go along for a year," Woojin said, then grunted at his next card, the four of spades.

"King still bets," Clive announced as he completed the round.

"Let's try a red one," Jeeves proposed, pushing the chip into the pot. "Personally, I think you'd get on well with Flower, Woojin. She'll appreciate the fact that you've had formal military training. The Dollnicks thrive on a rigid chain of command."

"You're taking advantage of the fact that I always stay in for the first hand," Joe complained, adding a red chip to the pot.

Woojin checked his hole card, shook his head, and slid in his own red chip.

"King still bets," Clive said after dealing each of the remaining players their fourth card. "One round to go."

The Stryx tapped the cards in front of him with his pincer, indicating that he was standing pat. Joe passed with a look of relief, but Woojin pushed a red chip of his own into the pot. Lynx exploded.

"You've got a three, a four and a six, all different suits!" she gritted out. "Jeeves wouldn't have stayed in if a little pair would beat him."

"And I'll call," Jeeves said, adding the equivalent of a half a cred to the pot.

Joe did the same, though he clearly would have preferred to fold.

"Pair of kings bets," Clive announced after dealing the final card.

Lynx shot her husband another disgusted look but didn't say anything.

"I'm afraid I have to do this," the Stryx said apologetically, pushing in a pair of blue chips.

"What you have showing beats me," Joe said with relief, getting out of the expensive hand.

"All in," Woojin declared, pushing his pile into the pot.

Lynx reached for her husband's hole card, but he swatted her hand away. Jeeves bobbed forward a bit, as if re-inspecting the man's up-cards, and then called.

"Finally," Woojin declared, grinning like the Cheshire cat when he flipped over the five of diamonds that completed his inside straight.

"Three kings," Jeeves complained, uncharacteristically giving away his own hole card. "What a terrible beat. I've never lost my whole stake before, much less on the first hand of the night."

"Buy yourself a new one," Joe said, passing the robot the box of chips. "I guess I can trust you to the extent of twenty creds, assuming that Dorothy hasn't spent you into the poor house."

"You still played the hand wrong," Lynx said in frustration as her husband stacked his winnings. "In what universe does it make sense to hold on for a low inside straight playing five card stud?"

Over in the living room area, the argument over the secondary characters in *Bleak House* was growing heated.

"Parasites," Judith growled for the second time. "I don't care if they're family. That woman spending all of her time on her charities while her children starve and her husband is going bankrupt. The fat old poser who kills his wife with hard work so he can pretend to be a gentleman, and then tries to ruin his son's life in her place. Somebody should do something about it!"

"Dickens does do something about it," Kelly said. "He holds them up to ridicule. I don't want to ruin the surprise for the people who haven't finished yet, but I think you'll feel better by the ending."

"I thought it was interesting that the daughter of the charity woman fell in love with the son of that old fraud," Donna said. "Dickens may exaggerate situations to make his points, but I think he really had a keen understanding of human behavior. I'm glad Kelly made us read this book."

"I didn't make you—" Kelly began to protest, but Chance cut her off.

"Sure you did. It was in the Galactic Free Press as your choice for the book club. Did you think we could ignore it?"

"Chastity is the one who made it a feature! And I'm happy to take suggestions for our next book."

"*Artificial People for Humans,*" Chance responded promptly.

"But you're the co-author."

"It would be a big help to sales," Chastity explained. "I subscribed to the Stryx service that reports register data for the publishing sector. *Bleak House* has sold over a hundred thousand copies since we announced that you chose it, and the on-demand printers are having a field day. When you consider that anybody can get the electronic version for free from a teacher bot, you may have influenced tens of millions of humans around the galaxy to give it a try."

"Not to mention alien intelligence agents," Blythe pointed out. "Did anybody actually understand the Jarndyce vs Jarndyce case at the center of the plot?"

"I sent the translation that the station librarian made for me to our family advocate to try to figure it out," Flazint informed them. "He said he'd need to see the original documents to offer an opinion, but that the practice of one individual producing multiple wills is always highly problematic. He also said that there was another inheritance case in the book involving a small farmer that was much more straightforward. A couple of brothers went to the law over centees and the legal costs ended up eating the whole estate. It wouldn't be allowed in Frunge court."

"They prejudge the conclusion?" Chastity asked.

"Litigation costs are limited by law to fifteen percent of the amount at stake in civil suits. In practice, lawyers just refuse to take those little cases, and the plaintiffs are welcome to appear before a magistrate and argue it themselves if they want to look foolish."

"I'm only about halfway through the novel but I do plan on finishing," Affie said. "It's just so foreign and sad. So many victims and not enough people who cared."

"You have to remember that most of the characters had very hard lives of their own," Kelly told the Vergallian woman. "If I recall, the British government had only recently passed laws prohibiting child labor, and that only applied to children younger than nine."

"But even if we prorate your ages for lifespan, the children still wouldn't be big enough to do much useful labor!"

"That was the curse of the industrial revolution. The mechanical looms did the heavy work, but children could change spools of thread and gather the lint."

"Well, I finished the book and you couldn't call it a romance," Tinka said. "Everybody just blushed a lot and the babies seemed to appear out of nowhere. It reminded me more of the sorts of books males read."

"I thought you said Drazen men are too lazy to read," Chastity tweaked her friend.

"I said most of them are too lazy to learn musical notation so they can't get the full meaning from true literature. They mainly read about wars and history before we joined the tunnel network. Come to think of it, wars and history were pretty much the same thing back then."

"Those sound like the sort of books that our people might understand if I have them translated," Blythe said. "Can you suggest any?"

"I can ask my dad or my brother," Tinka replied with a sigh. "I just hope they don't mistake it for interest on my part. Men do tend to go on about books they've read if you give them an opening."

"Speaking of the men, what are they shouting about over there?"

"Straight flush," Woojin crowed, raking in his second big pot of the night. "At first I thought it was just a bunch of small red cards, but when I arranged them, they turned out to be all hearts, all in a row."

"Do Humans have an expression about the sun eventually shining on a dog's behind?" the Farling doctor asked grudgingly as he turned to the bank for a new supply of chips.

"You're complaining?" Jeeves demanded. "I had four aces this time!" The Stryx flipped over his cards, and sure enough, the only hand that could have beaten him was a straight flush.

"New deck," Clive called. "We've got to do something to cool him off."

"New player," Lynx said, rising from her seat. "I can't watch this. I'm going to go listen to Kelly talk about books."

"What's she mad about?" Thomas inquired after his former spy partner left the table.

"She can't stand that I'm winning even though I play all wrong," Woojin explained. "You know that her father was a professional gambler. My poker playing is an embarrassment to her."

"And well it should be," the beetle rasped out on his talking legs. "Good timing, Herl. The seat is open."

"Thanks," the Drazen spymaster said, settling in between Woojin and the Farling, who didn't so much sit as lean forward over a chair to rest on the belly of his carapace. "No Daniel tonight? I see his wife over there."

"From what Kelly tells me, he's working around the clock on this colony ship thing," Joe replied as he began to send the cards around the table. "I guess my son and his student committee are creating a lot of extra work for Daniel since it's another group to coordinate with."

"Funny, the Stryx involving the Open University in the deal," Herl mused as he exchanged twenty creds for chips and put in his ante. "It's not clear to me whether they're doing it for your benefit or for Flower's."

"I am sitting right here," Jeeves said, peeking at his two down cards as Joe dealt a hand of seven card stud. "It has always been the policy of our Open University campuses to encourage students to tackle real-world projects."

"Let's move the bet in the opposite direction in honor of our Drazen friend," Joe said after dealing the third card, this last one being face-up. "Ace has control."

The Farling doctor turned his head to look past Herl and see what Woojin's hand was showing before he tapped his ace with a foreleg. Joe also passed, followed by Thomas, Jeeves, Dring and Clive in close order. Woojin slid aside the four of diamonds to check his hole cards again, then pushed in a blue chip.

"Fold," Herl said, flipping over his king. "Since when do we bet big on the first card?"

"I know you're bluffing," the beetle addressed Woojin, but after a moment's hesitation, he threw in his own hand.

"Too rich for my blood," Joe said.

"It's times like these that I wish I'd kept my gambler enhancement from Quick-U," Thomas commented, giving up his own cards.

Jeeves said nothing but flipped over his queen.

Dring munched thoughtfully on a stalk of celery for a moment. "On one hand, I concur with our Farling friend that you are most likely bluffing. On the other hand, with everybody else folding, the rationale for my staying in with such a poor starting hand is weak. I choose discretion," he concluded, and pushed his cards in the direction of Thomas, who was next in line to deal.

"Come on, boss," Woojin addressed Clive. "Baby needs new shoes."

"Then you should be talking to Jeeves," the director of EarthCent Intelligence said sourly. "He's the one with the fashion business. Take it."

As Woojin sent his cards towards Thomas and swept in the antes, Blythe's voice cut through the momentary silence, saying, "But I married a man who's older than me by almost ten years, and that's more than ten percent of my projected lifespan."

"Compared to Woojin and me, you're a cradle robber," Lynx informed her.

"Joe's a good deal older than me," Kelly said, and over at the poker table, her husband snorted.

"Shaina and I married young ones," Brinda boasted. "Men are like Cayl hounds. You want to get them early while you can still train them."

"That's not my point," Tinka said. "Jarndyce, the one that Esther kept referring to as 'Guardian,' never should have aspired to her in the first place. He was already a grown man when she was a little girl, and he paid to have her trained as a housekeeper. It's icky."

"I don't see the problem," Affie said. "We often marry men with more than a hundred years of age difference in either direction. I have an aunt who married a guy who was almost two hundred years younger than her and it's a very happy marriage."

"She probably keeps him in line with pheromones," Tinka said.

"It doesn't work that way," the Vergallian replied patiently. "They wear off too quickly. We aren't chemical factories."

"But Jarndyce realizes that himself and retracts the offer so she can marry the young doctor," Kelly explained. "He even buys them a house."

"Thanks for ruining the ending," Affie said.

Several of the other women who hadn't yet finished the long novel shook their heads as well.

"I expect to see all of you on our setup day for Flower's book fair benefit," Donna announced during the lull. "It's next Saturday on the park deck. As a bonus, anybody who helps gets first dibs on buying books before we let in the early-bird browsers."

Seventeen

"Sharf Industries demo," Samuel instructed the lift tube capsule. "It's funny, but I don't have a clue where we're actually going," he added for Vivian's benefit. "Do the Sharf even have their own deck?"

"I don't think so," the girl replied. "They aren't tunnel network members and I think that's the main criteria for getting the Stryx to grant a dedicated section of deck. Are you sure the others all know where to meet?"

"Lizant said she notified everybody and she's been a hundred percent reliable. We were lucky to get her as secretary."

"Does Yvandi have any relations in this factory that we're visiting?"

"I hope so, they'll treat us better. Libby. How long until we get there?"

"Three minutes and twenty-seven seconds. The factory is located in the heavy industries area where Gryph relegates the manufacturing facilities of some of the less cautious species. The Sharf are excellent engineers, but they are perhaps a little too comfortable with learning from their mistakes."

"Here," Vivian said, producing a small box from her purse. "Put this on."

"Are you proposing?" Samuel joked as he popped open the lid. His smile froze when he saw the ring. "Uh, is this

199

like an EarthCent Intelligence spy ring that does something?"

"Yes. It protects you from Vergallian vamps," the girl replied, and held up her left hand. "See? I have the same thing."

"Come on, really. What is it?"

"It's a couples ring. We're scheduled for the Vergallian deck after the Sharf factory visit, and if you think I'm letting you go unprotected with your perfect high-caste accent and your dancer's grace, you've got another thing coming."

Samuel felt the blood rushing to his face as he pulled the ring from its holder, but he hesitated at putting it on. "We're friends. Right?"

"Of course we're friends," Vivian said, and watched as he slid the band onto his ring finger before continuing. "You're my boyfriend and I'm your girlfriend. What's so complicated about that?"

"It's just—"

"Ailia gave you to me and I have the paperwork to prove it. Are you going to make her into a liar?"

"I just think I should have a say since I'm, you know," the boy muttered.

"The party of the first part?" she prompted, giving him a playful shove.

The lift tube door slid open on a brightly lit deck where a group of students stood waiting. Yvandi started off without greeting the late arrivals, and the others all fell in behind the long-legged Sharf girl, some of them finding themselves forced into a jog to keep up.

"Is she mad about something?" Samuel asked Lizant.

"You're two minutes late," the Frunge replied. "The rest of us were early."

"It was the long lift tube ride, over three minutes."

"Really? Did you ask it to go slow for some reason?"

Samuel turned sharply to question Vivian, but she had conveniently sped up to ask the Sharf girl something.

"Is that a new couple's ring?" Marilla asked the ambassador's son. "You guys seem kind of young for that."

"Oh, they've been together for a long time," Lizant said. "Didn't you know?"

"I don't see how she could when I didn't know either," Samuel objected.

"Men are always the last to find out," the Frunge girl said.

"Presents?" the Verlock student huffed from his trailing position.

"Good question," Grude said. "We wouldn't want to offend them."

"No presents," Samuel insisted, feeling like he was losing control over his destiny. "She just gave me the ring since we're going to the Vergallian deck later and she's got a thing about them."

"SHE gave the ring to YOU?" Jorb tripped over his own feet when he turned back to deliver this remark and would have hit the deck if he hadn't managed to grab one of the Grenouthian's arms with his tentacle. "Humans are weird."

"Halt," Yvandi declared, holding up a bony arm, and the group of students came to a disorderly stop. "I had to call in some family favors to get us into EOD, but you're still all going to have to sign the confidentiality agreement or they won't let you beyond the reception area. This is proprietary stuff."

The bunny sniffed loudly at the idea the Sharf could have developed anything the Grenouthians would possibly want, and the Dollnick exchanged an eye roll with the Verlock, but the students from the other species nodded seriously. Yvandi led them past a heavily armored door into a bland-looking reception area where a Sharf awaited them with a tab/clipboard combination in one hand and a pin cushion in the other.

"Use the Thark stylus to sign the tab, then prick a finger and put a drop of blood in the circle next to where your name is printed," he ordered.

"I can't read this," Samuel complained, feeling he'd been pushed around enough for one day. "Libby? Should I sign this?"

"It's a standard Sharf non-compete and confidentiality agreement," the station librarian informed them. "As the Sharf are not tunnel network members, it's nonbinding outside of this factory unless you visit Sharf space."

"What's the point of that?" Lizant asked the Sharf.

The skinny alien shrugged. "Procedure."

Eight signatures and pinpricks later, the students were allowed to enter the factory proper, which turned out to be a vast empty space at least as large as Mac's Bones.

"I don't get it," Grude said, staring about suspiciously. "Where's the equipment?"

"Outside the projection chamber," Yvandi told them. "I couldn't describe the technology to you before you signed the nondisclosures, but what you're about to see is the fruit of a collaborative project between my people and our AI that is being adapted for our colony ships. Engineering On Demand is still in Beta testing, but I have a classmate whose mother is the local sales rep, and she might be persuaded to send a prototype out with Flower for field trials."

"Engineering On Demand?" the Dollnick student asked. "How is that even possible? You have to know how to properly describe a problem in order to start working towards the solution. It takes a higher order of AI than your artificial people to figure out what's needed."

"Surprisingly astute," the Grenouthian concurred.

"Proof," the Verlock demanded.

"Very well." Yvandi checked something on a wrist controller and looked up with a smug expression. "What engineering problem do you want solved?"

"Say I have a river I need to cross," Vivian said.

In a blink the students found themselves in a life-sized hologram featuring a placid river winding through a flat plain. They were standing near the bank, and two parallel blue lines extended from just in front of them to the opposite bank, which was at least a two-minute walk away.

"Is the location appropriate?" Yvandi asked, consulting the wrist controller again.

"You didn't give me time to describe the problem," Vivian protested. "I was thinking more of a river with steep banks and a rocky cliff on one side, plus barge traffic."

As soon as she spoke, the hologram morphed to adapt itself to her description, and the projected bridge location shifted slightly to make room for access roads.

"I don't get the point," Grude complained. "Who uses bridges when they can license our floater designs?"

"I forgot," Vivian admitted. "I just remember my grandpa talking about the suspension bridges on Earth being some of our best engineering before the Stryx opened the planet. A few of the oldest ones are still standing."

"Give me something else," Yvandi suggested after glancing at her wrist again. "It knows how to do suspension bridges, but they take a long time to model because of all the wires."

"What difference does it make?" the Grenouthian asked.

"What you see isn't just a pretty picture," the Sharf girl explained. "The projectors use manipulator fields to mimic the physical properties within the hologram for testing purposes. Plus, you get a complete set of engineering drawings and mechanical plans. We don't use construction bots ourselves, but if you did, you could feed them the data, go away for a couple of years, and come back to a completed bridge."

"Dangerous," the Verlock student commented, taking a step back.

"How about a faster-than-light drive?" Samuel asked hopefully.

"Very funny. Think of something your colonists might need."

"A faster-than-light drive."

"For which you're more than welcome to buy our ships."

"A bowling alley?" the Dollnick suggested.

"Too simple, unless you want pin-setting machines," Yvandi replied.

Grude waved the idea off and the students all hesitated, trying to imagine what colonists might do with EOD. They came up with and dismissed a number of ideas as being too complex for an isolated community to manufacture, even with perfect plans.

"How about a school?" Vivian suggested. "Say it's a cold planet so it has to hold up in the ice and snow, with classrooms for a thousand students, all the usual stuff."

"EOD excels at architectural plans," the Sharf girl declared with obvious relief. A hologram materialized depicting a school thronged with tall, emaciated-looking students with bony crests. "Oops, I'll make them Human."

The image wavered and was replaced with a structure and holographic students that wouldn't have looked terribly out of place on Earth, other than the peculiar roof design. As the Sharf girl gestured with her wrist controller, the hologram began peeling off layers, showing the sheathing, the insulation, the structural members, cabling and plumbing. At each level, a riot of numbers appeared, some of them measurements, others referring to specific Sharf part numbers for items that would be available in a colony ship's stock.

Samuel noticed what looked like a puddle forming in the hologram and nudged Grude, who looked in the direction the boy was pointing and frowned. A moment later the peeling process reached the heating plant, and the whole hologram exploded outwards as the boiler failed with a tremendous sonic blast that almost knocked the students from their feet.

"Very realistic," the Grenouthian remarked dryly.

'I told you it's in Beta," the Sharf student retorted. "I'm glad you saw that, though. The system is always testing its own assumptions in various ways, so it makes sense that the boiler blew up when the vessel grew too thin."

"Could the system damage Flower?" Vivian asked.

"It's highly unlikely," Grude said. "The force, or the simulated force of any explosion would be limited to the energy being fed into the system, since there's no storage capacity. As long as it ran off of the ship's power, Flower would be able to set safe levels for herself."

"And for the people in the room?"

Grude and Yvandi both shrugged.

"I think it's fascinating," Lizant said. "I didn't realize you were so far advanced in field manipulations."

"The projection technology is licensed from the Stryx," the Sharf girl explained. "It's the application that's novel."

"Been there, done that," the Grenouthian said, affecting a yawn.

"Anyway, the Vergallians are expecting us and we better be on time since they're already offended by not having a member on the committee," Lizant pointed out.

"I don't see why that means we have to go to them," Vivian said.

"It's in the addendum to the student handbook as a right that any species without a committee presence can invoke," Lizant explained, as she led the group back towards the lift tube. "I thought they were joking at first, but when I checked with our admin contact, the Verlock told me that as the committee secretary, I actually had the duty to approach unrepresented species with an offer to tour their business incubators."

"Does this mean we're going to have to visit the Cherts and the Fillinducks as well?" Samuel asked.

"I already checked with them. The Cherts said it wasn't necessary and the Fillinducks said it wasn't desirable."

"Do humans have any tech-ban colonies?" Marilla asked.

"There's Kibbutz, which Paul has been to," Samuel replied. "It's not so much tech-ban as geologically active to the point that the kind of infrastructure we can build just gets shaken apart. Other than that, there may be some people living with minimal technology for environmental or religious reasons. I think Daniel mentioned a few groups, but they aren't members of the Sovereign Human

Communities conference because they try to avoid unnecessary space travel."

"Flower can go to them," Wrylenth suggested.

"I could always get in touch with the student who presented the blacksmith's wagon," Lizant offered.

The committee members crowded out of the lift tube when the doors slid open and were met by a waiting delegation of Vergallian students.

"Welcome," the flawless beauty who was obviously in charge of the reception said in a flat voice. "You're barely on time."

"Sorry," Lizant apologized for the committee. "There was—"

"No need to offer excuses," the high-caste Vergallian spoke over her. "I have an appointment with my hairdresser, but these gentlemen will take you around." Without a backwards glance, she walked away from the group.

"But her hair is perfect," Marilla pointed out needlessly.

"Sorry about Arinda," one of the Vergallian males said. "We only got here a minute ago ourselves but she's mad that we mistimed it. She's Empire, by the way, but we're Fleet. I'm Keena and he's Pojee. We think we have some really exciting ideas for your colony ship."

The student committee members all introduced themselves, and then the two guides led them down a long corridor to a section that looked surprisingly low-rent for the normally upscale aliens. Keena halted in front of a statue depicting a trader sitting cross-legged on a blanket and counting coins, an old fashioned beam balance by his side.

"Union Station Business Incubator," Samuel read the Vergallian inscription out loud.

"I see our information about you was correct," Pojee said. "I understand that both you and the young lady were competitive in our junior ballroom championships, and I hope that your experiences there don't prejudice you against our business offerings."

"We're honored by the opportunity," the ambassador's son responded diplomatically. Vivian scowled.

Keena took over from Pojee in what was apparently a rehearsed presentation. "We put a lot of thought into the sorts of businesses that might make sense for a circuit ship serving your scattered communities, and even though we're both Fleet, we concluded that low-tech might be a better match for your mission."

"We have a lot of isolated outposts of our own, and we're always sending out new groups of colonists, even though our ships aren't as big as Flower," the other Vergallian picked up the thread as he steered the group towards a curtained-off area. "You may be surprised to know that new colonies often adopt technology from tech-ban worlds because they don't require extensive infrastructure to be effective."

"How can you talk about technology on tech-ban worlds?" Vivian demanded.

"Ladies and gentlemen," Keena said, smiling broadly at the committee members, "I give you the humble windmill."

The curtain drew apart as if of its own accord, and the students gaped at a life-sized windmill that might have been copied from a landscape painter of Earth's Dutch Golden Age. The four sails consisted of fabric on wooden latticework, and the round tower was improbably constructed from dressed stones.

"Is this a joke?" the Sharf student demanded. "You expect space travelers to spend their time hand-building obsolete structures?"

"I like the stonework," Lizant commented.

"Wind!" Pojee cried, dramatically raising his arms, and a stiff breeze suddenly blew down the corridor, catching the sails and putting the whole mechanism into motion. "Lights," he declared, and the corridor lighting in the immediate area dimmed.

Marilla let out an "Oooh," as a string of colored lights arranged on the deck around the windmill flickered to life and then began to glow steadily.

"The modular construction and interchangeable parts of our windmills make them the ideal match for isolated farms or communities on outposts with irregular supplies," Keena said. "You don't need the full stone tower kit, of course. The most basic module consists of a rotor head, shaft, and transfer case. Add-ons, which are interchangeable through hot-swapping, include electrical generation, well-pumping, belt drive for machine tools, even a millstone kit for grinding grain."

"Aren't millstones a bit heavy to be transporting in shuttles?" Grude asked skeptically.

"The kit consists of templates for quarrying your own millstones from local resources," Pojee jumped back in. "The manufacturer offers standard mounts for the core mechanism that can be adapted to anything from a skeletal steel tower to the traditional stone building before you. The arms can be fabricated onsite using native materials in a nearly infinite number of shapes and sizes, or you can purchase premade arms in materials ranging from magnesium to carbon fiber."

"If you only care about electricity generation, they make all-in-one units that mount on the top of a tower with a vane to head them into the wind," Keena said. "But the flexibility of the standard kit is why it's the go-to back-up power system for our own outposts."

"Back-up?" the Grenouthian inquired.

"Well, you'd need a lot of windmills to power an asteroid protection system," Keena admitted.

"Thousands," the Verlock grunted. "Big ones."

"I think windmills could make a lot of sense in the right applications," Samuel said. "There are probably Earth manufacturers—"

"We checked," Pojee cut him off. "There used to be quite a number of them, but they all went out of business after the Stryx, er, opened your planet. The station librarian was able to retrieve their primary patents for us to review in the competitive technologies section of our written proposal. Although there were some interesting designs, nothing would have come close to the flexibility and durability of these units."

"Good sales pitch," the Grenouthian student remarked.

"You're all welcome to come back and examine this model at any time, but we have three more displays set up for you," Keena announced. "If you'll follow me."

The Vergallians set off with the student committee members in a row, and Vivian remarked to Samuel, "I guess it wasn't totally stupid."

"I don't get what you have against them," he said, followed by, "Excuse me," as he nearly ran down a lovely Vergallian girl around Affie's age, who favored him with a dazzling smile.

"I couldn't help noticing you," she said, batting her eyelids playfully. "If you're not with anybody, I'd like to—"

"He's with me," Vivian snarled, pushing between the two. Then she realized that the Vergallian was still talking, something about needing volunteers for a focus group to view a new drama and discuss alternative endings.

"You're standing inside her foot," Samuel said quietly. "It's more holo spam."

Vivian jumped back, but not before several of the other students noticed. Yvandi was the only one to put her thoughts into words.

"Wow," the plain-spoken Sharf student said. "Fighting over a guy with a holographic advertisement. You've really got it bad."

Eighteen

"Heavy one," Thomas warned the EarthCent Intelligence recruit who was next in line in the bucket brigade. "Must be hardcovers."

"Are you sure this is part of our training?" the man asked, wiping some sweat off his face with his sleeve before accepting the box.

"It's all for the benefit of humanity," the next recruit in line told him, then grunted when the box was passed to her. "It's in our oath."

"Looking good," Joe encouraged them. He leaned into the large cargo container that was welded to the stern of Kevin's four-man scout and did a quick count of the remaining boxes. "The mule bots I rented from the Little Apple Merchants Association can float eight of these at a go, so they're keeping right up with you."

"Why were you in such a hurry to get these books unloaded?" Judith asked, setting the heavy box down at the top of the ramp and giving it a push. It slid down to the bottom, where two more recruits picked it up and loaded it into a mule bot's suspensor field. "The benefit book fair doesn't start until the day after tomorrow."

"If the books are still here when Kelly gets home she'll never let them leave," Joe explained, then turned to the newcomer. "Hello, Jeeves. Paul is around the other side with Kevin helping to unload some of the kiddie rides we brought in for Libbyland."

"Did your daughter return with him or is she hiding on Earth?"

"You're the one who gave her the expense account," Joe replied, familiar with the Stryx's complaints about Dorothy's use of the company programmable cred. "Can you take a look at the new equipment and let Paul know if we'll have to break it down to move it to the Physics Ride? I know the corridors are wide enough but some of the doors aren't."

"Don't worry about that," Jeeves told him. "I can take the rides out into the core one at a time and then bring them in through one of the service shafts in the spokes."

The Stryx floated off to find Paul and Kevin and to inquire after Dorothy. He found her watching the men utilizing the crane on Mac's Bone's alien-built wrecker to unload a carousel featuring dolphins as mounts. Some of the marine mammals were painted in their natural colors, such that they might have just leapt from the ocean, while others were decorated in psychedelic pinks and oranges in concentric rings and swirls.

"Hello, Dorothy. Did you have a good time shopping on—"

"Holo spam," the girl cried and threw a wrench at her boss.

"Very funny," Jeeves said, catching the tool in his pincer. "However, the purpose of interactive marketing holograms is to encourage economic activity, which is the last thing you need. Are you prepared to explain your purchases on Earth, or do you need more time to make up the reasons?"

"I wouldn't abuse my company cred. Everything I bought has a business purpose, and taking a few wholesalers to lunch scored us a ton of free fabric samples."

"Fabric samples are free by definition," Jeeves thundered. "That's what makes them samples."

"Oh well, I'll know that for next time. Hi, Mom," the girl said, turning away to greet the ambassador. "You're home early."

"I heard that you were back and I thought I'd take a peek at the bookstore inventory your grandmother acquired for our sale. Where are the books?"

"We brought them, but wait," Dorothy added, grabbing her mother's arm. "You have to see the material I got for my dress."

Kelly fought against the impulse to break away and start looking through the books as soon as possible. But Dorothy had been putting off her formal wedding until she could design the wedding dress to end all wedding dresses, after which her mother hoped the girl would get down to business and deliver a grandchild.

"I bought bolts of silk Mikado, mousselline, chiffon and charmeuse because I want to experiment with how they drape and move—for our new bridal line," she added, in the direction of her boss.

"How convenient for you," Jeeves muttered.

"Kevin! Where did you store all of my silk?"

"I'll bring it out," her husband called back. "Those bolts are pretty heavy."

"And lace," the girl continued, ignoring the Stryx's theatrical groan. "I bought miles and miles of lace."

Dorothy made her mother feel the texture of every fabric sample and give her opinion on each type of lace, a drawn out process during which Jeeves got bored with waiting and moved away to help Paul and Kevin unload the kiddie rides. Eventually Joe came around the side of the ship behind Kelly and gave his daughter the thumbs-up.

"But you don't want to listen to all of this, and you'll see the dress while I'm working on it," Dorothy concluded suddenly. "Grandma sends her love."

"And the books?" her mother asked.

"Oh, they're all in the number three container around the other side."

Kelly walked around Kevin's ship as quickly as dignity would permit and was greeted by the sight of twenty exhausted recruits sitting on the deck while Thomas lectured them about aerobic conditioning.

"You're home from work early for a Friday, Kel," Joe greeted her. "You just missed getting stuck unloading a lot of heavy boxes."

"I submitted my weekly report early," the ambassador replied reflexively. "Where are the books my mother sent us?"

"I rented a bunch of mule bots and the trainees helped load them. The last one just left for the park deck where Donna arranged to set up the book fair. We've been at it for hours."

"You already moved all of the books from two second-hand bookstores?"

"They pack really well," Joe replied. "I guess one store was all paperbacks because the boxes were lighter. There were only around two hundred of those, and I'd estimate about fifty paperbacks in each, so ten thousand overall. Then there were another three hundred boxes of mixed paperbacks and hardcovers. Does that sound right?"

"All of them? There's not a single box left?"

"Don't forget that we're all going to help with the setup tomorrow," Joe said, starting to feel a little badly about having outfoxed his wife. "You'll get a chance to buy whatever you want before the general public gets in. It's for a good cause."

Dorothy passed in front of them with her arms full of lace, walking rapidly towards the ice harvester with Jeeves floating alongside.

"You could at least pretend that you had a business plan to start a bridal line for SBJ Fashions," the Stryx complained. "You don't even make an effort anymore."

"That's because I know I could never fool you. Besides, you're coming out way ahead of the game. You know that if I had stayed on the station I would have insisted on spending a lot of money on a special event for the launch of our basic ballroom shoe. How did we do?"

"The first batch sold out in four days, and the stores gave customers enough rain checks to account for the next two shipments coming from Chintoo," Jeeves admitted grudgingly. "We're getting great data back from the buyers who chose not to disable the reporting function, and you'll be pleased to know that practically every woman who bought a pair has at least tried the maximum height setting."

"I knew it! You said that I was making it way too high, but what does a floating robot know about heels? I can't wait to check my mom's data. I made her promise to wear the shoes for all of her official events and I'll bet that she cranked them up herself."

"Do you remember the embedded nano snap switches I insisted on?"

"Sure. You said there had to be a way of proving if anybody reprogrammed the heels and then hurt themselves, for liability reasons. Wait a minute," Dorothy said, breaking into a wide grin. "Do you mean that my mom went above the maximum height? I'll never let her hear the end of it."

"Actually, she went below the lower limit," Jeeves replied gleefully. "I checked the programming remotely, and whoever broke the encryption covered their tracks so well that it had to be another Stryx."

"Libby! Did you hack into my mom's shoes?"

"Welcome back, Dorothy," the station librarian replied smoothly. "I'm afraid that the information you have requested is confidential. Did you have a pleasant trip?"

"We spent most of the week with my grandma," the girl replied, knowing she wouldn't get any further by complaining. "She doesn't move around much anymore, but she's still interested in business, and she handled all the arrangements to ship the entire inventory of two out-of-business second-hand bookstores up to the elevator hub for us. She even made up a list of fabric wholesalers in the city who were interested in meeting with me."

"For lunch on my creds," Jeeves interjected glumly.

"And the president's office set up meetings for us with a librarian and a carnival guy," Dorothy continued unperturbed. "They both jumped at the opportunity to move their stuff off Earth and join Flower."

"I thought that might happen," Libby said. "Did your husband enjoy the trip?"

"He's not my husband until we have the wedding."

"You seem to have forgotten a certain affidavit which I submitted to the Frunge honor court myself," Jeeves said. "In accordance with the treaty EarthCent signed with the tunnel network, alien marriage certificates—"

"I don't know what you're talking about," the girl insisted, stalking up the ramp of the ice harvester and heading for her sewing room. "Instead of making up stories you could do something useful like fetch my silk. It's heavy."

"Silk is light. The fabric bolts are heavy because you bought so much of it." Nevertheless, Jeeves spun about on his axis and began floating away to retrieve his designer's purchases before coming to a sudden stop. "Did you just use my patented change-of-subject technique on me?"

"Is she claiming not to be married again, Jeeves?" Samuel asked, coming out of his bedroom. He turned to his sister. "You know he's the one who registered Ailia's affidavit."

"Welcome back, Dorothy," she said in a fair imitation of her little brother's voice. "I really missed seeing you for three weeks."

"You went somewhere? I've been so busy with school, work and the committee—"

"But I see you had time to get engaged," Dorothy said, staring pointedly at her brother's left hand.

"What?" Samuel turned bright red. "It's just a couple's ring. Vivian gave it to me for our visit to the Vergallian deck because she doesn't trust them or something." He tried to tug the ring back over his knuckle without success. "It won't come off."

"That's how they're supposed to work," Dorothy taunted him. "I'll bet Vivian bought one of those memory metal ones from the Verlocks. You'll need a bolt cutter to get it off, and that's only if you're willing to take the finger at the knuckle and then have the Farling glue it back on for you."

218

"Your husband's dog is about to get into trouble," Samuel retorted, pointing at Alexander, who had slipped into the ice harvester and begun eating out of his sire's bowl.

"Please don't tease each other," Kelly said, stepping off the ramp into the living area just in time to avoid getting knocked down by Beowulf, who could hear another dog eating from his bowl from all the way across Mac's Bones. Alexander leapt straight into the air as if he had been startled, and then collapsed unmoving to the deck.

"Nine," Samuel rated the younger dog's performance.

"Ten," Dorothy contradicted him.

"If you're going to play dead, you should stop chewing," Jeeves pointed out to the young Cayl hound.

Beowulf sniffed his prone offspring, shook his head, and thumped his tail on the deck six times. Alexander rose and performed a lazy downward dog stretch in lieu of bowing.

"I'm glad I caught you both at home," Kelly said. "Aisha invited us all to dinner at seven, and since we have a few hours, I thought it would be fun if you helped me rearrange my books to make room..."

"I've got a committee meeting, Mom," Samuel said, sidling around the couch towards the exit. "Libby said that Flower has approved all of the business cases we submitted so far, but Lizant just pinged me to say that we still have a backlog to work through."

"How about you, Dorothy?"

"Jeeves will kill me if I don't get cracking on my dress—I mean, our new bridal line," the girl said, backing towards her sewing room. "Isn't that right, Jeeves? Jeeves?"

"I just remembered that I promised to help Paul with something," the Stryx replied from the top of the ramp before shooting off at high speed.

The loud "pop" caused by the air rushing in to occupy the vacuum he left behind gave Dorothy the distraction she needed to slip into her sewing room and trigger the door lock. Kelly smiled to herself at having successfully emptied the room so she could work on her manuscript without distractions, and decided to treat herself to a quick massage session in her Love-U chair before getting back to the final chapter of *EarthCent For Humans*. She fell asleep almost immediately.

Jeeves found Paul in the section of Mac's Bones adjacent to where Herl was reconditioning Drazen carnival rides. The men were standing in front of a circle of eight brightly painted little cars, all connected to each other. A central arrangement of arms attached to linkages between the cars.

"So why do they have steering wheels?" Paul was asking Kevin.

"Morton, the guy who owned all of these rides, said this one is safe for toddlers. You paint two concentric circles on the deck at the limits of the steering, and then the kids feel like they're actually driving between the lines."

"And if they never touch the steering wheel?"

"They'll go in a perfect circle. We've got the same ride with fire engines, which are two-seaters, but they're longer so there are only six of them."

"Circular motion seems to be the theme with these rides," Herl observed. "I like the color scheme on this one, but I can't make out what the mounts are supposed to be."

"Bees," Joe said. "They don't actually grow to this size on Earth, and it's a little scarier for the youngest kids because they bob up and down as they go in a circle."

"And the one with the balloon-shaped fiberglass constructions over the baskets?"

"Gondolas. The idea is for the kids to play like they're going up in a hot air balloon. I think the hub on that one tilts as it goes around."

"Morton threw in some fiberglass biplanes we can swap out for the bees," Kevin told them. "Dorothy and I actually tried the ride with the giant teacups that turn slowly as the whole plate goes in a circle. We each took our own cup, but it would work for a parent and a child."

"Nothing that goes in a straight line, even for a little while?" Herl asked.

"He had a whole bunch of kiddie trains, some that ran on tracks, some on tires, but those are all being packed up for Flower, along with the adult rides. I couldn't tell him anything about the colony ship's height limits, so he's not sure which Ferris wheel to bring, or if there would be room for a rollercoaster. I told him he had a few months yet."

"Here's what you missed while you were gone," Paul said, handing the younger man a heavily dog-eared paperback. "I have it half-memorized already just from looking things up for Samuel's student committee."

"*Dollnick Colony Ships For Humans*," Kevin read the title. "The Galactic Free Press doesn't miss a business opportunity, do they? How's the ambassador's book coming along?"

"Kelly's been working on it every night, and I suspect she sneaks some writing in at the embassy as well," Joe said. "The bits she let me read were very good, but I'm not sure that she's sticking with the formula."

"That's not so surprising, given the difficulty we all have in getting a handle on EarthCent," Herl observed. "By accepting your ambassadors on the stations, the Stryx have established EarthCent as the default government for humanity, but it's unclear to us how many of your people actually see EarthCent as representing them."

"Other than the people living on Stryx stations, most humans are barely aware that EarthCent exists," Joe said. "I'm surprised your reports don't show that."

"We don't really expend any resources spying on you anymore," the Drazen intelligence head admitted. "Perhaps the idea floated by Krylneth has merit after all."

"Who?" Paul asked.

"The head of Verlock intelligence on the station," Joe said. "I've met him with Kelly at a few receptions. Fast talker for a Verlock."

"He suggested that tunnel network members pool our intelligence gathering efforts to a certain extent," Herl continued. "While we would all continue to focus our best efforts on our traditional competition, we could realize significant cost savings by splitting the remaining load among us."

"I'm not in EarthCent Intelligence or anything," Kevin cautioned the Drazen. "Are you supposed to be talking about this stuff in front of me?"

"It's all been reported on the Grenouthian network already," Herl said. "I suspect one of their interns was indiscrete in a bar. But the thought just occurred to me that a berth on Flower could be the ideal cover for a spy looking to keep an eye on your activities."

"I'll warn Clive," Joe said. "Most of the business schemes coming out of Samuel's committee involve taking aliens on board."

"Exactly," the Drazen said. "It's an excellent opportunity for you to enhance your revenue."

"You mean we should charge the other species for allowing their spies on Flower?"

"I don't see why not. It's typical for intelligence agencies to subsidize costs for their casual agents employed in cover jobs on alien worlds, but in this case you'll actually be providing transportation to all of your targets of interest. What do you think?"

"I just checked with Flower and she wants a cut of the action and a free ride for Dollnick agents if she can convince any to join her," Jeeves announced, and then added, "It didn't make any sense to let you waste your time discussing it if she wasn't going to go along."

Nineteen

"Where did you find all of the folding tables?" Shaina asked Donna. "I thought we'd just be laying all of the books out on blankets like traders."

"I'm guessing we'll draw a lot of older buyers, and readers tend to be nearsighted anyway, so getting the books up closer to their faces seemed like a good idea. Chastity asked the Dollnick who manages the Empire Convention Center to loan us the tables for the week. I think she made it part of a package deal when she rented the Nebulae Room for the Union Station book awards, but I didn't ask for details."

"I'm more interested in where you found all the volunteers," Daniel said.

"I pinged everybody on the notification list for the embassy's monthly dance mixer. It's really gratifying how many people are showing up, and quite a few who couldn't make it today came yesterday and dropped off books for the sale. I contacted Ian to arrange catering for lunch, and he rounded up a bunch of restaurateurs from the Little Apple to do it for free. I only hope the work holds out long enough so people don't wander off before the food gets here."

"I guess even twenty thousand or so books get laid out pretty quick when you have over two hundred pairs of hands on the job," Shaina observed.

"Can I go look for Fenna and Spinner?" Mike asked.

"I think I see Paul over on the box brigade," Daniel told his son. "Fenna and her mom are probably nearby." The boy darted off in search of his friends while the associate ambassador surveyed the park deck, looking for an activity that wasn't already overstaffed. "Who are those alien kids?"

"You've never met the students from Vivian and Sam's committee?" the embassy manager asked in surprise.

"It's all been correspondence so far. That Dollnick kid can sure empty a box of books in a hurry. Where's my brother-in-law?"

"He and Chastity are meeting right now with representatives of the alien publishers to finalize the award categories."

"How are the judges going to have time to read the books and vote on the winners?" Shaina asked.

"Chastity said not to worry about it, which means she's not telling."

"And what's Blythe doing over there with Jonah?" Daniel said, pointing to a nearby table. "Setting up to recruit more intelligence analysts? I suppose she could do worse than starting with avid readers."

"She brought copies of some translated alien books she printed to give away for the sake of feedback. I don't know why she got so caught up in competing with Chastity's new publishing business," Donna added. "I guess with the twins almost grown she doesn't have enough to do with her time."

A few tables away, Kelly crouched protectively over a box of Victorian hardcovers which included all six volumes of Trollope's Palliser novels and a nearly complete set of the works of Thomas Hardy. "Fenna," she whispered loudly, motioning to the girl who was crawling through the grass under the next table over. "Do you have Spinner with you? I want to ask him if he can carry something for me."

"Mikey, Spinner," the girl called. Shaina's son crawled through a forest of adult legs to join Aisha's daughter under her table, and Spinner came floating around a stack of empty boxes, skimming just above the grass. "Grandma Kelly wants help moving something."

"Nuh uh," Mike said, crossing his arms. "I'm eight."

"But you're a big strong boy," the ambassador cajoled him. "I bet you and Spinner could move this box easily."

"Mommy said you told her that children under nine don't have to work, 'cept for acting, like me and Spinner did on Aisha's show," the boy explained.

"Spinner and I," Fenna corrected him, a habit she'd acquired from her own mother.

"Your mother told you I said acting—you must mean the Factory Act," Kelly interrupted herself. "It's illegal for you to work in a factory at eight years old, or it would have been around two hundred and fifty years ago, but it's okay to help an old woman move a heavy box."

"I can do it," Spinner volunteered. "I've been practicing picking things up in a suspensor field. It's safest if I know the exact weight, though. Do you have a scale with you?"

"What are you doing down there, Mom?" Samuel asked, coming around the table. "Do you need help putting out the books from that box?"

"These aren't going out. I'm invoking, uh, ambassadorial privilege."

"As long as you pay Donna for them. I'll carry the box to the register for you."

"It's heavy," she warned him, but the seventeen-year-old easily lifted the box to his shoulder and carried it to the check-out table.

"Your first customer," he said, setting down the box.

"Does that mean I get a special discount?" Kelly asked her office manager.

"For everybody else it's a cred for hardcovers and fifty centees for paperbacks, but I can let you have ten of each for fifteen creds total," Donna offered.

"Thanks. Wait, that works out the same!"

"It's a benefit, Kelly. You're lucky I'm not charging you the early-bird fee. You spent the whole morning picking out books rather than helping."

"I'll come back and take the box home in a minute, Mom," Samuel said. "I've got to go tell my committee members so they don't think I disappeared." He headed over to where he had left the other students arranging books on the tables and found the Horten girl engaged in an argument with the Drazen student, as usual.

"The ones that are all the same size have to go together," Jorb was insisting. "You're messing up my arrangement."

"You're mixing fiction and nonfiction," she told him. "Lizant said that Humans have enough trouble figuring out the difference without the books being jumbled together."

"Like you know which is which."

"I read English, unlike some tentacled—"

"Hey, guys," Samuel interrupted just in the nick of time. "There's a heavy box of books over at the checkout that we need to deliver, Jorb, and I thought with your teaching at the dojo and all..."

"I'm on it," the Drazen said, seizing the opportunity to show off his physical prowess to the Horten. "If I'm not back before lunch comes, save me something with hot sauce."

"You're getting to be pretty good at managing aliens," Vivian observed, as Jorb departed and Marilla returned to rearranging the books the Drazen had set out. "Maybe you should consider a career in EarthCent yourself."

The Grenouthian student signaled Samuel and Vivian to come over to where he was unloading a fresh box of books onto a table and using a hand-held translation wand to scan the titles. "There may be some mistake here. I've counted fifty copies of what appears to be the same book, though some of them are obviously from different printings."

"That's funny, let me see one." The ambassador's son accepted a paperback from the alien and read off the title, *"How to Win Friends and Influence People."*

"It must have been pretty popular," Vivian observed, "but then again, maybe stocking fifty copies of the same book is how the store went out of business."

"Do you think anybody will mind if I borrow one to skim through?" the Grenouthian student asked, gesturing with his translation wand. "It sounds surprisingly practical for a Human book."

"Keep it," Vivian said. "I'll put fifty centees in the donation jar for you. I'm just surprised you're interested in anything published on Earth."

"Thanks," the student said, tucking the book into his belly pouch. "There's a rumor going around that you guys might actually know something about marketing. It makes sense if you think about it. Other than InstaSitter and the newspaper, none of your products or services are any good, but you still manage to sell them to each other."

"Thanks, I guess," Samuel acknowledged the back-handed compliment.

"It looks like we're pretty much finishing up here," Vivian said. "I'll ping Lizant and tell her that all the book handling is done so she can come for lunch and we can go over some more proposals."

"Good timing. That's Ian coming out of the lift tube with those mule bots, and I saw Shaina and Brinda setting out plates and silverware over on the tables we set up for food."

The volunteers held off mobbing the buffet until the cling wrap was removed from the trays, and then they claimed their reward for a hard morning's work. Samuel fulfilled his promise to the Drazen student by loading a plate with anything that looked chewy and then dumping over it the entire contents of a bottle of hot sauce Ian had thoughtfully provided. There were a few folding chairs for the older volunteers, but everybody else sat on the park deck grass and attacked the food with gusto.

The caterers were just beginning to clean up when the first group of early-bird shoppers stormed the cashier's table and queued up to pay ten creds each for the chance to shop before the sale officially opened the following day. Kelly flagged down Paul to take another boxful of books to the register for her, and congratulated herself on her decision to skip lunch in order to beat the competition.

"How did you hear about early entry to our benefit sale?" Donna asked each of the eager shoppers as she took their donations and gave them a badge fashioned from the supply of nametags she kept for the EarthCent mixers.

"Galactic Free Press," the first woman answered tersely, and practically ran for the loaded tables.

"Some bookish-looking guy in the corridor told me," the next shopper said, handing over his ten creds and accepting the early-bird badge. "Didn't know him."

"I heard about it from one of the other parents as I left our school meeting just a few minutes ago," another woman replied as she paid. "At least, I think he was one of the parents, but I didn't really recognize him."

"Libby," Kelly subvoced while she waited for her turn to pay for the box of books that Paul was holding, and to buy a badge so she could get back to shopping. "Are you using holo spam to send people to our book fair?"

"Just doing my part for the cause," the Stryx librarian replied modestly.

"Couldn't you have waited a couple more hours?" Kelly complained. "They're going to buy all of the books!"

"You look a bit jittery," Donna said to her friend as the ambassador stepped forward to pay. "I think I should cut you off."

"What!"

"Two boxes of books is plenty for one day, especially when we both know you have no shelf space. Why don't you go home to relax a bit and you can always come back tomorrow. Besides, I thought you said you were starved for free time to finish writing your manuscript."

Kelly looked over at the rows of tables laden with books, back to the box Paul held, and chewed her lower lip. "One more box," she promised, shaking off the embassy manager's skeptical expression. "I'm not an addict. I'll prove it. One more box and I'll go home."

"Libby," Donna said. "You heard that, right?"

"The ambassador promised to limit herself to one more box," the station librarian confirmed.

Kelly handed over an additional ten creds and snatched the badge, favoring her friend with a glare before heading back into the scrum. She retrieved an empty box from under a table and resolved to take her time and select only the choicest gems of English literature, but strictly in paperback, so she could fit more of them.

A half an hour later, a loud noise like a loose sail flapping violently in the wind cut through the quiet murmur of conversation and the rustling sounds of books being examined and replaced on tables. Somebody shrieked in alarm. The ambassador pushed her half-full box of books under the table where she hoped it would be safe and headed for the commotion.

"What is it?" she asked Blythe, who had abandoned her own post to investigate.

"I think it must be the Farling," she replied. "I saw him browsing the books, and then suddenly he was gone."

Kelly stayed behind the younger woman who pushed through the crowd, and there on the ground, between the tables, the alien doctor was flat on his back, his wings beating against the grass.

"I think he's having a fit," a man gripping a stack of books told them. "We called for a med bot, but it seems to be taking a long time."

"The Farling doctor is sick," Kelly subvoced the station librarian. "Why haven't you sent a med bot?"

"There's nothing wrong with M793qK," Libby replied. "He's just a bit—hysterical."

"Hysterical?" Kelly cautiously extended a hand to gently touch one of the antennae on the giant beetle's head. "Are you all right, Doctor?"

The wing-beating ceased the instant her fingers made contact, and for a moment, the ambassador was afraid that she had somehow killed the Farling. Then he levered himself onto his side by opening just one of his hard forewings, rolled onto his legs, and slowly rose.

"Oh, my," the insectoid physician rubbed out on his speaking limbs. "I haven't laughed so hard since I heard that Gem changed her mind about being a clone and was soliciting us for genetic samples of her former race. I made my retirement nut on that one."

"What are you doing here?" Kelly demanded.

"Shopping. A finely rendered holographic representation of a high status Farling approached me as I left my office and told me about the early-bird sale. I shall miss the excitement of Union Station."

"You're leaving?"

"I have accepted Gryph's offer to accompany Flower on her maiden voyage in the service of your people. Thus, my visit to your charming book sale."

"I get it now," the ambassador said. "You figure the more money we raise, the more you'll get paid."

"Hardly," the beetle replied, rubbing out the equivalent of a long suffering sigh. "Once aboard the Dollnick colony ship I will not have the same access to the resource materials useful in conducting a medical practice that I enjoyed here."

"You came looking for medical books?"

The Farling clamped a limb to the underside of his carapace as if he had been shot through one of his major organs, and weaved drunkenly in an attempt to remain upright on his hindmost legs.

"Stop it. You're killing me. I was looking at one of your so-called medical texts when I suffered my undignified loss of control. How did your people ever survive when they think everything is a disease, including their moods?"

"You seem to have made quite a stack for purchasing," Kelly observed, pointing to the pile of medical books. "Besides, since when do you read English?"

"I picked it up reviewing the charts brought by patients who wisely fled the barbaric care on your Earth," the alien doctor explained. "As to these books, I'm buying them as gag gifts for my friends when I eventually return home. Even advanced biologicals such as Farlings get sick on rare occasions, and laughter is the best medicine."

"I'm surprised to hear you have any friends," the ambassador muttered.

"I also require books for my patients," M793qK continued as if he hadn't heard. "Perhaps you would enjoy explaining the process of biological reproduction to adolescents of an alien species, but I've always left that to your station librarian while working here. She informed me that I would likely find a number of books that do a reasonable job illustrating the procedure for youngsters whose parents aren't up to the task."

"You're here to buy sex education books?"

"Yes, and old magazines if I can find any. I understand that they are an expected accoutrement in the offices of Earth physicians, and I want to make my patients feel at home."

Kelly couldn't help but be impressed by the giant beetle's sincerity and offered a suggestion of her own. "I saw several tables of children's books over near the cash register. I bet you can find a copy of *The Very Quiet Cricket* or *The Very Hungry Caterpillar*. Come to think of it, anything by Eric Carle would be good. My children loved the same books their grandmother and I read at that age."

"Do all Human children enjoy reading about insects?" the Farling inquired.

"I just thought that with you being a, uh..." she stumbled to a halt.

"Were you about to compare me to Earth bugs?" the doctor rubbed out in disbelief.

"There is a certain superficial resemblance," Kelly backpedalled, figuratively and literally before the towering alien. "It might help the children get comfortable with you."

"I should think that nothing would relax them more than discovering they will be treated by a physician from an advanced species rather than a Human quack!"

"Of course, of course," the ambassador agreed in hopes of mollifying the doctor, but then another thought occurred to her. "Please don't take this the wrong way, but you might want to consider hiring a human nurse."

"A nurse? For the suckling infants?"

"No, for all the patients," Kelly replied.

The Farling stared at her for a moment and began to sway on his hind legs. The hardened forewings that formed the top of his carapace began twitching rapidly.

"Easy, big boy," Jeeves said, floating up to the pair. "It's just a translation glitch. Humans also call trained medical personnel nurses."

"Thank you, Jeeves," Kelly said. "What are you doing here?"

"Helping to fit out Flower seemed like a worthy cause," the Stryx replied, though he sounded a bit squirrelly. "I'll be over there if you need me for anything."

The ambassador suddenly recalled her half-full box of books waiting under the table where some other unscrupulous early bird might poach them, and left the Farling to his own devices. A short distance away, a trio of Fillinducks were holding up leather-bound volumes, whispering to each other, and placing them in large shoulder baskets. After quickly exhausting the available supply, they began creating stacks of books by color, alternating red, white and black in one pile, and light blue, light green, and other subdued pastels in another.

Hours later, the ambassador was engaged in the third repack of her box to make room for new prizes at the expense of the old when Donna made the announcement that the book fair was closing for the day. Kelly found herself last in line behind the Fillinducks, who discreetly held perfumed handkerchiefs to their noses to mask the odor of humanity.

"With all the books you brought up earlier, that makes four-hundred and eighty creds," Donna told the aliens after tallying up on a tab. "You must be some serious readers."

"How dare you!" the shortest Fillinduck hissed.

The dominant partner of the trio smoothed the ruffled feathers of the shorter alien and informed the embassy manager, "None of us have the slightest interest in reading Humanese. We're interior decorators and I have just the place for these ornaments picked out in my mind's eye."

Kelly felt a flash of anger at the waste, but then again, Dorothy had told her about the fiery fate that awaited unloved books on Earth, and perhaps a curious alien might one day open one of the volumes and fall in love. Then something Kevin had related about the visit to the abandoned university library came to mind, and she inserted herself into the conversation.

"Excuse me, but if you're looking for books for strictly decorative purposes, there used to be an entire industry on

Earth dedicated to manufacturing them. My embassy can supply the contact information, and my understanding is that you can get them much cheaper than these."

"What is the name of this product?" the Fillinduck demanded.

"Monographs."

After the aliens moved off, Donna tallied up the paperbacks in Kelly's box and added the money to the large jar she was using for a till.

"Who ever knew that Stryx creds were so heavy," the embassy manager commented.

"How much have we raised so far?" Kelly asked.

"A few thousand, at least. I know that even if we sell all the books it's not a drop in the bucket of what the refit is costing, but I still think it's important to get people involved and interested in Flower's mission. Jeeves even overpaid for his books, though he wouldn't let me see them."

"How do you know he overpaid, then? He might have tricked you."

"No, he opened the box and let me pull one out a little to see how thick it was. They were all large paperbacks, but he had packed them with the spines down. I guessed there were around thirty in the box, and he paid a hundred creds, even though they would have been just a half cred each if he let me add them up."

"You couldn't see what they were at all?"

"I could only see the cut paper edges and a bit of the cover on the one I pulled out. The color scheme reminded me of that kiddie ride Kevin brought back from Earth. My two-year-old grandson learned how to say 'Bee' when Chastity put him in it."

Twenty

"Aren't you glad we came early?" Kelly asked her husband as they browsed through the displays in the lobby of the Empire Convention Center. "I've never seen so many different alien books in the same place before. Somebody should open an all-species bookshop."

"I wonder what this one costs?" Joe looked around for the Dollnick in charge of the booth, but the alien was with another customer. "These illustrations and technical diagrams of colony ship engineering are incredibly detailed. I'm not sure if I'm looking at a work of art or a technical reference."

"Take a snap of the back cover with your visual implant and ask Libby to translate it."

"I don't know if Dollnicks put prices on the cover." Joe lifted the book closer to his face and he squinted to focus at the short distance. "I can't even tell what it's printed on, though the fibers—you're not going to believe this, Kel. I think it's woven."

"That would make it more expensive, but I'm sure I've heard of handcrafted books from Earth printed on woven paper."

"No, I mean with different colored threads of some sort that have been dyed to spell out words and form pictures once they're woven in place. I'm sure of it. If you look at the edge of each sheet, you can see that it's really two back-to-back weavings sewn together along the margins."

"That's unbelievable." Kelly accepted the book from Joe and confirmed his assessment. "These books must cost a fortune."

"Because they're worth a fortune," the overdue Dolly salesman declared, looming over them. "However, the naval architecture book you've wisely chosen is a reprint edition produced on machine looms for the consumer market."

"How much is it?" Joe asked.

"Let me tell you about our financing program for first-time buyers, for which I'll assume you qualify." The Dollnick drew a laminated reference table from the over-sized pocket of his immaculately tailored suit as he spoke, and ran a finger along the columns. "If we spread the payments over a hundred years—no, I see that won't work for your species. May I ask how old you are?"

"Skip the actuarial tables," Joe said. "What's the cash price?"

"Eighteen hundred creds is a pittance when you con-sider—"

"How about fifteen hundred?" Joe interrupted. "That's more than I earned in a month before I retired."

The salesman looked quickly to both sides to see if anybody was listening in, then flapped all four hands in a gesture of good-humored submission and declared, "Done."

Kelly bit her tongue while Joe completed the transaction with his programmable cred. It was the most money she had ever seen him spend on anything, but she could hardly complain given her own book habit, especially since she was counting on him to build her a new bookcase. Then she spotted Walter and Brinda wending their way through the displays and moved to intercept.

"So?" she demanded.

"Do you really want to do this now?" the editor of the Galactic Free Press asked with a sigh. "All right, then. It won't fly."

"What do you mean? Libby read my manuscript and she was very complimentary."

"Exactly," Walter replied. "It's too good."

"What?"

"You completely ignored our outline and wrote the book you wanted to write. I'm sure you'll have success with a different publisher, but it's not a *For Humans* title."

"I have a contract!"

"Which includes a fitness for publication clause. You're lucky you didn't sign the first contract I offered or you'd have to return your advance payment."

"But I haven't been paid yet," Kelly pointed out.

"Really? Well, I wouldn't spend the money in that case," Walter warned her. "Seriously, it's a fine manuscript and I read every word. Perhaps we could serialize it in the paper, but it's not the book we hired you to write."

"It doesn't count as hiring if you don't pay me," Kelly groused, but she was secretly relieved to be out of the contract and had been expecting something of the sort for weeks. "If you need help finding another writer to finish the book with your outline, one of my colleagues might be interested."

"I've already engaged the author of *Economics for Humans*, and he's promised me a completed manuscript by morning," Walter said. Then he pointed at his ear to indicate that he was being pinged, and turned to his wife.

"I'll see you after the awards. Chastity is waiting for me in the ready-room."

Kelly chatted a bit with Brinda and then made her way back to Joe, who was showing off his purchase to Bork and Czeros.

"Yes, the Dollnick page-weaving technology is very advanced," the Frunge ambassador acknowledged. "My own people experimented with a similar approach due to our aversion to paper but we never got the cost down to a practical level for books."

"Neither did the Dollys," Joe informed him.

"I'm looking forward to our prize for illuminated scrolls," the Drazen ambassador said to Kelly. "It's nice to see one's cultural heritage draw the respect of other species."

"I never expected that literary prizes would be such a big hit with everybody," Kelly admitted. "Chastity told me that several of the alien publishers have already asked why the Galactic Free Press can't host an annual awards show every week. The Grenouthians are broadcasting it live on their network."

"And I've arranged for a pop-up shop featuring all of the winning titles in our deck's boutique section," Aainda announced, gliding up to Kelly's side and taking her arm. "I believe it's important to foster interest in the other species among my people, and I hope you honor us with a visit."

"Are you sure the empire knows you're here," the EarthCent ambassador asked half-seriously. "You're not like any of the Vergallian ambassadors I've ever met."

"I had the pleasure of participating in a mission to your Alt cousins before assuming my post. They made such a favorable impression that I decided to throw away the briefing materials about Humans provided by my intelligence service and go with my childhood experience and instincts."

"So you'll be instructing your spymaster on the station to meet with Herl and Clive as I proposed?" Bork asked the Vergallian.

"Already done," she replied with a gracious smile. "The potential for cost savings alone would have convinced me, and the opportunity to contribute to Flower's worthy mission just adds frosting to the cake. Excuse me, I've been ignoring Ambassador Ortha and he's looking a bit pink."

"What proposal?" Kelly asked the Drazen ambassador.

"Hasn't Clive briefed you yet? It only trickled down to me this morning, but apparently the Verlock intelligence head has followed up on his scheme for sharing intelligence targets with a suggestion to run a trial on your colony ship. If Aainda has convinced her people, that means that everybody is onboard."

"Onboard with what?"

"We're all going to send agents along with Flower, undercover of course. It will save everyone quite a bit in transportation and lodging costs, since they'll be able to recruit local sources on all of your outposts worth mentioning without leaving the ship."

"May I enquire what we get in return?" Kelly asked, somewhat taken aback by the news that the head of the EarthCent spy agency, for which she was nominally the Minister of Intelligence, had agreed to host alien spies on a guided tour of humanity.

"Paid," Czeros chipped in to the conversation. "The agreement is that all of the species will contribute half of their savings over what we would have spent spying on you otherwise. It's not a tremendous sum of money as you don't have anything worth hiding, but it's a bit of a diplomatic coup for you since nothing like this has been tried since the Drazens and Hortens joined the tunnel network."

A loud bell dinged in the Empire Convention Center lobby, indicating that it was time for the awards show attendees to enter the Nebulae room and find their seats.

"I suppose I'll get an earful if I don't sit with our publishers and scribes," Bork said, taking his leave of Kelly and Czeros.

"Same here," the Frunge ambassador excused himself, though he made a sharp detour for the lobby bar before entering the Nebulae room.

The EarthCent ambassador and her husband delayed for a few minutes, Kelly to avoid getting caught up in the alien crush, and Joe to admire his purchase under the bright lights. They were just heading in when Blythe and Clive arrived along with Chastity's husband, Marcus, and accompanied by Shaina and Daniel.

"Great timing," Blythe greeted them. "We're all sitting together with mom and dad. Chastity sprang for our table."

"I wondered about that," Kelly said. "I didn't see a seating chart or name cards with table numbers."

"That's mom's style. With all the interest from aliens, Chas went with selling whole tables. We're at a big one up front, and Dring bought a table for everybody who didn't fit right behind us. Vivian and Samuel are with the kids from the committee. Didn't you get a ping from the Empire Convention Center?"

Kelly frowned, activated her heads-up display, and navigated with eye movements to her incoming message queue. "Oops. I really cranked down on my spam filter after Libby started with the holo ads, and the seating notification got filed as a commercial solicitation."

"Those ads work phenomenally," Marcus told them. "Chastity did a trial spend for my dance studio, and by the third day I was turning away new students and we had to cancel the ad. She's still arguing with the station librarian over whether we should have to pay for sales that we turned down."

"You're fashionably late," Jeeves greeted the group when they reached their round banquet table right in front of the raised stage. "I took the liberty of ordering your drinks so the poor waitress wouldn't fall behind."

"Thank you, Jeeves," Blythe said. "Have you seen Lynx?"

"She just ran backstage a minute ago to help Woojin get ready. Something about 'wigging out,' if I understood her."

"I'd be wigging out too if I was him," Kelly said sympathetically. "How did he get stuck reading the names of the award winners?"

"Flower wanted to see how he interacts with aliens in a formal setting before accepting him as captain, and this is the best opportunity we could come up with on short notice," Clive explained. "It's surprising that an AI would care so much about appearances."

"Hey, everybody," Lynx said, looking a little nervous as she took her seat next to Shaina. "I hope Wooj doesn't screw this up."

"I didn't know you were so anxious to leave the station," Kelly addressed the embassy's supposed cultural attaché.

"I'm not, really, but I think Woojin likes the idea of being in command again more than he'll admit, and then when I heard that our doctor had signed on, that clinched

243

it. We'll probably come back when Em is old enough to start at Libby's school."

"Shh," Brinda said. "They're starting."

Walter stepped up to the podium and began, "Welcome to the first annual—"

"Semi-annual," somebody at the head Dollnick table interrupted.

"Quarterly," a Horten called out.

"Weekly," a Grenouthian publisher bellowed.

"Thank you for your enthusiasm, but as I already told you, that's a discussion for another time," Walter said. "Welcome to the first celebration of the Union Station Book Awards. We are gathered here to recognize the best efforts of our industry and to confer status on those authors and publishers who have produced these exemplary works for the benefit of tunnel network members. But first, a word from our sponsor."

There was a polite round of applause as Walter and Chastity exchanged positions, and Joe took the opportunity to show his Dollnick book to Clive, who was duly impressed.

"I'd like to thank everybody who purchased tickets for a table tonight, the proceeds of which are being donated to Eccentric Enterprises for the Flower project. I also want to request that audience members hold their applause while the presenter is speaking. The winning books were chosen by our three-judge panel, whose identities we are keeping private for obvious reasons. The Galactic Free Press will be publishing a book supplement tomorrow which will list all of the finalists, including a special section for runners-up, second-runners-up, and honorable mentions. Official artwork of an award medallion suitable for inclusion on book covers and other marketing materials is available on request."

"Request. Request," a number of rambunctious aliens cried out.

"The official presentation will be done by Pyun Woojin, who will serve as Flower's captain for her maiden cruise as a circuit ship. Woojin?"

The unfortunate ex-mercenary reluctantly climbed the short stairs onto the platform and strode to the podium, drawing choked laughter from the humans. The aliens reacted quite differently to Woojin's elaborate uniform, with the Dollnicks whistling in admiration and the Grenouthians patting their bellies, while Kelly distinctly overheard Bork at the next table saying to Herl, "Not bad at all."

"Why is Woojin dressed like George Washington?" Joe whispered to Daniel. "And I know that's not his real hair."

"Didn't Dorothy mention it to you? Flower insisted on uniforms, and to prevent her from designing them herself, Blythe agreed to let SBJ Fashions come up with proposals based on historical uniforms from Earth. Jeeves did the negotiating in the end, and Flower really went for the buttons, wig and colonial hat."

"Now I know what Jeeves meant about getting even one day after Wooj cleaned him out three times at our last poker game."

"The first prize tonight," Woojin read from a tab, "is for the longest running serial novel written by members of the same family."

"Huh?" Kelly muttered.

"And the winner, with no runners-up, is, *Irrational Numbers*. This mathematical thrill ride has held Verlock readers enthralled for over a thousand generations, so let's have a big hand for Hylneth, accepting for his extended clan."

A Verlock who was conveniently waiting at the foot of the stairs shuffled onto the stage and accepted the heavy medallion mounted on a marble slab. Hylneth graciously deferred when offered the opportunity to make a speech, and Woojin began announcing the next prize the moment the slow-footed alien turned ponderously to return to his seat.

"In the category of novels based in an imaginary universe where all of the inhabitants have belly pouches, the winner is, *Warren Master*. Beloved by Grenouthians and sophisticated readers of all species, this recent release is destined to become a new classic. Other titles making the final cut include, *Furry Warrior, Pink Stripe*, and *The Producer's Daughter*."

"Who came up with these categories?" Kelly asked Brinda, as the Grenouthians in attendance broke into loud arguments and flung accusations at one another.

"I'm sworn to secrecy," Walter's wife replied. "Let's just say that it was complicated."

The unnamed bunny who accepted the prize for *Warren Master* thanked his extended clan for their efforts to influence the judges on his behalf, and hopped back to his place.

"In the category of best translation of a romance to the languages of three or more different species, the winner is our station librarian, for her renderings into Drazen, Frunge, Horten and Vergallian of the Bea Hollinder novel, *Her Only Choice*."

"You have a side job translating romance novels?" Kelly subvoced.

"Later," the Stryx librarian replied. "I want to enjoy the moment." The figure of a little old lady who looked almost human, except for a hint of vines about her hair, a tentacle bump in the back of her dress, and downy fur growing on her four arms, ascended the stage.

"Show-off," Jeeves muttered. "She's using data from my holo advertising business to appeal to everybody."

The hologram shuffled across the stage like a Verlock, all while the color of her fur and bare skin shifted smoothly to a cheerful brown. The overall effect somehow produced a sense of beauty that could make a high-caste Vergallian jealous.

"Can I give you this?" Woojin whispered to the holographic projection, not wanting to ruin the illusion or his chances with Flower by dropping the heavy award on his foot.

The hologram nodded, and the presenter placed the stone-mounted medallion in her hands.

"Double-show-off," Jeeves grunted. "She's using manipulator fields to make the fingers solid. You wouldn't believe the math involved."

"I just want to thank everybody for all of the nice things you've said about my work, and I hope the Galactic Free Press gives me the opportunity to translate the new Bea Hollinder that they'll be serializing over the next five cycles," Libby spoke through her avatar.

"She means that she hopes Chastity doesn't balk at her price," Jeeves continued bellyaching to Kelly.

"Are you jealous of your parent?"

"They only asked her in the first place because I turned it down. Romances," the young Stryx snorted dismissively.

"In the category of illuminated scrolls with an axe motif, we have a longer list of candidates than I have time to read," Woojin continued after the station librarian's holo-gram moved off with her trophy. "The winner is, *A Hun-dred Axes*, by Truk. Is the scribe here?"

The fortunate Drazen made his way out of the section of tables reserved by his compatriots, though he almost lost his balance from shock when he passed the table pur-chased by Dring, and the Maker called out, "Fine work, Truk."

"You saw his scroll?" Paul asked.

"I read it," the Maker replied. "I'd like to think that the other judges did as well, though I have my suspicions about—I promised not to name names."

"Is this what you expected, Dring?" Aisha asked. "It reminds me of the broadcasting award show the Grenouthians put on."

"Finest book awards event I've attended in thousands of years. In fact, it's the first time in recent history I can recall so many species competing for the same prizes."

"It's not exactly a competition when they all got to add categories where their authors are the only ones with a chance of winning," Dorothy pointed out.

"It strikes me as a novel way to sell books," the Farling declared, eliciting a round of groans at the feeble pun.

"Don't pay any attention to them, Doc," Kevin came to the alien's defense. "I haven't forgotten how you fixed me up after that radiation poisoning, and I hope to see you at our wedding, if Dorothy ever finishes the dress."

"Are you trying again because the first marriage didn't take? You're welcome to come and see me as a couple if you're experiencing trouble mating. I recently purchased a whole collection of books you might find useful."

At the adjacent table that Chastity had provided for the student committee, Marilla nudged Samuel and said, "I think your sister is really angry."

The teen glanced over at Dorothy before responding, "No, we mainly turn red when we're embarrassed about something. When people really get mad, they usually go pale."

"Weird," the Horten girl said.

"Look at this," the Grenouthian student exclaimed, shoving his tab into the center of the table. "Sales of all of the books mentioned for our imaginary universe prize began spiking within seconds of being announced. You guys really do know something about marketing."

"Fashion design too," Grude said. "That uniform your captain is wearing demands respect. I wouldn't be surprised if those three-cornered hats catch on with other navies. You know, Sam," he added thoughtfully, "You might consider one of those grey wigs with a ponytail yourself."

"I got an offer from Frunge Intelligence to go out on Flower when I graduate next cycle," Lizant told the others. "They said that my work as the committee secretary demonstrates how well I get along with other species. They seemed to think that I'm the brains behind you guys," she added apologetically to Vivian and Samuel.

"Have you thought about joining the ship yourselves?" the Sharf student asked the young couple.

"My mom says that just because I'm old enough to boss people around doesn't mean I'm ready to live on my own," Vivian replied.

"But you wouldn't be alone," Yvandi said, pointing her bony chin at Samuel. "Aren't you getting married?"

"The Sunday after I turn eighteen," Vivian replied, intentionally not looking in Samuel's direction. "You're all invited."

Up on the podium, Woojin regrouped after butchering the pronunciation of a number of untranslatable Frunge titles, and announced, "In the category of new branded nonfiction published on Union Station within the last three cycles, the winner is, *Economics For Humans*. Humans and aliens alike have voted with their pocketbooks to make this title the business category bestseller in the authoritative Galactic Free Press list."

"What are you doing, Jeeves?" Kelly asked the Stryx as he elevated above their heads.

"Shortcut," he replied, and then floated over the front of the stage to accept his prize.

"I thought Walter said that the author was an anonymous academic," Kelly whispered across the table to Brinda.

"Jeeves decided to take credit after he discovered that Libby would be accepting the translation award. Shh, he's going to speak."

"I want to thank my Human friends and business associates for their help in steering the development of my book, though some of the lessons they've taught me have been costly. And speaking of giving credit where it's due, I want everybody to know that I got the idea for the targeted holo-marketing service we've been beta-testing on this station from my research into early twenty-first-century advertising on Earth."

"We're in for it now," Kelly said. She gave Jeeves the evil eye as the Stryx launched into a sales pitch for his advertising service, complete with holographic charts detailing the before-and-after sales of various Union Station businesses. "The aliens will never forgive us."

"I think you may need to read *Economics For Humans* again," Blythe told her. "The other species are going to start taking us more seriously now that they know we're good at something that matters. Have you forgotten that it was our success at the Verlock's Raider/Trader game that got them to start talking with us twenty years ago?"

"But it's advertising," Kelly protested. "Everybody hates it."

"Love it or hate it, it works," Brinda told her. "My dad actually sold out of egg beaters for the first time ever after we started advertising Kitchen Kitsch with the holograms."

Up on the stage, Jeeves wound up his marketing spiel with, "In conclusion, to borrow a phrase, it is the view of the Union Station Stryx that our investment in Humans is coming along handsomely. You can learn all about it in the soon-to-be released bestseller, *EarthCent For Humans*, the eventual award for which will give me one more than—"

A manipulator field disguised as an enormous holographic candy cane materialized around Jeeves and dragged him from the stage.

EarthCent Ambassador Series:

Date Night on Union Station

Alien Night on Union Station

High Priest on Union Station

Spy Night on Union Station

Carnival on Union Station

Wanderers on Union Station

Vacation on Union Station

Guest Night on Union Station

Word Night on Union Station

Party Night on Union Station

Review Night on Union Station

Family Night on Union Station

Book Night on Union Station

LARP Night on Union Station

About the Author

E. M. Foner lives in Northampton, MA with an imaginary German Shepherd who's been trained to bite bankers.
The   author   welcomes   reader   comments   at
e_foner@yahoo.com.

Other books by the author:

Meghan's Dragon

Turing Test

Lightning Source UK Ltd.
Milton Keynes UK
UKHW03f1005120418
320928UK00002B/287/P